Other Art

Other books by John Harris

FICTION

Small Rain (1989)

NON-FICTION

George Bowering and His Works (1992)

Tom Wayman and His Works (1997)

Other Art

John Harris

NEW STAR BOOKS
VANCOUVER
1997

"Other Art" appeared in *Capilano Review*. "Mending Walls" appeared in *New Directions* (Vancouver). Ian C. Johnston of Nanaimo originated "She Done Spun and Donut."

This is a work of fiction.

New Star Books Ltd.
2504 York Avenue
Vancouver, B.C. V6K 1E3

Edited by Audrey McClellan
Cover by CARDIGAN.COM
Book design and production by Carolyn Stewart

Printed and bound in Canada by Webcom Ltd.
1 2 3 4 5   01 00 99 98 97

New Star gratefully acknowledges the support of the Canada Council and the British Columbia Arts Council.

THE CANADA COUNCIL | LE CONSEIL DES ARTS
FOR THE ARTS | DU CANADA
SINCE 1957 | DEPUIS 1957

CANADIAN CATALOGUING IN PUBLICATION DATA

Harris, John, 1943–
Other art

ISBN 0-921586-58-2
I. TITLE.

PS8565.A6488O83 1997   C813'.54   C97-910704-0
PR9199.3.H3459O83 1997

Contents

Other Art

L illa and Harvey have been living together for three years. This
is a big change in Harvey's life. Lilla is a colleague of ours
whose job it is to look after the "mentally disadvantaged," "challenged," or "other-advantaged" who are dropped off at the college
every morning by the Peter Pan bus. Down the hall they come, an
intimidating phalanx, shuffling, staggering, and running, their
toques pulled down over their eyes, gloves hanging by strings
from the sleeves of their coats. Lilla is there to greet them, take
their coats, ask after them. They gather around her, pat her on
the back, hold her hand and say hello, a bunch of giant, dis-
torted, affectionate children. They attend some special lectures
that she arranges, take books out of the library and dump them
immediately into the outside book drop, do aerobics in the gym,
attend classes to ask unanswerably profound questions, and sit by
the entrance to the cafeteria greeting incoming customers.

"Hi, guy, what's happening?"

Looking after them is a tough job and getting tougher as, due
to budget cuts, the number of organized activities for them goes
down and the amount of "free time" goes up. During this "free
time," Lilla sits in her office and talks to the ones who want to

talk and waits for the phone to ring about the others, *viz.*, "Lilla, we've got a student up here in the Bursar's office. He says his name is Danger Man."

"Oh yes. Bill. What's he doing?"

"Collecting paper. He says he needs paper. We've given him some memo pads, typing paper, graph paper, but none of it seems to be the right kind. He emptied out the wastepaper baskets, but now he wants to look in the filing cabinets."

"I'll be right up."

Lilla also has to put up with faculty meetings where the appropriateness of having the disadvantaged at the college is sometimes (usually obliquely) discussed. While they have their uses, like bolstering attendance at noon-hour lectures and poetry readings closer to figures likely to be respected by the Arts Council and other funding bodies, they are generally considered to be a "distraction," even more so (somehow) than the flamboyant co-eds who are presently into majorette boots and very, very short miniskirts. The college is, after all, some faculty argue, an institute of higher learning dedicated to providing opportunities in the professions to students of proven academic ability. Is it really a suitable place for people who need ... special care? These discussions generally revolve around a number of specific complaints — someone who wandered into the psychology lab and released the white rats, someone who popped up during a geology lecture with the assertion that the town still *was* under water, someone (it had, with his interest in office procedure and uncanny ability to penetrate the administration complex on the third floor, to be Bill) who stuffed the mailboxes with the contents of a garbage can taken from the principal's office, creating a flurry of confusion, anxiety, false hope, and anger.

Lilla's good at her job and she's been working at the college for a long time. So last year, when Harvey decided to go into business, informing us that an artist should "put his money where his mouth is," we naturally assumed he meant Lilla's money.

But we did worry that Harvey *could* have meant our money. Consequently, during the planning stages we avoided him or, whenever we ran into him, talked incessantly about our Visa accounts and bills for sending kids to university. We reminded him of all the failures that had already taken place in town, everything from perogie bars to bookstores to chopstick factories. Only the franchises, we pointed out, appealing to the lowest common denominator of human taste, have ever survived, and some of those, we suspect, exist only for tax purposes.

It was not so much that we minded putting in a few hundred, or even a thousand, on an even chance, but we knew that Harvey would fail.

The trouble is, Harvey gets bored very easily, and he cannot abide boredom. He refuses to accept it, as the rest of us do, as normal. During boring conversations he is apt to sigh loudly, announce that something interesting must be happening somewhere, and leave. He is famous for abruptly and forcefully changing the topic of a conversation, or insulting people by telling them straight to their faces that they are boring, or staring hard at them while they talk and then asking them questions like, "Are you happy?" As a result of this low boredom threshold, Harvey has never been able to work at a regular job. He has been a mailman (eight months), a tree planter (three summers), a waiter (part time for two months), a surveyor (one week), and a disk-jockey (six months). Of the eleven years of his working life, he has put in approximately two. Also, he has never been able to complete any schooling. He took college courses from Barry and me, got straight A's, and went to university, but got bored and came home. He got within six months of certification as a journeyman printer, but he got kicked out of his work experience for refusing to typeset a boring textbook.

For most of his adult life, and it is a matter of local speculation as to whether Harvey ever really was a child or, conversely, ever became an adult, Harvey has lived as a man about town, a man not of leisure but of taste: an artist, poet, philosopher. He writes poetry, practises the saxophone, serves as emcee for most local cultural events except, of course, those run by the Symphony Orchestra and Art Gallery group, and does graphic designs for anyone who needs them. Also, he is much sought after for personal advice; he finds it boring to be anything other than perfectly candid. Over the years, no matter what happened to the rest of us in our lives and jobs, Harvey was always out there, creative, intelligent, free. Of course he was bored most of the time, but at least it was not at our expense.

Harvey convinced us, however, that he was a changed man. He was finding it embarrassing, he said, to be in his thirties and kept by his parents or girlfriend, accepting an allowance, especially from Lilla, where it was less than what her kids got and not nearly so well managed. And he had panic attacks about the future, which would hold no financial security, no children, no place of his own, while the rest of us, it seemed, would be wearing soft hats and whistling back and forth across the continent in our electric Winnebagos. He implied, too, that his feelings for Lilla and her kids were at the point where a serious commitment of some sort was called for. And he told us that Lilla was willing to remortgage her house, so financing would be no problem.

So we waited and watched. After an extensive period of study and thought, Harvey decided to start a cappuccino bar and art gallery. This actually sounded feasible. As Harvey explained it, we thirsted for his cappuccino, which we understood was some fancy kind of coffee traditionally consumed in a bohemian atmosphere of serious philosophical and artistic discussion. We were less sure about the art, but Harvey was convinced that there were enough local patrons willing to buy it if they only knew what and where it was. Certainly there were plenty of local artists producing it. All he had to do was get these two groups together. Naturally most of us assumed we were members of the latter group, producers rather than consumers, and we would not actually have to *buy* any art. But there was some uncertainty about this.

There was no uncertainty in Harvey, however. Harvey is never uncertain when he is being driven by an idea, a concept. His concept was embodied in the name and logo that he quickly produced for his business. The name would be Other Art, indicating a whole new world of artistic experience or a whole new approach to art. The logo incorporated an O placed on top of an A to make a human figure. The figure had spidery arms, one of which held a sickle aloft in position to strike. The logo was actually, Harvey explained, an icon, discovered by him in the course of his studies of Finno-Urgic mythology. The icon denoted a new, militant phase of artistic capitalism. Harvey was indeed serious about putting his (or someone's) money where his mouth was.

I confess that this worried me. Did "artistic capitalism" mean something like creative bookkeeping or financing? Did it mean crime? I didn't ask Harvey. It was more interesting to sit back and watch.

Location was Harvey's final problem. The business had to go downtown because Harvey hates the new suburbs and never goes there, even for parties where the drinks are free. Anyway, he couldn't afford shopping centre rentals. But the downtown is tricky. It is in a natural bowl where two great rivers join, and it shares this bowl with forty large lumber mills, three pulp mills and two hundred acres of railway tracks. The mills and railways got here first, took almost all the river frontage, and have seniority, which entitles them to dump into the river and shower the town with fly-ash that turns everything a dirty grey and contains totally reduced sulphur that, on bad days (which is most of the time), burns your eyes and nose and gives you a headache. The government is still trying to figure out what else it does, but it is generally understood that this study could take a long time. It will probably not be completed until the bush and the mills are gone and nobody is around to care.

The downtown core, as it is called, is made up of hotels with stripper bars along with other businesses (cafes, junk stores, pawn shops, and boarding houses) that serve the population of drunks, bums, and drifters who make up the seasonal workforce of the logging industry and are the town's original class of inhabitants. Around this core are the bank buildings (with offices of lawyers and accountants) that went up in the sixties when the pulp mills came in and the town advertised itself as the world's fastest growing city next to Calcutta. Then there are the older suburbs where Joy and Barry and Lilla and Harvey live, and then, on and over the hills around the bowl, the new suburbs and their shopping centres, dental clinics, neighbourhood pubs, and auto sales centres.

During the day, when the suburbanites commute to work, the downtown is busy and safe. At night it is dark, silent, and (except for the hotels) locked up. Lonely drunks wander up and down the streets, shouting at ghosts and looking for open doors. The city has put a library, swimming pool, and ice rink in the downtown, and the provincial and federal governments have put the offices of their various departments there, but most of these facilities are closed at night, creating large dark areas. In the downtown, the closure or removal of one respectable business, or the shifting of a government office, can turn an entire block into a place where you are guaranteed to step into fresh barf or broken glass or come face to face with a panhandler or a drunk. If you are a business that gets isolated in one of these areas, you are done for.

Harvey found a place above an Italian cafe run by people with diversified interests who use the cafe more as a family kitchen and training centre for their kids, so customers are a secondary consideration. There is a major government complex nearby, occupying most of a huge hotel that was abandoned on completion after the coal mines up north went broke. The bank buildings are within range for those energetic secretaries or professionals who, on their lunch hours, go looking for the bohemian touch.

Harvey decorated the place tastefully, slashing the floor space dramatically, placing black-and-white checkerboard linoleum squares with glass-topped tables and wrought-iron chairs on one side, and on the other a grey rug and racks for clothes, sculpture, jewellery, tapes, and books. By the entrance was the cappuccino machine and an appealing selection of muffins and cakes, and all around were pictures, paintings, and sculptures by local artists, displayed on consignment.

The opening was a great success. Most local artists participated. Vivien, for example, had two of her South American photos, enlarged and framed, on display. There was lots of pottery and painting. People came in from the suburbs and wandered around the statues, montages, clothes racks with hand-painted T-shirts, and jewellery and pottery display cases. They circled the room looking at paintings. They sipped lattes and chatted. I bought some earrings for Vivien, who couldn't make it due to a meeting of the canoe club. A doctor from out of town paid $300 for one of Vivien's pictures. Word went around the room like wildfire. Barry and I slipped out and ran home and got some copies of our books and broadsides and put them in the book racks. But at the end of the evening they were still there.

The newspaper, on the following afternoon, said that Other Art was "a bold new enterprise that heralds a new age of sophistication for the area."

As it turned out, Harvey's business paid the rent but did not provide him much of a salary. And, as we predicted, it was hard work for him. Harvey is not used to catering to people. Some of the artists became irate when their work didn't sell and Harvey insisted on returning it, in their opinion, prematurely. They pointed out that other stuff sat around a lot longer than their stuff did. The three-quarter-ton, cast-bronze cockroach with the human head in its mouth became a sore point. The main reason that Harvey left it so long was that he threw his back out getting it there and did not look forward to spending another two weeks immobilized after he moved it out. But the other artists accused him of favouritism. Harvey told them to fuck off, and many did. Other customers, like Barry and I, wanted more food.

"You have to have something on your stomach when you look at some of this stuff," we explained. "How about a crock pot with soup or beans?"

I suggested frozen yogurt and even got Harvey a pamphlet explaining how to get the franchise and machine.

But Harvey was firm. "If you want meals," he said, "go downstairs."

Mainly, however, Harvey got bored. There was no escape from the place. He became irate with customers. He would have trouble suppressing a snicker when they asked if he had the latest Elton John tape or described the colour scheme in their living room or bedroom. He was a sitting duck for the lonely, wounded, and/or crazy. Pete, for example, an accountant whose wife had left him, made the place a kind of headquarters so it was unsafe to go there unless you liked looking at the photos of the house and kids that were in dispute, or the Land Rover in which the wife had (simply) driven away, or the antique gun collection that she had (if you could believe it) hauled to the junk shop and sold for next to nothing. One day Harvey saw Pete, with a coffee in his hand and his photos in his breast pocket, making for a table of secretaries on their coffee break. Harvey took him aside and told him that the subject of his divorce was, from that point on, in Other Art, banned, verboten, closed, taboo. Pete never came back, and neither did some others with stories to tell who heard about his fate. Then Harvey threw out a woman and her three kids who were running around and around the tables screaming at the top of their lungs. Other customers sympathized with the woman and thought Harvey was too heavy handed, even if the kids had broken a Guatemalan vase and were not inclined to say they were sorry, let alone pay for it.

Those of us who knew Harvey understood when he let it be known that he was starting to get very tired of a couple of unnamed college instructors who spent most of their copious spare time sitting around his place talking about how to escape their easy and lucrative jobs, or a certain railway worker who regularly enumerated the worth of his pension plan and the buyout he was sure to get (at taxpayer's expense) at age fifty, or a certain local artist who had made so many mugs with cute faces on them that he was starting to look like a mug himself. But there were others who took it hard. The tree planters, for example, who regularly sought out civilized comforts like cappuccino, were hurt when they learned that, in Harvey's opinion, planters, while they usually looked interesting, were actually as boring as most urban professionals and sometimes a lot more boring.

And then there were the bad days, when the mere request for a cappuccino would get you nothing from Harvey but an unflinching, incredulous stare, and you had to sit under that stare, coffeeless, trying to read the newspaper or look at the art.

Lilla stepped in. She hired Rob, a painter who used to be a bartender, to watch the tables. Rob was efficient and could stand polishing a cup or spoon for hours and even manipulate his eyebrows to look interested while customers told him their stories. He liked everything that people purchased, even when they chose it off the wall from right beside one of his own things.

Other Art started to prosper as soon as Harvey left. He is now more or less banned from the place, though he still uses the studio in back to arrange consignments, paint T-shirts and ties, and do graphic designs for various businesses around town. He is actually making money from some of this work, though he finds it boring. He is allowed out front briefly, in the afternoon, for coffee, and if Rob knows you know Harvey and thinks it's okay, he will let you go back into the studio for advice.

As an owner of Other Art, Harvey has a new social presence and more places in town where he can legitimately hang out. He is a member of the Downtown Business Association and the Chamber of Commerce. He goes to meetings and votes on such matters as parking meters and garbage pick-up. He has taken to wearing a sports coat that he bought at the Sally Ann and carrying around an empty attache case. He is being courted by the Kinsmen. When asked how things are going, he inevitably says that he is "in a new phase." He implies that there is lots of movement "under the surface." He says there are opportunities everywhere, "just waiting to be picked up." Other Art, he suggests, is about to be "revolutionized" or to "come into its own."

"Jesus," Barry will say, "you'd almost think he meant it. Maybe he's reading Lee Iaccoca or something. If you think about it, he's even starting to look like Lee Iaccoca."

None of this could've happened, however, without Lilla. Harvey is the first to admit it. "She's the muse," he says. "She inspires idiots." Presently, he's trying to talk her into quitting the college and devoting herself entirely to the business. He's also looking for a job.

Kissing
My Money
Goodbye

I'm awake early on a beautiful July morning due to a dream about money. I'm drenched in sweat, trying to stay still so as not to awaken Vivien, who is breathing deeply and steadily, her pillow scrunched around her head. Outside, the birds are singing and the white stems of poplars are clearly etched into an orange dawn.

In my dream, Randy, whose $8000 loan I guaranteed three years ago so he could buy a truck and some equipment so he could get more work as a forestry contractor, missed a payment. The $289.26, automatically "scooped," as the bank puts it, from my account, brought down the delicate economic house of cards that I've spent the past two months building.

Item 1: Last month my older daughter Victoria, after two years of deep consideration about what she "wants out of life" and an emotionally charged break-up with a long-time, live-in boyfriend, finally found the perfect house for her and her menagerie of chickens, ducks, rabbits, dogs, and cats. The house is attractive, fairly new, and only twenty minutes away from the hospital where Victoria works as a nurse. The house is on six acres of land with a barn, toolshed, and covered barbecue pit. Best of all, it is on the road that leads out to my homestead. She will be safe there (so long as she keeps her distance from the neighbours) and will enjoy all the benefits of electricity, natural gas, and city water. One of my nicer dreams is where I, a grey but active old man in retirement, wearing heavy bifocals and smoking a pipe, drive my beat-up Mazda (of which more later) into her yard, picking my way through a litter of toys, wagons, and tricycles to be surrounded by some joyous grandchildren who want to go to McDonald's.

Of course I never mention this dream to Victoria, especially when Vivien is around, not wanting to "run Victoria's life for her" and being sensitive to the exorbitant influence that a father can have, especially in the months immediately after he has borrowed $7000 from the bank and signed it over "as a gift" to his daughter, who signs it back over to the bank as a down-payment so that a mortgage for $57,000 can be duly processed. There is also the question, Vivien would point out, of whether or not, if I keep *spoiling* my kids, I will be able to *afford* in my retirement to take anyone to McDonald's. Maybe my grandchildren will have to pool their allowances and take me.

As part of the deal, however, I now have a room at Victoria's house for the years that it takes me to pay the loan, a place where I can store my stuff, shower on the way to work, wash clothes, and generally bunk down when blowing snow or marauding beavers block my road and keep me off the homestead. I also have Victoria close by and thus able, when I'm away, to check in on the homestead and pick up my mail — tasks she will take up as of today. Vivien and I are off for the rest of the summer, our travel packs already stuffed and waiting in the kitchen below.

Item 2: During my annual May trip to Vancouver to recover from the teaching year and visit my mother and my son Wes, while driving my mother to the White Spot for a Mother's Day breakfast, I swung a sharp right off Willingdon onto Broadway, which forced the seat on my side down through the rusted-out floor of my Datsun pickup, leaving me flattened against the door, barely able to see over the dash, and my mother a foot higher in the air and barely able to see under the roof. It occurred to me then that I needed a new truck. Surely, I thought, a 46-year-old man, after twenty years of steady and relatively lucrative employment, should be able to get his mother to breakfast on Mother's Day with some dignity — especially a mother who, after decades of dedication, asks for only a $2.50 Mother's Day Breakfast Special (With Surprise Gift). We continued on our way, despite the discomfort, parking in the back of the lot out of sight of all the other mothers and their more visibly prosperous sons and daughters. Later, when we got home with the gift (an African violet), I used Dad's old jigsaw to cut a piece of half-inch plywood to shape. I jammed the plywood under the seat and, a few days later, returned north without incident. I could've convinced myself that there was another winter left in the old Datsun, but an ominous, increasing racket from the timing chain kept me resolute. As soon as I got home I purchased a two-year-old Mazda pickup from Victoria's ex-boyfriend, who was "restructuring" his finances as well as his life. I happened to encounter him in the driveway of Vic's new house. He seemed to be at the end of what was an evidently unsuccessful attempt to reconcile with Victoria, and we closed the deal there and then. I borrowed $6000 off Vivien to pay the boyfriend and retired the Datsun to the homestead, from where it was promptly (one evening when I was in town at Vivien's apartment) stolen, driven to a power-line cut near town, and torched. This was a significant loss. The Datsun would've been useful in moving gravel, hay, and firewood around the homestead. To add injury to injury, it cost me $100 to have the Datsun carted from the power-line cut to the crusher. To add insult, the people at the crusher paid me $2 for it.

Item 3: My younger daughter Jennifer has just been accepted into university in Vancouver after last fall at the college here where she got straight A's, and this past spring at the college in Kamloops where, despite an emotional break-up with her forester boyfriend (who was the reason she went to Kamloops in the first place), she got straight B-pluses. She will be in Arts and not the coveted Commerce program, due to a deficiency of one semester of calculus, but at least she will be at university with a single room in residence, which will be safe so long as she doesn't jog along Marine Drive at night, and with five courses including the missing calculus. The bill, totalling $5500, arrived early in June and the bank was happy to see me again. I didn't, when reviewing my liabilities, mention the loan from Vivien, but I did (and proudly) add the Mazda to my list of significant assets.

Total: $18,500 in debt accrued over a dizzying period of about two months at roughly 10 percent — cheap because Vivien's loan is interest-free on the condition that we use the truck for all hikes and ski trips. The debt is to be amortized over three years at about $650 per month.

There are also, of course, future expenses to worry and dream about, but they are (so far) minimal. Fortunately Jennifer has a job this summer, working in a western supply store at Spruce Centre for an East Indian guy named Cactus. She minds the front, does adjustments on boot-length jeans, and tries to lose (somewhere, anywhere) the Eddie Rabbitt tapes that Cactus provides as appropriate mood music for his customers. Jen's job means that I won't have to give her a monthly allowance, at least not until next spring.

Fortunately Wes, who presently works for a Victoria company that installs hot tubs, an activity he refers to as "soaking the pensioners," also seems happy with his job, non-unionized and poorly paid as it is. He seems happy with his recently acquired basement room near the ocean, his beat-up Datsun 510 (for which I buy the insurance out of fear that, if I don't, he will drive without it), and a case or two of beer on the weekend. He seems disinclined to return to school. Of course I know that this cannot last.

Eventually he will get tired of being ordered around by the tattooed bikers who form the bulk of the hot-tub company's employees, and watched every morning on his way to and from the shower by his landlady, who is either horny or timing him to see how much hot water he uses. I also like to think that, having been raised in a highly literary environment with parents in the professions, he too will gravitate to the professional end of the employment spectrum. Law, I think, would be a natural for him. If he succeeded at it, my legal as well as my financial and medical needs would be met gratis and in perpetuity by my own kids. With luck, though, he will hold out for two more years before the desire to go to university becomes overpowering. Having two kids in university at the same time would kill me financially.

Randy's problems arose some three or four years ago and are, of course, much more serious than mine. Randy is a musician and songwriter. I first met him a dozen or so years ago when he appeared in my freshperson composition class at the college. He was noticeable because he carried his guitar everywhere. We soon became friends. After college, he went on to university but dropped out in the middle of his first year, largely because he couldn't (and still can't) write standard English despite a C-plus in my course. I passed Randy largely because of his wildly inappropriate but still somehow charming use of figures of speech. "My knowledge of Canadian poetry," Randy wrote in the first paragraph of his book report on Margaret Atwood, "is slim, and Slim lives on the other side of town." Or, from his editorial on a topic of local concern, "In this town a university has about as much chance of success as a dog humping a football."

I wasn't the only person who pampered Randy. His indulgent but visibly long-suffering father, who had put up with Randy's sporadic attendance at public school and college and then at various jobs, and with his in-no-way sporadic dedication to songwriting, finally used his influence with the railway to get Randy on full time as a dispatcher. Randy disappeared to a small town in the Rockies where he got married, built a house, and had kids. He was, as they say, made. He even prospered, largely due to the local backyard marijuana industry in which he quickly became an eager participant.

Unfortunately, Randy continued to write music. He wired some sound equipment into the radio shack and practised. There was a problem some years ago when, in the heat of creativity, he put two trains on a collision course. Luckily the engineers figured it out in time and Randy's father stuck his head out again and Randy kept his job. The recording equipment was ripped out of the shack and replaced with a colour TV so Randy could stay awake by watching football games. Randy promptly put two more trains on a collision course — as an act of rebellion (unconscious I'm sure) against the TV set. Again the engineers figured it out.

Randy was booted out of the shack and into yard work. Then he and his little band went, at their own expense, to Edmonton to cut a demonstration tape, invited there by someone who'd heard them at a local dance performing some of Randy's original songs, including the ever-popular rockabilly tune, Randy's only real hit so far, "She Done Spun a Donut on the Ice-Rink of my Heart."

Randy's demo tape got as far as Santa Fe, where Randy went (at his own expense) to meet a producer. Shortly after this trip he quit his job, which he said he "couldn't stand anymore," to devote himself to writing songs. Shortly after quitting his job he had to destroy his marijuana crop when the police started dropping into the area in helicopters. And shortly after destroying his crop he was, of course, broke, his pension fund (accumulated over five years) spent, his unemployment insurance used up. He had twenty years left on two mortgages and two kids in kindergarten and elementary school. He had stepped out onto that dreaded edge.

And I owed him. At the time that Randy was at college, I was in the process of breaking up with my wife. He helped me make it through. I was finding the light in the classrooms too bright, my courses and assignments meaningless, and my life futile. At my wife's insistence, I was attending weekly sessions with a shrink and then a counsellor, both of whom were, while personable, clearly a lot more fucked up than I was. They kept forgetting why I was still visiting them. "*Politics,*" I'd explain, over and over again. "My wife *believes* in you people." Randy inspired me just by continuing to be himself, skipping classes and tests, ignoring all assignments except those he found interesting, packing his guitar around as if it were still the sixties, playing some new song for me in the college cafeteria while incredulous but hurried future managers, accountants, nurses, and lawyers steered their trays around us.

Just when he was about to lose his house, which was still mostly owned by the bank anyway, he was rescued by the drummer in his band, a forester who'd split with the Forest Service and started his own contracting company. Randy was good at forestry and liked the bush. It was, he claimed, a big improvement over the railway, where you had to talk to all the lost-boy unionists for whom a membership button and a large paycheque were passports to the never-never land of eternal childhood. As Randy described it, you had to discuss, endlessly, the positive and negative features of every available brand of pickup truck, rifle, skidoo, boat, and motorcycle. You had to listen patiently to repetitive fishing, hunting, drinking, and fucking stories, every one of which was mostly lies. You had to explain, over and over, the intricacies of income tax, the pension plan, the list of deductions on the paycheque, and women.

However, if forestry was more interesting than railroading, it wasn't nearly as lucrative. After a year, hoping to increase his wages, Randy started getting his own contracts. About three years ago there was the loan, that I co-signed, to purchase a truck and some necessary equipment. Then there was a payment he couldn't make that he phoned to warn me about. I paid it and then Randy paid me back. A year later there was a payment that he warned me about and that I paid, but then Randy didn't pay me back.

After this, Randy didn't warn me anymore.

Nor did he pay me back anymore.

Then there was what Randy described as a "big break." He won a song lyric contest and was invited to Vancouver to do some recording. He came through town in a van that, he said, was more useful than the truck but was also (I noticed) much older. Randy was clearly cashing in his few remaining chips to finance this latest musical venture.

While he was visiting, I influenced Harvey to put Randy on stage at Other Art. I came right out and explained my financial involvement with Randy and the fact that another monthly payment was overdue on the loan. Harvey sympathized. He rounded up a drummer and bass player and rehearsed Randy, and decided to put him on with two other local singer-songwriters. This would make, Harvey said, for some variety.

"Are you saying that Randy doesn't have variety?"

"Hugely. Are you coming?"

"Do I have to?"

"You can get your ticket off Lilla in a couple of days."

Harvey didn't have to worry about an audience or about Randy's performance.

"He does have a kind of persistent sincerity," said Harvey admiringly as we sat over coffees in the very back of the crowded space.

"Is he any good?"

"Roy Forbes he's not."

"Who?"

"Never mind. The trouble is, there's no money in the bar and coffee-house circuit. You'd better hope he gets a steady job soon."

One day last spring, when Vivien and I were walking down the road out of the homestead to our vehicles, Randy and his whole family appeared in the van. My heart skipped. I started calculating what it would cost to feed a family of four. I congratulated myself on having started a large garden. But there was no immediate problem. As a matter of fact, Randy had landed a steady job in Vancouver via an ex-girlfriend whose father owned an art gallery. Randy and his wife were full of hope and exuberance. Randy would be closer to the music scene. They would be away from their small town where they owed almost everyone money. The house was rented out at just over half the mortgage payment, and they had free accommodation in the ex-girlfriend's house because Randy's wife was going to do the housework and some babysitting.

That's the last I saw of them, fading out of my driveway in a rusted van full of kids, the youngest in kindergarten, amplifiers, keyboards, guitars, speakers, and hope. My heart glowed.

"Maybe he's going to make it this time," I said to Vivien.

Vivien shook her head. "Give me a break. They're going to live with an ex-girlfriend? His wife is going to cook and babysit for this girlfriend? He's going to wish he was back in a logging cut. You can kiss your money goodbye."

But I haven't heard from Randy since then, except indirectly through the bank over the occasional missed payment. One of the reasons that Randy has given up warning me in advance is that there is no real urgency about missed payments. The bank has a certain, somewhat lengthy, procedure for collecting overdue accounts. It takes them at least a month to scoop my account, and sometimes in the course of that month Randy does make the payment. So far I've made only four payments for Randy, all at convenient times when I hardly missed the money.

I don't hear anymore, either, from the congenial Phil, the local bank manager who originally signed Randy and me up for the loan. Once you have missed payments, your local bank refers you to an office in Vancouver where a team of "consultants" (in our particular case "Jason," who may be Asian) is engaged in tracking you through the jungle of your financial life and extracting overdue payments. Probably this is hard work. Randy, for example, seems to be forever on the move, so Jason always needs to know his most recent address and phone number. Since Randy has never thought (or decided not) to inform me of these things, I always express deep sympathy with Jason and promise that when Randy phones or turns up next, I will prod him for the payment in question and get his phone number.

Jason's moods swing violently, though it may be that these swings were studied by Jason in loan-collecting (or rather, I suppose, *consulting*) school. Sometimes he is jovial and we discuss Randy as if he were a sort of younger brother, unversed as yet in the ways of the world and needing our guidance and protection. Sometimes Jason is impatient and excessively colloquial: his supervisor is on his ass, there are too many jerks on his list, he needs the money now, and Randy should, like, wake up and smell the coffee. Last Christmas when Jason phoned, he was hurt. He said he had phoned Randy to wish him a Merry Christmas and Prosperous New Year and remind him that one payment was overdue and the next one coming up soon. No one had answered the phone. He knew that Randy was around, however. Randy had been at a bank machine at Granville and Georgia the day before Jason had phoned (the machine had told Randy that his account was overdrawn and refused to give him any money). He'd also, Jason said, only a couple of days previous to *that,* been in a finance company office trying to get a "loan consolidator" loan. The finance company had contacted the bank (which had contacted Jason) and then turned Randy out onto the street. Jason was deeply hurt that Randy was avoiding the phone and hadn't come to him with his financial problems.

I assured Jason that I would have a long talk with Randy. Randy, of course, never called, but he must've made this particular overdue payment fairly soon after because a few months later, when Jason phoned, he was jovial again, informing me that Randy was a week overdue with his latest payment and that it might be a good idea for me to remind him.

I don't talk much to Vivien about any of this because if I do she gets angry and makes a speech. While she is generally sympathetic to starving artists (her favourite is Dostoevsky) and the downtrodden masses, especially the fighting ones led by Castro, Guevara, and (especially) Ortega (who she saw recently at a rally in Nicaragua), she cultivates her investment portfolio with the incisiveness of a brain surgeon. "When in Rome," she says. *Her* daughters are responsible (i.e., married or on the verge of marriage to eminently responsible men) and *her* friends bite the bullet and indulge in their hobbies *when they can afford to*. She tells me how lucky I actually am that the bank is harassing me and Randy for the money rather than trying to suck us into more loans or into allowing them to tack missed payments onto the principal amount.

She usually sums up her speech by warning me that if Randy's problems ever affect any travel plans we might have, there will be trouble.

Fortunately, our plans for this summer are mostly paid for; we are leaving today for Mexico, Panama, and Peru. Vivien has assured me that the cost of the plane tickets was 90 percent of the cost of the trip. Where we're going, she tells me, hotels are five dollars per night, beer is twenty-five cents, and meals are one to two dollars. I have columns of figures on my kitchen table showing that I will actually earn back the cost of the tickets by the time we arrive home in September. Not only will I save on beer and food, but I won't be buying paint, nails, lumber, and (I'm always tempted this way) machinery for the homestead. I won't burn up $200 in gas every month going to town for cappuccinos at Other Art. Most importantly (in Vivien's view), my kids won't be able to get at me.

These prospective savings are important to our even-more-distant-future plans. In two or three years, depending on when I come up for sabbatical leave, we are going to Guatemala and maybe India. Vivien will take an unpaid leave for that year. When

I express concern that I may not have enough money for this trip because my salary on leave is cut by one-third, she volunteers to collect $100 per month from me, starting now, and even to pay interest on it. Then she will buy me the tickets. She recently suggested that I give her a pile of post-dated cheques. I have agreed to cooperate, but so far I don't have the $100 and so have delayed writing the cheques. In March, Wes, due to a number of hot-tub installations (the payments for which have not yet been received) up-island, had some heavy gas bills that I had to pay for him, and this month I may have to buy some roofing materials for Victoria's house as her auto insurance is due and the roof is leaking right above the kitchen sink.

As always, Barry is the only one who really understands my financial situation. It is only natural, he says, that a roof will start to leak shortly after you buy the house and just when you need auto insurance. It is natural that your kid will win ski and/or BMX bicycle races and need new boots and skis and/or a new chrome-alloy bicycle, and that your other kid will fall in love with some dipshit with a ponytail and earrings and quit her job at Pizza Palace and go off with the dipshit to, if you can believe it, hairdressing or photography school. It is natural to spend all the money you earn and more.

Barry also understands how Randy got into his situation. It is natural that someone with artistic pretensions will hate his or her job no matter how good it is and will quit or spend the rest of his or her life whining and complaining. Barry sees himself as a prime (but inspired) example of this syndrome. Barry believes that it was stupid of Randy to quit and naive of him not to realize that whining and complaining can be sublimated into great art. The railway, after all, thanks to the pluck and brains of early unionists, is one of the few places left where you get paid a fortune for doing nothing and complaining about it. Randy actually had it made in the radio shack. He had lots of time to write and practise his instrument. However, Barry also understands that

Randy is in his thirties and so still in danger of misjudging (usually in the sense of overestimating) his abilities, harbouring romantic illusions, and making impulsive decisions.

And Barry's opinion is that Randy *did* massively overestimate his abilities. Barry has followed Randy's musical career to some extent. He has been forced to. Whenever I get a new tape from Randy, I take it to Barry's to play it on Barry's super stereo. I want to hear Randy at his best. Barry has never stayed in the room with Randy's music for more than thirty seconds.

"Leonard Cohen he ain't," says Barry. "You were generous when you gave him a C-plus. You were stupid when you loaned him money. If he doesn't land a good job soon, you can plan on kissing your money goodbye."

I do plan on kissing some money goodbye, but not too much. Randy, with a little help from me, has gotten his loan paid down to $3000 or less. With luck, he will get it down even further before Phil or one of his successors calls me in for that final reckoning at the bank, with Jason or one of his successors testifying, no doubt devastatingly, over conference-call phone. At that time, if I'm lucky, none or at most one of the kids will be in school. If I'm not lucky, I'll cash in an RRSP when Vivien isn't looking and pay the price on my income tax and during my old age in Guatemala or Peru.

I still think that Randy's a good investment. This morning, on the verge of our flight to Mexico City, watching the poplars and listening to Vivien breathing smoothly beside me, I'm convinced of it. After all, Randy did write "She Done Spun a Donut" — though I have to admit that the lyrics and music don't quite live up to the promise of the refrain. Randy's genius may be limited to metaphor.

Imagine it as I heard it at Other Art and on successive tapes at Barry's. It has a thundering bass beat, a raucous, howling male chorus, a guitar imitating the sound of tires spinning on ice:

She's the one who spun a donut
on the ice-rink of my heart
and now the grass is growing through
and spring is sure to start,
and when it's here we'll marry,
and I know we'll never part,
'cause she done spun a donut
on the ice-rink of my heart.

That, in my books, is poetry.

Mending
Walls

Just into my mother's driveway — waving at Mother who's waving at me from the basement window and, yes, there's the other matching small white head now in the living-room window above, waving at me, my Auntie Irene — when Vincelli is on me, pumping my hand, handing me a card. "All kinds of cement work" it says in italics. "Contracting and Repairs." He's saying something about a wall, about his nephew who plays for the Canucks, about running a line into our circuit box for power, then about a wall again, and he waves his arms and I see, finally, my mind learning to focus again after a ten-hour drive (the last half spent mostly in erotic fantasies) from the Interior, that the big old house next door is missing, poof! along with the willow and cedar that shaded its porch, and there is only empty space beside our house, blue sky, just the chimney of the next house down the hill protruding above the far edge of the front lawn.

"She wanted this wall out too," Vincelli says, pointing toward the street, and sure enough, the old retaining wall along the front, put in by my father and brothers when I was (luckily) at university back east, is also gone, very neatly, like it was plucked out by a giant thumb and forefinger. "Your aunt tell me you come, you take care of it. Eleven dollar a square foot, cheap. We go half and half. I like to be good neighbour. This house for me and the next one for my son," and he's guiding me now across the lawn to the edge of what appears (and turns out) to be a huge hole, and I see that the wall down the side is gone too, right out to the back alley, and our house is on the edge of a crumbling, eight-foot sheer drop, with a panoramic view of Burnaby (Metrotown, Central Park). "We blast those," he said, pointing down at three colossal boulders that must've been sleeping beneath Capital Hill for ages. "We do it in stone. Looks very nice. I talk to you again tomorrow."

Then he's in his truck and gone in a roar and cloud of blue smoke, and the old peace settles around me again, the peace that I remember from (in particular) my late teens, those last years with my parents, when I commuted to university (winters) or the waterfront (summers) on the Puch-Daimler two-stroke motorcycle that I bought out of the Sears catalogue and paid on every month. Back to the hill in the evenings, the tall cedars (which were everywhere then), little old houses on huge lots with orchards and gardens, empty streets, and (at night) the glittering carpet of city below.

So now it's finally come, and to my mother of all people. Progress. Colossal houses built shoulder to shoulder. Sundecks. Cars parked solid on both sides of the street. New people. Italians. East Indians. Chinese. Of course Franke, the owner of the house that used to be next door, was German, but he came just after the war and kept to himself, which was always the unwritten law. Will the new neighbours do the same or will they want to talk, tell stories, make deals, borrow sugar, break the silence that my mother loves, especially now that she is eighty and has her lottery tickets, cable TV, the *Province*, the bus downtown, seven grandchildren (so far) from four kids, and the likelihood of great-grandchildren in the near future?

And then my mother and aunt are bunching up on the front steps to greet me (they've been hiding), and there is that evening no talk of Vincelli or the retaining wall but only of children and grandchildren, while the TV game shows run and Mom and Auntie Irene, settled under quilts, guess the answers (they're good at it, too) and sip hot water, and I read a book. I'd prefer to take them out to a movie or for a walk, or (this evening in particular) I'd like to sit with them outside in the back yard, but my mother and aunt would do none of these things. We all recognize this and that I am here only to be with them and will be able to stay around for only so long before I bolt for home like a cat let out of a cardboard box.

Meanwhile, Vincelli and the wall will be discussed tomorrow, downtown at the Woodward's coffee shop. My aunt will not participate but instead will spend the morning alone in the house, playing old show tunes and bits and pieces of famous concertos on the piano, pitting skill against arthritis. Mother will allow me to drive her to Woodward's, but she will leave me and go off to do her banking and shopping while I write and read and visit the bookstores. She will return home by herself on the bus. At Woodward's, she will tell me what she wants, and I will deal with Vincelli.

When the game shows are over and the news comes on, my brother phones. This call is expected, a regular evening event. Mom and Auntie do not watch the news but leave it on as a kind of social responsibility while waiting for Mark's call. Any comments are not on the news itself but on the personal lives of the anchorpeople. Mark is fifteen years younger than me, the baby in the family, a teacher, and he lives quietly in an apartment overlooking Kitsilano Beach. Since my other brother and my sister all live, like me, in other parts of the country, he has assumed most of the responsibility of checking in on Mother and helping her on Sundays with any jobs around the house that she cannot do herself. There is a tacit agreement that he is to be relieved of this responsibility whenever any of us are in town. After Mom and Auntie talk to him (nothing about the retaining wall), they give me the phone, turn the TV down, and head upstairs to bed.

Mark knows about the sale of the house next door and is not surprised to hear that it has been bulldozed.

"It was Vincelli's wife who actually bought the house," he informs me. "She's a real estate agent but she told Franke that she was buying the place for herself. They were moving right in and needed the stove and fridge. I think Franke gave them most of the furniture, which is probably in a second-hand store on Hastings Street right now."

Mark is surprised, however, when I tell him about the wall. "Why did she let him rip out the front one?" he asks.

"I don't know," I say. "I'll find out in the morning. Probably she didn't understand. He's too fast."

Then I tell him that, based on my knowledge of the cost of cement work, our half of a new retaining wall down the side could cost up to $3000.

Mark whistles. "I think he took advantage of her," he says.

I agree and tell him that I will try to make a better deal. If worst comes to worst, I can always come up with some money to help out. He says he could too. Then he lists some jobs that I could do. The main one is an outside light.

"She saw an ad for one on TV," he explains. "I think she thinks it would be good to install one above the sidewalk between our place and Ken's."

Finally he asks me what I've got planned and I tell him that we're going to Victoria, probably on Sunday.

"Watch it. Uncle Oliver's gone Baptist, though he still has one foot in the Presbyterian. I think Mom and Auntie Irene would be worried that he'd start to babble. Better make it Uncle Fred. Are you going to see Wes?"

"That's the main objective."

By the time I hang up, the sounds from the upstairs bathroom have stopped. I glance up the stairs and notice that the lights are all off. I close the door softly, snap the TV off, and lift out the hide-a-bed.

I learn in the morning at Woodward's that yesterday, very early, Vincelli informed my mother (in the presence of a nodding surveyor) that her retaining wall was four inches onto his property and would have to be righted, which was easiest done by busting it up, carting it off, and replacing it, and that this should be done while the machinery was still around and before any construction started and that he would be willing to split the cost of this and building a new wall fifty-fifty, and maybe at the same time they could replace the one along the street and do it in stone. My mother said she guessed that would be alright and fled inside, then watched in dismay as the wall and the flowers along it were instantly demolished. Then Vincelli came to the front door and, when it was not answered, the back door, and when that too remained unanswered he opened the door (!) and told my aunt (who was advancing to meet him while my mother fled to her bedroom) that he needed my mother to sign a statement to the effect that she'd given him permission to remove the wall. My aunt said that that was impossible at the moment and that her nephew (Mrs. Harris's oldest son) was arriving later in the evening and would be taking care of everything. Vincelli repeated that he only needed a paper signed stating what had already been agreed upon, but my aunt (who is older but feistier than my mother) interrupted him and said that nothing could be done until the aforementioned nephew and son, who was a college professor up north, arrived. Vincelli then asked if he could have an electrician come in a day or two and wire in a breaker box and plug-ins so they would have power to build the house, and my aunt repeated that all such matters were now in the hands of the oldest son. Vincelli seemed, according to my aunt, quite angry at this development. His face turned red and he left very abruptly without so much as a goodbye.

As Mother and I sniff our coffee and butter our scones, we admit to one another that we're both out of our element. We don't know anything about the laws on these matters. She isn't interested in anything that will cost $3000. That would be "too permanent." She can see maybe $1000, at most. So far as she is concerned, the yard can slope down the way it did before the wall was built. This strikes me as a good idea, a bargaining point. I'd forgotten that the yard did, originally, slope. Mother reminds me that there is, on the upstairs mantle, a colour photo of Dad pushing a lawnmower down the slope. However, a lot of dirt would have to be removed. I tell her that it seems to me that the wall wouldn't have stayed up anyway, righted or not, because Vincelli excavated so deeply and so closely, and we agree that it is all very mysterious as to why the wall is our problem to begin with. However, it *was* leaning into Vincelli's property. I promise to contact the municipality in the afternoon and, in the evening, to ask the neighbour on the other side about it. Ken is a contractor and his wife is a nurse and they got along well with my father (which wasn't that easy) and even did mouth-to-mouth on him when he had his final stroke (but he was stone cold dead over his crossword) and called the ambulance and all of us. Since then they have kept a watchful eye on Mother.

She leaves me in Woodward's among the menagerie of generally antique weirdoes that haunt the place. She understands that, being a professor and (it seems) writer, I need time to brood, preferably in a place that is populated by weirdoes and serves strong coffee. When she was last visiting me in the north, I took her to Other Art where she met Harvey and Lilla, enjoyed the latte, and tried to be polite about the art.

I brood about why my mother, even when she's alone, always comes to Woodward's. The cafe is a touch seedy, as she'd put it. Probably she has always come here, ever since the Depression when she worked as a secretary at B.C. Sugar. I remember, too, after the war, coming here with her myself. We made regular trips to Woodward's for groceries, in particular for peanut butter, which was freshly roasted and oozed warm out of a grinder into a cardboard tub. Probably the place is a comfortable reminder of the past, though my mother is not particularly nostalgic. Anyway, there's no doubt that this is the closest thing to a bohemian atmosphere that she knows. And I do feel comfortable here. Right next to me there's a pensioner with dreadlocks having a conversation about salmon fishing with another pensioner who looks equally unlikely in a nautical hat, blazer, white pants, and canvas shoes. The nautical pensioner is smoking a cigarette that is stuck (a bit crookedly) into a jaunty holder. I am pleasantly reminded of Other Art and even the Sears cafe where I work and/or write almost every day.

After Woodward's I go to see Bill in his Gastown bookstore, but he is back east buying books and his assistant is going nuts trying to cope and has had it up to here with writers, so we talk about her horses which she boards in Abbotsford. Then I have a late lunch with my publishers, who inform me how my book is selling. We decide that there will be enough royalties for another lunch when I come back in September. They also inform me that it is high time I do a reading in Vancouver. I have been avoiding this. I hate readings myself, only slightly less than sermons and political speeches. I point out that Barry read in Toronto once in front of five people, and that only his mother and two of her friends came to one of his book launchings in Calgary. My publishers say that this is because he is a poet. As a writer of short stories, my readings could attract at least six people. Anyway, they say, the audience doesn't matter as the real benefits come from the free notices in the newspapers and the possible presence of a reporter. They also remind me that I signed a contract agreeing to do a certain amount of promotion and, in two years, haven't done any. By the time we've argued our way from the cafe back to Stan's house, where their office is, I've agreed to do a reading in September if they can find someone who wants to put it on.

I use their phone to call the municipality about the retaining wall, and the guy there tells me that a wall is an agreement between two neighbours. If only one neighbour wants it, he/she has to build it. This is what I wanted to hear. He also tells me that if I let Vincelli wire into our house, I should ask for a cash advance on the bill. There have been a lot of rip-offs lately.

Back home, I find Vincelli conveniently available, sorting and stacking lumber on our front lawn. The lumber will be there, he informs me, for only a few days, at most a week. I tell him that I am not sure we need a retaining wall as there wasn't one there before, and maybe we will just dig out the extra dirt and create a gentle slope. Vincelli, getting more and more excited as I speak, suddenly bursts in and says no, it wouldn't work, it will cost us plenty to get rid of the extra dirt, that he had an understanding with my mother, that if he finishes his house and we then realize that we need the wall it will cost plenty to build it, that there will be a bill in the mail for the entire cost of removing the old wall because the Drott 4000 doesn't work for nothing and, in fact, costs $85 per hour, and the pieces of the wall had to be trucked, at $45 per hour, to a landfill site way over in Surrey, and (by now he has scrambled far below me in the hole, gesturing at the ground at his feet as if he were trying to embrace it) that later on, if any dirt gets down onto the sidewalk he is going to put right there, he will hire someone to clean it up and send us the bill. Then he is gone, his arms still waving, over to the surveyor who is pretending to be busy staking out the foundation.

I go in and dinner is set (they must have heard the shouting), and I notice that there are two of my special favourites, baking powder biscuits and apple pie. I eat and gently shoulder my aunt away from the dishes and wash them and watch my mom and aunt settle in front of the TV with hot water, and then I go next door to talk to Ken.

Ken has been watching the action from a distance, waiting for a sign to get involved, and when I give him the details he gets just as excited as Vincelli. The wall, he says, leaning or not, would certainly have caved in when Vincelli excavated, and when it caved in it would have been his responsibility to set our property right again. Also, the wall that Vincelli wants is necessary only because he's excavating so deep for a sidewalk. The new wall will be three times the height of the old one. So Vincelli is taking advantage of my mother, making her pay half for something that he would have to build anyway. Ken knows guys like that, he says. He works with them every day. They'll do anything to save a buck.

I agree with him, but what I hear is a fine legal point. Mother did agree to have the wall removed. It was on Vincelli's property. It started to lean (I remember my father explaining) the day after it was poured, but nothing was said because (he further explained) Germans and Englishmen are brothers, sort of, and fight only over abstract considerations like whether or not Poles, Frenchmen, Chinese, Africans, etc. should be treated like humans, with the Germans traditionally believing that such people are certainly not human and the English believing that they should be treated as decently as possible just in case they are. I decide that if there's one thing I'm not interested in, it's getting a lawyer after Vincelli, who is probably a millionaire. Also, while I don't believe that Vincelli plans to live for long (if at all) next door to my mother, it is a possibility that good neighbourly relations would be beneficial. I decide to pay for one-third of the wall on the grounds that the new one will be much bigger than the old one.

That night during the game shows I answer a phone call from Vincelli's wife. She sounds worried and insists on talking to my mother. Mom takes the phone but keeps her eye steadily on the game show (and Auntie Irene keeps on giving the answers). Finally she says, "I'm afraid you'll have to talk to my son about that," and passes the receiver to me. I do my line about not needing the wall, there wasn't one there in the first place, and Mrs. Vincelli is saying yes, she understands that (I can hear her husband shouting in the background), but that there was an understanding. Then I tell her that we will certainly pay for removing the old wall and that it would be helpful if they could give us a written estimate on the total cost of a new one, but my mother is on a small pension and doesn't have money to throw around. She then asks me about the power hook-up. I tell her that it would be better to run a power line into the neighbour's place on the other side, as it would be too much of a bother to my mother to figure out the bills. Mrs. Vincelli says she understands and will talk to her husband (still shouting in the background, only closer now, like maybe he is trying to wrestle the phone away from his wife) and then she will get back to me. Then it's back to the game show, my mom and aunt informing me that the fat lady, who is just an ordinary housewife, beat out the schoolteacher and car salesman. The fat lady is up to $13,000, a car, a sailboat, and a living-room suite that you would have to sell if you could. I go upstairs to put on the kettle for more hot water.

In the morning the table is not set, which means that Mom and Auntie are agreeable to breakfast at the White Spot. I go outside first, ostensibly to warm up the truck, but really (we all understand) to intercept Vincelli should he want to talk. Sure enough, he has been laying for me. He has a long roll of paper in his hand — the plans, it turns out — which he spreads out on the hood of my truck. He explains that he has a new idea. He will reverse his house so that the sidewalk will not go between his house and Mom's, but rather between his and his son's house. This will mean that only some sixty feet (instead of a hundred and fifty feet) of retaining wall will be needed, twenty feet at the front and forty at the back. The ground between the two houses, and his portion will be much longer than ours, will be level. Costs will be much less, maybe $1000 each, including removal of the old wall. The front and back yards will then be level, which will be better for Mother. I'm impressed by this idea and say so. I notice that, in addition to making for a cheaper wall, it will ensure (with the sidewalk on the other side of Vincelli's house) more privacy. I especially appreciate the fact that Vincelli is treating me seriously, consulting with me as if I can actually read the plans and understand the fine points. I try to figure out if Vincelli's kitchen will be directly across from Mother's. I note that the sundeck extends out back almost to the alley. I tell him that I'm sure now we can agree on the retaining walls, but I want a written price. My mother can't get into something without knowing how much it will cost. He says it will still be about eleven dollars a square foot, cheap because his friend will do it, split two ways. Once the friend comes to do it (after the houses are finished), it will be easy to figure out the total price.

"We have to have a price in writing," I say, but he has already rolled up the plans and turned away.

Breakfast at the White Spot takes almost two hours because the waitress (trying to be extra nice) puts two teabags instead of one into the small stainless steel pot for my aunt and then has to produce what seems like gallons of boiling water so my aunt can thin it enough to drink it. My aunt tells me that they didn't waste tea like that when she was young, and one bag served a family of nine. My mother nods in agreement. I tell them about Vincelli's new idea and that it sounds very conciliatory and maybe a deal is in sight. I also tell Mother that his house, including the sundeck, will extend to within twenty feet of the back alley and effectively shade out the small garden she has always had along that side of the yard. She says that is alright as Mark had to do most of the work anyway and she's at the age where she won't be spending so much time back there. My aunt says that this is a good thing, as she might get hit on the head by a falling geranium pot or wine bottle or something.

We go to the hardware store to get the automatic light fixture and all the wire, junction boxes, etc. needed to install it. My mother and aunt comb the store and come up with a paring knife that has a wooden handle and the proper shape, and then they try to pay the whole bill but I refuse to let them. When we get back home we have a snack (by now it is mid-afternoon) and I walk down the hill to the supermarket and a cafe and a store that sells used books and then I walk back up with a chicken which I cook for dinner, Mom and Auntie making sure the chicken is properly elevated from the bottom of the roasting pan so it will shed grease properly. This is my turn at dinner, but they won't let me throw the potatoes and carrots in with the chicken. Instead, they cook them in a steamer. They shove a cake in beside the chicken. Mom and Auntie Irene do the dishes (on the grounds that I made supper) and then we settle again in front of the TV.

Through the game shows, we arrange the Victoria trip. We decide that we will head over on the first ferry, brunching on the other side at the White Spot because the food on the ferry is terrible, and then checking into the Dominion Hotel which the family, I am reminded, has been patronizing since the turn of the century when Grandfather first went over for an Orange Order convention. (He later became Grand Master, and a photo of him in full regalia is made available after a quick search through the albums which I fetch from upstairs.) The hotel has a decent cafe, particularly for breakfast, and there is a bakery around the corner that produces cakes that are not all icing as so many cakes are these days. One of these cakes might be purchased and taken to the hotel or to the relatives for tea. We will visit Wesley who, they both agree, looked "very thin" when they saw him at Christmas. Contact will be made with Uncle Fred and Auntie Violet if time permits. Mom and Auntie Irene half-heartedly question the necessity of breakfast at the Empress (too expensive) but give up when I state that it will be a good experience for Wesley. In reality, breakfast at the Empress is a necessity for Auntie Irene, who stayed at the hotel when she and Uncle Joe (who fixed trains for the CPR) got married and who still has a pass that gives her half price on all company services but not their food.

The Victoria trip is a big success, though Mother develops an ominous limp ("a slight swelling," she says and immediately changes the subject) and I notice that her left foot is swollen. We spend a day with Wes, who is living with two guys and a girl in a rented house. Wes is very gallant with his grandmother and great aunt and at the same time knows enough to joke with them and accompany them through any stores where they buy him socks, tea towels, pillow cases, and hankies. They are ecstatic about the drywalling he has done (in lieu of some rent payments) in the attic of the rented house. They are amazed at how talented he has become. The fact that there is a girl connected to the whole arrangement, whose cot is in the newly finished attic room that also houses a drum set, amp, and various guitars, goes unmentioned. So too does the motorcycle in the living room and the massive stack of beer cases full of empties in the kitchen. We go for dinner at a place that Wes recommends. He is careful to make it very British, though he tells Mom and Auntie that the atmosphere would be more genuine if there were waiters on strike, football fans rioting, and skinheads chasing East Indians up and down the street. He produces, and introduces with all due formality, his girlfriend, a quiet blonde. Mom and Auntie Irene find that the meals on the menu are suitable and the tea excellent. After test questions to elicit the fact that the girlfriend lives at home and has a father in the Navy (and therefore cannot possibly be the occupant of the cot at Wes's lodgings), they decide that she is nice.

Next morning at the Empress (with Wes but not his girlfriend, who is at school), the tea is good and the cream, jam, butter are not in little plastic containers with peel-off lids. However, the seats of the chairs are very low and Mom and Auntie Irene have to reach up to eat. They have fun joking about how they were small before and are now shrinking to insignificance. Soon they will have to use booster seats, or picnic beneath the tables. They note that the silverware at the Empress is stainless steel, but that is, after all, more efficient. We return to the Dominion, with

Mom limping so badly that Wes volunteers to carry her. Wes hugs and kisses them goodbye and he and I leave them in their room and go to buy Wes some clothes. Then I drop him off at work and say goodbye.

Back at the hotel, I find that Mom and Auntie Irene have rested and arranged the visit to Uncle Fred. Auntie Irene has gone to the bakery so we have cake to offer. We get there and drink tea and listen to Uncle Fred talk about recent church events and how much they cost or earned. We hear about all the marriages of my cousins' kids, and there is talk of a family reunion this summer back in some Ontario township where, Uncle Fred implies, some of the less progressive relatives are still clinging to the original farms. Certainly no one plans on going back there; it is too muggy to sleep.

After the visit we are full of cake and tea and decide to forego dinner and spend the evening resting. I watch one game show with Mom and Auntie Irene and then go off to my own room. I phone Mark and ask about Mom's leg. He says that she believes she sprained it a couple of weeks ago when stepping off the bus. The trouble is, it's not getting any better. I tell him I will get her to the doctor when we get back to Vancouver. He asks me about the relatives in Victoria, but when I start to tell him about the reunion he begins to hum "Shall We Gather at the River" louder and louder until I give up and say goodnight.

Back home, we are amazed to see that the foundations for Vincelli's houses have already been poured and the forms removed. We hustle into the house and, looking down into the concrete maze below, see Vincelli, alone, knocking the metal strapping off the cement with a hammer and cold chisel. He is burning scrap, too, and it is so smoky that Mom can't open the back door to air out the house. I start to install the light fixture. Later, when I am running the wire out through the siding and up the wall, Vincelli appears and tells me he will move the pile of lumber (which has tripled in size) off the lawn soon. He also informs me that if I put the wire inside a plastic pipe, it will look legal when the man comes around to read the meter. Those bastards, he says, will report you to the building inspector. We talk about where I live up north and he asks about the hunting. When I say it is very good, he talks about coming up and asks for my phone number. I tell him I have no phone but will draw him a map, which I do (sitting now on the lumber pile on the front lawn), warning him that my road is a bog. He says that is okay as he has a four-wheel drive and hauls a couple of all-terrain cycles with him, one for him and one for his wife.

Our friendly conversation is interrupted by a huge firetruck with three rubber-suited men riding on the back. It rolls quietly down the street and stops in front of the building site. "Shit," mutters Vincelli, and he scrambles over to talk to the firemen. I go inside and learn that Ken, on returning home from work, saw the smoke and phoned Mom and asked her if Vincelli had a large fire going, and Mom said that, yes, it was fairly large, and then Ken said "he can't do that" and "it's smoking up my house" and "I'm going to report him." We watch the firetruck leave and Vincelli douses the fire with a bucket and some rainwater that has collected in the excavation. Then Vincelli leaves too.

I leave two days later, after getting my mother to the doctor who reports that she has only sprained her leg and should stay off it. The outside light works fine, though I should have taken my mother's height into consideration (instead of just following the instructions) when I mounted the scanner. We discover when we test it that she has to walk ten feet into the passageway before it clicks on. Auntie Irene suggests that we place a bamboo pole at each end so Mom can wave it in front of the scanner, but Mom demonstrates that if she takes her hat off and waves it above her head as she steps into the passageway, the light goes on nicely.

Over the next couple of months I phone regularly and get reports on the building. Vincelli's house is huge and entirely shades out Mom's back yard, and she and Mark start the process of moving prized flowers out to the front lawn. The wall goes in and, including the piece along the front, looks "very nice" and costs only $800. Mark starts seeding grass. Then one day Mom reports that "for sale" signs have gone up in front of both of Vincelli's houses. She doesn't sound surprised. I can't tell if she's disappointed.

Elgin

My cousin Elgin's ashes are in a standard-issue cardboard box in his parents' basement on the table with his train set. My brother Mark saw them there recently when Uncle Clarence took him downstairs to inspect two hundred stainless steel teapots, all set out on the basement floor. The teapots had been fished out of a dumpster in an alley off south Granville Street. They were the kind of teapot used in restaurants. The main features of such a teapot are a hinged, flip-up lid and a tendency to dribble its contents onto the table. This tendency, Uncle Clarence explained to Mark, was because people failed to lift the lid up an inch or so when pouring, to allow the pot to "breathe." He demonstrated this in the basement sink. In short, there was nothing wrong with the pots, only with the majority of people who used them. Nevertheless, Uncle Clarence hadn't been able to donate them to the church, the Sally Ann, or even the soup kitchen down on Powell Street. He was wondering if Mark had any ideas. But Mark had none, short of returning them to the dumpster without further delay. He found it hard to concentrate on Uncle Clarence's dilemma and was instead glancing at the box of ashes, thinking about Elgin and getting, as he put it, "royally depressed."

The reason for the disposition of Elgin's ashes is that my family on my mother's side, the side that is rooted deep and wide in Vancouver where I grew up, is mostly religious and Elgin, as it turned out, was gay. He died of AIDS and, while dying, confessed. He even introduced everyone to his "friend," Clifford, a good-looking Jamaican who hovered solicitously over Elgin's hospital bedside while we came and went. A few months after Elgin's death, Clifford crawled into virtually the same bed and died himself.

There is some talk in the family now that Elgin wasn't *really* gay but only deduced he was, possibly on the grounds that he was never interested, sexually, in women, which was evidently the case. But does that necessarily mean that he was *therefore* interested in men? Maybe he just thought he should be. Elgin always did have a tendency to mull things over too much, so that they got to seem more important than they really were. In fact, Elgin never, as an adolescent, seemed to be interested in sex at all, never spoke about it, never asked any awkward, groping questions or told any tentative jokes about it, and never hovered over porn magazines in the drugstores — and some of these did, doubtlessly, have pictures of naked or near-naked men in them. As an adult he was always the perfect bachelor, the one person you could count on for birthday and Christmas cards and to be home alone whenever you were in town and felt like phoning. The only things that interested him in any obvious way were the church and electrical gadgets like train sets, organs and pianos, telephones, breaker boxes, radios, televisions, and (especially) computers.

Probably Elgin was sexless. There is some talk that Elgin might have been "out of his head" by the time he was taken to hospital, and also that his "friend" (Clifford is seldom referred to by name) might have been manipulating him for his money, of which there was very little but it might have seemed like a lot to Clifford. As for AIDS, he could have picked that up by accident. He was in the hospital for a serious heart condition some four or five years previous to his death, and the doctors gave him a lot of blood transfusions.

This sort of speculation is normal in the family and will, in the long term, resurrect Elgin sufficiently to permit the proper burial of his ashes. It is, after all, weird to have a son's ashes in the basement, and Uncle Clarence's basement is weird enough. Uncle Clarence, in retirement, got into driving around in his Volvo picking up bottles. He took the valueless bottles to the glass-recycling depot and collected deposits on the beer and pop bottles, donating the money to the church. However, he was possessive about his bottles, letting them collect for long periods of time in the basement and counting them over and over, and they stank up the basement and the Volvo. Auntie Milly put her foot down, so he switched over to the salvage business, purchasing a new Datsun pickup for the purpose. He started in the dumpsters and still finds it hard to pass one up, but he is so well-known in Kerrisdale (they've been in the same house for forty years and at the same church for fifty) that people will simply phone him up when they have something they want to throw out but think is still good. It's amazing, Uncle Clarence always says, what people will throw out — near new Electrolux vacuum cleaners that need only $20 retractable cord spools, electric stoves with burnt-out switches, etc. Uncle Clarence fixes this stuff if it needs it and then donates it to the church or Sally Ann. Or he sells it out of his basement and donates the money to the church. He keeps only those items that he thinks have artistic or historical value — opium pipes, rare bottles, coins, jewellery, old books, and plug-in neon signs of the sort that used to sit in store windows and flash messages like "Rose's Ice Cream." Even this exotica is starting to pile up.

There is concern among the relatives that Elgin's ashes could get lost in it all, accidentally shipped out and taken for fish food or kitty-litter. Every once in a while a friend or relative visits the basement, as Mark did, and is reminded of Elgin's ashes. Uncle Nelson once told Mother that he was over there helping

Uncle Clarence load some stuff up for a church bazaar, lifted the lid off a box to see what was inside, and came face to face (as it were) with Elgin. Sometimes at a family gathering, someone will forget and ask where Elgin is buried and there is silence until someone starts the conversation again on a completely different topic.

So there is pressure to arrive at a solution. In the short term, however, there is a problem. Elgin did say that he was gay. Clifford was the main beneficiary of Elgin's will — a will that Elgin's parents had to administer. As a result of this incriminating evidence, the church that Elgin and his parents attended was unsure as to whether or not it could in good conscience stage Elgin's funeral. The minister wasn't sure he could officiate. There was a lot of fairly conspicuous scurrying around in the hall outside Elgin's hospital room in the last days of his life. Some sort of compromise was struck with the congregation so that Elgin could have some kind of service and his wasted body could be cremated, but proper disposition of the ashes, in particular their burial in Mount Pleasant Cemetery, where many of the family now rest, remains a problem. Elgin's ashes will have to sit by the train set until my aunt and uncle sort things out.

They will sort things out, and properly. They are good, practical people, and a son is a son and gayness or assumed gayness is some sort of unfortunate technicality, like socialism, atheism, poverty, disability, catholicism, and being foreign or weird. These things can be difficult, but if one simply ignores them and carries pleasantly on, they will eventually disappear or just not matter anymore. That seems to be the overall faith of most of my relatives, one that they would probably follow had they been born Moslem or Buddhist or even atheist, though that speculation is meaningless as in that case they would not be who they are. They are, most of them, Presbyterian, strongly so, unimpressed by the United Church compromise and every year more certain of the correctness of this attitude. They have no inclination to dwell much on philosophical matters, but were they to do so they would probably reason thus: the urge to carry on (pleasantly), which is endemic to all higher forms of human existence, does imply a certain order of things, in harmony with which one carries on, and this in turn implies a Divine Orderer, one who, while always wanting to be pleasant, has enough testosterone in His (Mother's relatives always imagined a beard on the Divine Orderer's face) system to see to it (as He evidently does if you take an overall look at the world) that those who stick with the script (Christians, especially Presbyterians) live pleasantly in neat houses in temperate climes and those who don't (Hindus, Moslems, Buddhists) get (for their own ultimate good of course) war, plague, volcanoes, piranhas, drought, and famine. It is further obvious that such a Divine Orderer would have expected Elgin to put up more of a fight against his tendencies or lack of them than he evidently did. So Elgin got the plague.

But I don't really understand how my relatives think. Sometimes it seems to me that they agonize or get belligerent over silly things like evolution and papal infallibility, and are complacent about important ones like the environment and books. Some of the relatives seem too complacent in general, others too belligerent, and others (like Elgin) too agonized. Religion was never important to me. There was little of it at our house: no prayers over dinner or before bed, no mandatory Sunday school attendance, though such attendance was clearly approved of, no prominently displayed Bibles, and no prohibition against playing outdoors on Sunday, though we were told not to go looking for our cousins on that day. My father had no religious background at all, claiming that he had gone to church once to meet Mother and once to marry her, and he hoped he wouldn't have to go there again for her (and didn't). My mother either followed his lead in this (but she didn't in much else) or decided on her own (or more likely in consultation with her sister, my Auntie Irene) that enough was enough.

However, I grew up in the (ample) bosom of my mother's family and spent a fair amount of time trying to figure them all out. My father's family was small — one brother in the airforce who lived mostly elsewhere, and a mother from the English Midlands who boiled cabbage and onions and fried bacon and pork chops (the kind of cooking I didn't get at home, where any kind of grease and fat and anything soggy or spicy was rigorously expunged), wore black for my long-dead grandfather, and bought the first TV that came on the market so we could go over on Sunday and watch *Toast of the Town* on a tiny, circular screen in snowy black and white. I got to enjoy her only until I was about eight, and then she died, leaving me Grandfather's Navy hat, some mess items from the HMS *Dreadnought,* and some souvenirs from World War I, all of which I lost. My mother, on the other hand, had five brothers and a sister, most in Vancouver and close by. When I was a child, Elgin and his family lived five doors down the street. Uncle Fred and Auntie Violet and two cousins were just over on the other side of Little Mountain. Grandfather and Grandmother were only a few blocks away. Also, Auntie Irene lived with my mother and helped to look after me until my father got back from the war. Later, when I was a teenager, Grandfather and Uncle Cecil came to live with us.

I deduced that these relatives had inherited their Presbyterian religion from Grandfather, whose namesake Elgin, as the first grandson, was. Grandfather was a saint in Calvinistic clothing. He was a model of integrity, patience, devotion, and diligence, and he attended church regularly, paid his tithes, pumped out hymns on the church organ or family piano, and taught the Bible to Sunday school classes. He was also a model family man and a druggist. I have, via Auntie Irene, his daily journal for the year 1903, and his minor and major term certificates (1901 and 1902) admitting him "to a full course of lectures upon all the subjects, including Elementary and Pharmaceutical Chemistry, Pharmacy, Materia Medica and Toxicology, Botany and Practical

Instruction in Dispensing and Reading Prescriptions." The journal is uninspiring reading unless you are interested in the minutiæ of day-to-day life in Birtle, Manitoba, including daily temperatures, sales at the drugstore, hymns sung at church, topics of sermons at evangelical meetings, and prices for everything from stamps to haircuts. Grandfather was very lonely there; he wanted to be back in Winnipeg with the family and wrote them every other day. His dream, short of becoming a doctor, was to own his own store, "God willing." God was clearly a major figure in his life — consulted regularly re: going home, buying a store, dedicating himself to Christian "service," getting a loan, and combatting some unspecified "temptation" that at least once a week proved to be a "sore trial" that seldom ended in "victory."

Anyway, God was certainly with Grandfather on most things. He did well in the drugstore business, married, had five boys and two girls, and quickly made his way to Vancouver, where the older members of the family had already begun to settle. He worked as a druggist right into his seventies. The store I remember was on Kingsway, a place of polished glass, varnished wood, and subtle, foreign smells, where I would get candy when I visited if I was good (and I always was, according to my mother, who still refers to me as "the politician") and would hear about the people in — I don't know — Africa somewhere, who were very thin and sickly (there were framed pictures of them on the wall), for whom Grandfather would collect, box, and mail off all the samples that salesmen gave him. It was a matter of principle — tested regularly by my father (who made a point of testing, to the limit, all of the principles of all of Mother's family), who felt that the Africans would have no need of, for example, after-shave lotion — that no one get these samples except the Africans. Grandfather was also a lay founder of Ocean View United Church, an institution that I attended fairly regularly until I was about ten years old, to the obvious satisfaction of, though with no active encouragement from my parents. I had an interest in religion in general and enjoyed the church because I got special privileges there as a result of Grandfather's influence. I was allowed to ring the bell, pass the collection plate, store away hymn books, and generally *do* things around the place instead of just sitting bored in one spot and maybe singing, which I don't do well. I got the impression that I was a suspected repository of holiness which, while certainly not evident at the time, would show itself later. I prided myself on this, but spent little time speculating on what form this holiness would take. I wasn't interested much in any form of holiness that I had encountered up to that time, not Livingstone's, Schweitzer's, or even Grandfather's.

But if Grandfather was a touch formal and suspiciously good, he was also a nice guy. All my memories of him are pleasant ones. On my fifth birthday, for example, he and Grandmother gave me a wagon, a good, solid, and fairly large one that would last for years and serve me well for pleasure as well as useful pursuits like hauling things. I insisted (this is the part I remember clearly) that Grandfather give the wagon its inaugural ride, and to my great pride he did, in the basement, kneeling one leg in the wagon and pushing it with the other, round and round until he crashed it into a support and cut his head. This sent me into a paroxysm of concern from which I refused to be extracted until I saw him safely bandaged and seated in a cosy chair with a cup of tea. Then I got my father to put the offending wagon into the trunk of our car where it couldn't do any further damage.

Grandfather's appeal was augmented by the fact that my mother and Auntie Irene obviously loved him very much. They fussed over him even more than they did over me. When he was with them he smiled a lot, and he seldom ever smiled. This was important to me, as my mother and aunt were (with, of course, my father, sister, and younger brothers — but they all turned up after the war and when I was in school) the most important people in my life and the only two of their family who, in my opinion, had any significant sense of humour. I never thought they inherited it from Grandfather, though they always assured me that he had a sense of humour. They said it was a "quiet" one, but that designation made me doubt. Grandfather even lived with us for the last few years of his life, and it was obvious to me that he did so in order to be near Mother.

Finally there was Uncle Cecil, Grandfather's constant companion. Uncle Cecil was, as some of the relatives put it, a "burden." He was a "sore trial." He was "simple." Either that or he was, as my father suspected (Uncle Cecil never having had to work a day in his life), a genius. Family legend was that one morning, on his way to Grade 1, where he was a promising student, Uncle Cecil fell down the front steps of the old house on Sophia Street, banged his head on the cement sidewalk, and was never the same again. He couldn't function except on the simplest level. I remember my father trying to teach him how to ride a bicycle — for what purpose I don't remember, but Father regarded Uncle Cecil as a challenge and experimented endlessly to see if he could be made to do things that might be useful like digging the garden, feeding the chickens, delivering newspapers, shagging golf balls, and caddying. It was all hopeless and in some cases (like shagging balls) near-disastrous. Uncle Cecil got beaned on the head while shagging; he apparently watched the ball coming, as instructed, but failed to step out of its way. He was knocked out cold but woke up unchanged, to the great disappointment of my father who, up to that point, had been nourishing a theory that if Uncle Cecil got hit — hard — on the head again, he would revert to normal.

Something like this theory may have been behind the bicycle lessons, but Uncle Cecil escaped any serious injury. My father held the bike up, ordered Uncle Cecil onto it, pushed the bike down the street, ordered Uncle Cecil to pedal, and, when he seemed to be pedalling efficiently, let the bike go. As soon as Father let go, Uncle Cecil veered off to one side or the other and crashed into the ditch. This went on for the most part of an afternoon, the neighbours all out on their porches watching Father and Uncle Cecil go back and forth on Quebec Street. Finally Father was exhausted, the front wheel of the bicycle bent, and Uncle Cecil dishevelled and wild-eyed (but still obedient) and so covered with dirt and grass stains that Mother had to get his clothes off him and wash and dry them before she could send him home to Grandmother and Grandfather.

As I got older, I spent a good deal of my time watching over Uncle Cecil. I never minded; it got me considerable credit with Mother, especially when I took him off and out of Father's vicinity on Saturday afternoons. Besides, like Father, I regarded Uncle Cecil as an interesting case. He could talk, but his responses were all formulaic. If you said, "How are you?" he would say, "Well ... alright I guess," very slowly and wearily, as if he was not alright but would trouble you with the details only if you were good enough to ask, and very few of the people who knew him were good enough to do that.

If you were stupid or careless or just feeling virtuous and you *did* ask, you got an endless list of ailments, the most interesting of which (to him) involved his bowels. You got to hear the opinion of numerous doctors — Uncle Cecil went from one doctor to another until he had been to every doctor in Vancouver and some way out in Burnaby and then had to wait for new ones to turn up before he could get more appointments and prescriptions. Half the doctors presently practising in Vancouver started their careers with Uncle Cecil. At home, Uncle Cecil would spend hours struggling with his bowels in the bathroom — this in the days when even a very large house had only one such room — and the only people who could eject him (apart from my father, who once did it physically, kicking the door in, and after that had only to walk up to the door and say "Time's up") were my mother, aunt, and grandfather. It took a good half hour to do it by pure persuasion, and then it was understood that Uncle Cecil was not yet finished and so everyone in the house who had, or even thought they had, to go would troop in past him while he waited (in evident discomfort) by the door. He moaned a lot, and loudly, when he was in there, a kind of litany, rising and falling, gradually absorbing the attention of everyone in the house until Father started muttering and Mother went to talk Uncle Cecil out.

Other than talking about his ailments, sitting on the toilet, and waiting in doctor's offices, Uncle Cecil walked. He could cover most of downtown Vancouver in the course of a day, dropping into Woodward's or the White Lunch for tea or soup. Sometimes Mother and Auntie Irene and I would meet or run into him down there, and sometimes we would have lunch with him, or they would spot him from the streetcar (he couldn't manage public transit) and try to guess where he was going or if he was going to get rained on.

There was a business side to my relationship with Uncle Cecil. At first he was useful only for getting through unfamiliar areas of town without getting beaten up, or for intimidating some of my friends, which I did by telling them that Uncle Cecil, while he looked passive, would do anything I told him to do. Uncle Cecil's nearly absolute silence and his vague smile were intimidating. But one day as Uncle Cecil and I walked up Oak Street along Shaughnessy Golf Course, Uncle Cecil reached down into the grass and produced a shiny new golf ball, which he handed to me. I was amazed. I'd done a bit of caddying (didn't like it much and went for a paper route instead) and knew what a good golf ball was worth and how hard it was to find one. So we veered off into the golf course that day, beating our way up and down the rough along the fairways, and Uncle Cecil netted a half-dozen quality balls. After that it became a regular thing, so much so that if Uncle Cecil didn't turn up on a sunny Saturday afternoon, I was asking after him. We'd hunt balls for a couple of hours and then I would take the balls to the caddymaster (who was usually Uncle Clarence) or preferably (since Uncle Clarence took a cut) to some golfers standing around waiting to tee off, and then take the money home and split the take with Uncle Cecil, an arrangement which I considered fair since I had, in effect, "discovered" him, and since he would never hunt for balls if I didn't tell him to and do it with him, and since I had to make the sales. My mother seemed satisfied with this arrangement. She held onto Uncle Cecil's money if it was more than a few dollars. If he was downtown and approached by a panhandler, Uncle Cecil would simply fork over every cent that he had. He was also, like his father and brothers, religious, and sometimes wandered into evangelical meetings at the Exhibition Grounds or services at the missions down on Powell Street, where he would be stripped of his money. Of course, I never exactly told my mother that Uncle Cecil really found *all* the balls. She might have guessed; I was so shortsighted that I was instantly tagged in Grade 1 and fitted with Coke-bottle lenses. Even with glasses, though, I had to accidentally kick a ball out of the grass while walking before I could see it.

Hunting golf balls with Uncle Cecil was a lucrative sideline that kept me in pop and chocolate bars and led me to appreciate father's attempts to teach Uncle Cecil something. I got the idea that if he would search for balls while I sat under a tree and read a book, it would be like the brooms that the Sorcerer's Apprentice activated. I wasn't greedy, except to sit and read. There was (thank God) only one Uncle Cecil, and the number of lost balls on Shaughnessy Golf Course was finite, so I wouldn't be swamped with money, which could get me into trouble. Instead I would be the recipient of a nice, steady income, and I liked that idea (and still do). So I tried some of my own small experiments. It was no use. When I stopped looking for balls, Uncle Cecil stopped. When I sat down to read, he sat down to stare at the ground. When I looked at the sky, he looked at the sky. When I got bored or hungry and went home, he came with me. I started to wonder if he might be making fun of me.

Uncle Cecil's religion didn't bother me much; if he started to talk about God or something he was easily deflected, and it took him a long time to get back to the subject. His religion did concern Grandfather, and it infuriated some of the uncles because Uncle Cecil's religion spilled over from the conventional to the bizarre. Strange people would turn up at the house, or engraved wallets, key chains, pen holders, belts, and Bible covers would arrive in the mail, and everyone would know that Uncle Cecil had wandered into some meeting or heard a service on the radio, copied down the address, and sent a donation. The people at the door would have to be sent away, the wallets, etc. returned with a letter stating that Uncle Cecil was nuts and shouldn't be taken advantage of, and the source of money had to be plugged. Usually it was Grandfather, who let down his guard with admirable regularity. Sometimes it was another of the relatives and sometimes even me, rewarding Uncle Cecil under the table, as it were, for a good day at the golf course. After the source of money was cut off, Uncle Cecil would have to be deprogrammed so he would stop talking about the healing shrine in Georgia where they (among other things) unplugged people's bowels (I imagined a toilet seat placed among other trophies at the shrine), or the key chain that brought special blessings from Jesus every time a door was opened.

The main thing about Uncle Cecil, however, was that Grandfather, as long as he lived, cared for him, a long, constant, and sometimes frustrating task. Others, even my mother, talked about getting Uncle Cecil into a home or hiring a nurse so that Grandfather could "do things," but Grandfather would hear nothing of it. Maybe he had nothing to do. Certainly he loved Uncle Cecil and maybe even liked him, as I did, sort of, so long as I had to deal with him for only one or two afternoons a week. Uncle Cecil was always pleasant, always agreeable to any proposition unless he happened to be heading for the bathroom. I saw them together often, especially when they lived with us, walking slowly along the street, side by side, talking (it seemed), or I heard the hum of their voices in their downstairs bedroom (it was hard to say if they were praying, singing, or talking). I never once heard Grandfather raise his voice at Uncle Cecil (like father and the uncles sometimes did), and thought then (and think now) that they were an ideal father and son, parent and child, sticking together through everything. I hoped my parents would treat me in exactly the same way if I ever fell on *my* head and turned simple.

The trouble with Grandfather, if I can properly put it that way, was that his saintliness had, in my opinion, a seedy side. What he referred to as "service" included things like missionary work, the Orange Order (of which he was, for some time, Grand Master), and other forms of Protestant politics. He pondered and then passed on to his sons (not to his daughters, unless they simply ditched them) hundreds of pamphlets on the iniquities of the papists and the Baptists and on various church missions around the world and the incredibly virtuous people who lived among the savages. I doubt his sons read these pamphlets, but they certainly kept them, and conspicuously, and so Elgin read them, all of them, and carefully. Worse, Elgin read them to me, an oppressive business (the train set was waiting downstairs) that I put up with only because I could see it was important to him. He seemed to want to convert me, and I think now that this was the case.

The trouble with Elgin was that he had no skepticism. He accepted everything he fell heir to. He studied the Bible, attended church, helped out at church functions, and forked over his 10 percent tithe. This last was, it seemed to me, an especially cruel levy, and I spent hours trying to convince Elgin that the tithe should be taken after, instead of before, essential expenses like a pop and chocolate bar after a hot afternoon's work at the golf course. Elgin would hear nothing of it. He believed the pamphlets. However, without skepticism, while there may be faith, there can be no conviction of the sort that Elgin understood — *viz.* that one and one adds up to two and that a current of electricity will ... whatever it will do. Elgin could never be a scientist or even an inventor. All he really could do was follow instructions. He became an engineer, a sort of tradesman with a good memory for abstractions, a kind of walking slide-rule. He specialized (as time went on) in computers.

I, on the other hand, had tons of skepticism. Elgin attributed this to my father, so that it wasn't entirely my fault. He liked my father, but was also afraid of him, and with good reason. Elgin was the perfect mark and while Father, liking Elgin, tried his best to restrain himself, there were situations that were simply beyond his control. Once, at a family picnic in Stanley Park, Elgin (then in first year university) was explaining to Father and me that he found the idea of people descending from apes to be ridiculous. Unfortunately for him, he was eating a banana at the time. Father grinned away at him, barely stifling his laughter when Elgin meditatively pulled the peel down another inch and took a bite, and then I caught on and had trouble controlling myself. Finally Elgin stopped talking, obviously confused. Later he asked me what Uncle Dudley and I were so "happy" about. I tried to explain — apes, bananas, evolution — but only succeeded in hurting Elgin's feelings. "Humans share the same food with mammals, birds, reptiles, and even plants," he said. "That doesn't prove an evolutionary connection." I finally agreed that Father had a tendency to be easily distracted from serious considerations. Elgin probably figured that if he could convert me, with my background, he had to be on the right track to salvation.

When he wasn't reading the pamphlets, mulling over the objectionable features of Buddhism or Irish Catholicism, or trying to convert me, he was a lot of fun. We wired incredible things into the train set. At Hallowe'en we put car horns and/or light bulbs behind masks or inside pumpkins, hid them in the shrubbery beside the front door, attached the horn or light bulb to the doorbell, and surprised (Elgin would never really try to *scare*, the trick-or-treaters and their parents. We built forts in just about every impenetrable patch of bush we could find in Vancouver. We went to the beach and put out pieces of driftwood at intervals and came back the next day to measure the tide. We went on long bicycle rides and even week-long camping trips, specifically to Roberts Creek on the Sechelt Peninsula, a wild spot that was, for some reason, Elgin's favourite place outside of the church. Because Elgin was a couple of years older than me, I easily got permission to do these things with him. My parents knew they could trust him. For the long trips, Elgin would always provide a carefully planned and prepared itinerary, complete with a menu, *viz.*, "Dinner: boiled potatoes and carrots, cold ham, milk, and two chocolate-coated cookies," and "Activities: secure iron bolts to rock outcropping to hold raft." My parents knew that the itinerary would never be deviated from, not even the two chocolate-coated cookies, which Elgin would distribute with brutal consistency, or the last items for every day, "8:00, go to bed; 8:15, say prayers; 8:30, go to sleep."

Elgin, being older than me, was a kind of advisor, and I always took his advice seriously even when I understood that it wasn't entirely practical for me. It was always, at least, interesting. Once he upbraided me for "taking the Lord's Name in vain." It was a sure way to damnation, he said. He then told me that whenever he was inclined to commit this sinful act, he would immediately convert the Lord's Name to "Jeez," thus avoiding condemnation. I tried it but found that it lacked impact. I also had doubts that God was stupid enough to fall for a mere ruse; it was clear from the Bible that He took a penetrating look at motivation. At the same time, I thought that He would have appreciated the fact that Elgin was at least (unlike, say, me) trying. There was an attractive humility, too, in Elgin's tactic, an acceptance of the fact that we humans were so far gone that we needed mechanisms to make us act properly, just as we needed them to make books, govern ourselves, and get from point A to point B.

Elgin also introduced me to a great way to clean my glasses, which were always cruddy. It may have been Elgin who pointed out to me that I could wash them, didn't have to stare at the world through a film of grease, dandruff, loose eyelashes, and dust. The technique was simple. After you'd gotten out of a soapy, warm, weekly bath, you grasped the glasses by the bridge, between the thumb and forefinger of your right hand, swished them up and down the full length of the bathtub, and then dried them on a towel. As well as making the lenses shine, this loosened the dirt that built up in cracks and crevices in the frames. Elgin also convinced me that using kleenex or toilet paper was more sanitary than using handkerchiefs. He was concerned because I had a very runny nose and suffered horribly from what I called "snot burn" (Elgin thought the phrase was accurate but objected that it included slang). This experiment was a failure. I found out that while Elgin could walk into any garage or cafe and secure permission to use the washroom and load up on toilet paper, I would more often than not be told to beat it. Also, I was careless, leaving soggy wads of toilet paper all over the house and yard. One day Father came into the house, sat himself in front of me and, without saying a word, lifted his foot and stuck it in front of my face. Embedded between the sole and heel of his shoe was a lump of toilet paper that (since the foot remained steadfastly in front of my face) I was obviously expected to remove. I removed it and went back to using the pile of hankies that Mother kept clean and pressed for me in my dresser drawer.

The last years that I spent with Elgin were at university. When I got there, he was in third-year engineering (electrical), with the exception of the mandatory first-year English, which he was attempting for the third time. He had grown a beard, which in my opinion improved his looks (he had a weak chin), and he wore his slide-rule, inserted in its slipcase and hung from his belt, with the elan of a Roman soldier. He even wore his red jacket, though only for special events (when it was dangerous to be without it). He thought his fellow engineers were overfond of liquor and obscene language, but he liked their cohesiveness and approved of many of the articles in their relatively conservative philosophy. He was already hooked on computers, and one of the first things he did was take me into the Engineering Building (the heart of darkness for any freshman, particularly during the initiation rites) to show me the computer that he worked on. It filled an entire room, and Elgin was busy programming it to calculate payments (interest and principal) that Grandfather would receive over the next ten years from the sale of his house.

I fell into Elgin's habit of staying on campus for dinner and studying late into the night in the army huts that lined the Lower Mall. This was more efficient than going home and trying to study in my basement room while the rest of the family watched *Gunsmoke* upstairs. Elgin and I would join up with some friends from the old neighbourhood, especially Frank, my bosom buddy, who went through school with me from Grade 1 to the master's degree (his in Classics), and go off to the cafeteria. Frank and I ordered meals with coffee and gave Elgin our milks, which he used to wash down the last of the peanut butter sandwiches that he fed on all day. Then we would find an empty army hut. The huts were quieter than the library and you could use the blackboards. You could also horse around a bit when you got bored, which Frank and I invariably started to do at around nine o'clock. Elgin would look on patiently or propose a game that involved figures on the blackboard instead of jumping around and knocking over desks. Then, at about ten o'clock, we would walk together to the parking lot, first to the motorcycle sheds where my moped was located, and then (me chugging along behind Frank and Elgin) out into the vast, dark, and deserted reaches of C lot in search of their cars. Both Frank and Elgin had ancient Studebakers (Elgin's the more compact "Lark" model) that had been given to them by their parents as high-school graduation presents. After starting both cars (which sometimes involved push-starting one of them and driving it over to jump-start the other) we proceeded out Twelfth Avenue to Granville Street and went our separate ways.

It was during those first two years in the army huts that I made my decision to stay, forever if possible, in the university. I had to face the fact that, unlike Frank or Elgin, I couldn't do math. In order to get my required math credit, I had to take the "dummy" course in probability and statistics. Calculus was beyond me. This shut me out of engineering or the sciences, which was crucial as I was modelling my career roughly on Elgin's, on the grounds that some professionals had real power and others had none. Law and medicine were, of course, supreme, but my parents regarded lawyers as that sort of human scum that rises to the surface, and I hated the sight of blood and had to sit down and put my head between my legs whenever I cut my finger. Teaching was the obvious way to go, but teachers were, I knew from my public school experience, the lowest form of professional. So I looked around at my professors and decided that theirs was a reasonably acceptable fate. I liked the university setting, especially at night with the yellow gleam of office lights viewed between the leaves of the luxurious maple trees that lined the malls. I loved the gorgeous sunsets and even the steadily drizzling rain. I imagined myself becoming a famous poet-professor and having a statue built in my honour of me staring contemplatively out over Georgia Strait.

Elgin couldn't understand my troubles with math and tried to help. With his help, a lot of memorization, and a promise to my professor that I would never attempt another math course, I got through the dummy course with 51 percent. At the same time, I tried to deal with Elgin's bafflement with literature. This was a more serious situation, as Elgin was nearing the end of his studies and would not be able to graduate if he didn't pass English. I could see, by looking at his assignments from the previous years, that he started with the fixed idea that literature was evil, a sort of antithesis to the Bible. In between was a kind of apocrypha (hymns, prayers, sermons, and devotional poems) by people of proven saintliness like John Wesley. However, none of the sacred stuff and very little of the apocrypha was on the English 100 reading list — only people like Yeats, Eliot, and Conrad. And who knew what they were talking about? Nobody, it seemed, including the professors, as Elgin could prove by the use of computer print-outs of contradictory comments that he had gleaned from the copious notes he took during his first two years in the course. However, even though the professors were obviously confused, they still didn't want to hear that Yeats, Eliot, and Conrad were "mistaken" in everything they wrote.

We started with Elgin's third annual attempt at "The Second Coming," a poem that offended Elgin because it described the birth of the Sphinx or Anti-Christ as the "second coming" and had the Sphinx being reborn in Bethlehem. When I suggested that Yeats was simply expressing the uncertainties felt by most people when facing war, famine, disease, and other forms of anni-hilation that might signify (at least for them) the end of the world, Elgin would point out that he should have explained this by calling the poem something like "A False Prophecy." But Yeats' title has more impact, I'd explain. It leads you into expecting a successful fulfillment of the prophecy and then experiencing dis-appointment. Then the title is just a cheap trick, Elgin would say. I tried, unsuccessfully, to explain why cheap tricks were okay in poetry.

I gave up on this and finally convinced Elgin that while he might be right, he didn't have to beat his professors over the head with it. Taking a less belligerent approach, *using Christian patience,* might get the message across more effectively. I got him into tak-ing the poem apart, like a motor, explaining the gyres (which Elgin could do in great detail), falconry, the building of the pyra-mids, and ancient theories of history. Once he got through all this stuff, some of which really interested him, he had no or few words left over to fulminate against the poem. In other words, he ended up saying everything but what he really wanted to say. The professor gave him a C-plus. I continued the process right through to the end of the year. The only thing I couldn't control was the final exam, but Elgin restrained himself and cleared a 50 percent for an overall C average. When he got the transcript and realized he had made it, he took his poetry text to a garbage can and unceremoniously dropped it in.

When he graduated, he entered the "private sector," a job with the telephone company that took him north to the small town of Kamloops. I continued on through my masters and married just before I took it. Frank was my best man. My wife and I visited Elgin in Kamloops one summer before we headed to Ontario, where I'd landed my first teaching job. He was "working his way up," but so far as he was concerned it was taking a long time. He objected to the work, which was mostly outdoors telling uncooperative and profane workers what to do, and he badly wanted back to Vancouver. Elgin drove us around, in the same old Studebaker Lark that he had at university. The Lark had acquired a second life as a result of a rebuilt engine, new brakes, and other improvements. We visited his office, where he had a desk that was crammed, with ten other desks, into a big industrial trailer. The shelf above the desk contained binders full of wiring diagrams, a daily diary, and a Bible; the drawers of the desk contained a hard hat, clip-on phone, and tool pouch. That's when I learned that engineering wouldn't have been a good choice for me even if I could've done calculus; the bravura of the engineers at university was a sort of long stag party that ended with a marriage to the system more stifling than that enjoyed by teachers. We visited the house where Elgin boarded and met the landlady who told us how she just couldn't sleep until Elgin was home and in bed. We went to the church, in which Elgin had recently installed a huge electric organ. He implied that the installation had been tough, politically. The congregation had wanted a nice organ but had no money, so Elgin had convinced them to purchase a kit, which he would assemble. Costs mounted on the assembly, and the centre of the church had to be gutted for some months, and there was a lot of talk whether they were "making a joyful noise" or merely "indulging Mammon." Elgin ended up making most of the payments on the organ itself, though he was sure the church would eventually pay him back. It was all worth it, he figured, and to prove his point he played a half-dozen hymns for us, the ponderous, slow, swelling ones that he favoured, while we sat in a pew and listened. In the course of playing, his face lost the worried look that it seemed to me it had taken on while he talked, and was lost in peace.

Elgin finally got back to Vancouver, but he had to quit the phone company to get there. I was still back east at the time. I heard that he had purchased his own computer and gone into some kind of business. This worried me, but by then I had three kids and no time to think about Elgin. Then there was an attempt on the part of his congregation to marry him off to some other member who had lost her husband to cancer and had a couple of kids. Mark, who was just finishing a teaching degree then, met her at the annual family Christmas party and reported that she was fat and bossed Elgin around. Somehow Elgin got out of that one, but apparently he disappointed a lot of people including his parents. His computer business didn't amount to much. He hadn't taken progress into consideration and his mainframe was soon outclassed by smaller computers that cost much less. It came to a point were Elgin was making a living by doing short-term repair jobs.

By that time I was back in B.C. But I'd gotten a job in the far north, and my marriage was falling apart, so I was not inclined to come south much and I was especially not interested in visiting relatives. Through my parents, however, I heard "complaints" about Elgin, mainly originating with his parents. He didn't have any money. He wasn't getting anywhere. Quitting the phone company had been stupid. He had no pension. I saw Elgin one Christmas and he had now, in addition to the beard, long hair, which (I told him) made him look patriarchal, prophetic. He seemed to like this idea. While we talked, he operated the train set for all his cousins' kids, mine among them. He gave me his card, which listed "electric organ repairs" alongside "industrial computer contracting."

Later I heard about the heart attack but was told that Elgin was recovering nicely. The heart attack surprised me; members of my mother's family generally lived to a ripe old age. I sent flowers.

Three years ago I saw him, for the last time walking around, in the northern town where I live. He left a message for me at the college — he was at the United Church fixing their organ and wondered if we could meet before he flew back to Vancouver. After work I picked up Vivien and we drove over to the church. We arrived a bit late because I got the Presbyterian confused with the United and we ended up out in the suburbs instead of downtown, me regaling Vivien with Stephen Leacock's story of the rival churches of St. Asaph and St. Osaph, which buried their religious differences (which seemed trivial anyway) and amalgamated in order to corner the lucrative religious market. We found Elgin waiting outside on the front steps of the church, everyone else having left for home. He had a small tool kit with him and was wearing an old pair of jeans and a windbreaker that was too light for the season. The long hair and beard were gone. He looked exactly as he had at university, only thinner and with a few flakes of grey in his hair.

There wasn't time for dinner, only enough to get him to the airport and have a coffee (or milk, in Elgin's case) in the cafe there. He explained his heart attack, and Vivien (who'd worked as a medical lab technician before becoming a college instructor) queried him on the pills that he sheepishly lined up on the table to take with his milk. I asked him if there was much money in fixing organs and he said no, but the people at Knox United had been kind enough to pay his fare and expenses. Vivien stared at him in disbelief. Finally he had to board his plane.

"He doesn't look very good," said Vivien as we watched him disappear. "He's not very clear on what happened to him in the hospital. He's also very depressed about it."

"He seems the same to me," I said. "A bit thinner."

"I can't believe that he would work for nothing."

Then my father died. I flew down for his funeral and in the course of making the arrangements, learned that Elgin was in hospital, dying of AIDS. He'd been there for a month or so before anyone knew, and Mark, Father, and Mother had visited him just a few days before Father died. They took a bowl of Mother's custard, which had always been a big favourite of Elgin's. Father, who had been in and out of hospital all year and was feeling tired all the time, took a close look at Elgin and then bet him ten dollars that he (Father) would die first. They shook on it.

What had happened, Mark and my parents learned from Elgin and later from a tearful Auntie Milly, was that Elgin had gone home one afternoon and told his mother that he was sick. She figured he had the flu or something and put him to bed in his old room. When Uncle Clarence came in from the dumpsters, Elgin confessed to both of them that he had been under treatment for AIDS for almost a year and that he was now dying. Auntie Milly had, she told us, broken down; Uncle Clarence said nothing about it and, so far as we know, never has said anything. Elgin stayed in bed for a week with his parents nursing him, and then he told them to phone his doctor. The doctor sent an ambulance and Elgin went to the hospital.

I don't know if anything was resolved between Elgin and his parents in the week they spent together in their little house. I think something was, some acknowledgment of love on both sides, because Elgin seemed calm and even happy when my sister and brothers and I visited him (I carried the custard). No one else seemed very calm. We met Clifford and the minister of Elgin's church. Elgin presented us to them in numerical order: "John is number one, Lynne is number two, Paul is number three, and Mark is number four." The minister said hello and then left. Clifford remembered Father's bet. "Your father won," he said, "but how can he collect?" Elgin smiled. "It was just another one of Uncle Dudley's jokes," he said. "If I'd died first, I couldn't have *paid*."

Elgin was shocking to look at. His face was covered with sores that had been closed by stitches. It was the result of a blood disease, which he explained in some detail. He spoke slowly, sleepily. Then he ate the pudding. Clifford explained that the minister of Elgin's church had been "hanging around all day, wringing his hands because the congregation won't have the funeral service at the church." Clifford sounded bitter. Elgin said nothing. I took the empty bowl from him. "Your eyes still have that old sparkle," I said to him. "Maybe you're in remission and we'll have you around for a few more years." Elgin smiled. He was clearly too tired to talk, so we said goodbye and left. Clifford followed us out. "He's asked me to tell everyone not to bring flowers to the service," he said to us out in the hall. "He'd like anyone wishing to do so to make a contribution to his estate."

We all stared at him, saying nothing. "Nice to have met you," he said, somewhat discomforted, and bowed very formally before turning and going back into Elgin's room.

I discovered the empty bowl in my hand, walked over to one of the plastic-lined garbage pails that were prominent throughout the ward, and dropped it in. Then I wondered if I should have done that; it was part of one of Mother's better sets. But I wasn't up to retrieving it from among the tissues, stained cloths, paper cups, plastic spoons, and heaven only knows what else was in the garbage pail.

Mark, Paul, and Lynne came over to me. "I should've warned you," said Mark, staring, with me, down into the garbage can where the bowl had disappeared. "Elgin's collecting money for his estate. It all goes to Clifford and Auntie Milly."

"Not a particularly attractive prospect," I said.

"I know. Anyway, they've sold all of Elgin's stuff, including the computer. They had to pay someone to take away the Lark. It's been rusting in the underground garage at Elgin's apartment for all the years he's been there. He's never driven it, but he kept paying the extra rent for the space. According to Auntie Milly, there's about $10,000 in the estate, but half of that will go to pay for the service and cremation. She says that if Clifford gets any, it'll be over her dead body."

Clifford did get some, but that was much later, after some legal action, and it was over his dead body. I think it went to a sister. We saw him for the last time at Father's funeral; he attended, but didn't hang around after.

Father's funeral took place a week before Elgin died. I'd gone back north, my "compassionate leave" time used up. Mark wrote to tell me about Elgin's funeral service. It was at the church and well attended. Mark and Mother took flowers.

The
Bjørne-Again
University

Barry sees the new university, presently being built on a hill overlooking our town, as just another battle zone in the war between himself and the ex-Principal of the college, a Scot whose bright idea the university initially was.

Most of Barry's friends think he's paranoid.

"The government isn't going to spend two hundred million dollars to build a university just because some guy, who isn't even employed by them anymore and has no official position with the university, wants to get you laid off," Barry's friends say.

Usually, Barry just shrugs. However, when fortressed in his living room with a case of beer, he argues: "So what was the little git doing giving a speech about the university last week at the Chamber of Commerce?"

Or, "So how come somebody's decided that the haggis-sucking little fucker's portrait, significantly entitled 'The Founder,' is going to hang in the foyer of the new administrative building?"

Sometimes his friends, worried, approach me. "He takes it so personally," they say. "A lot of people get laid off. Hell, everybody gets laid off. And not many get laid back on like he did. There must be something else wrong with him. He's too angry."

"Most great artists are manic-depressive."

That there at least was a war between Barry and the Principal, and that this war involved at least one serious attempt by the Principal to get rid of Barry, is undeniable. Legend has it that the war started as a case of mistaken identity. In one of our first faculty meetings, shortly after our Principal arrived, our historian, a young man sporting (as we almost all did then) a beard and wearing (as we almost all still do) a tweed sportscoat with patches on the elbows, stood up and called the Principal's plan for reorganization (a process called "clustering") "fascistic." The Principal leaned over to the Vice-Principal Financial (one of the few survivors of the purge in management that followed the Principal's arrival) and asked, "Who's that?" or (depending on who was telling the story), "Who's that fucking asshole?" The Vice-Principal Financial uttered Barry's name.

A few months later, our historian found another job down south, leaving Barry holding the bag.

But there are problems with this story. Why would the Vice-Principal Financial finger Barry? Anyone who had been at the college for any length of time knew that Barry would never say anything at a meeting where managers were present. Nor would he ever use an abstract and inelegant word like "fascistic." He would instead, and did, go around making jokes like "cluster's last stand" or "nuns fret not in their clusters' narrow walls." He would acquire a burr just like the Principal's and say things like "Crrreative wrrriting has goot to goo!"

Maybe some of this had gotten back to the Vice-Principal Financial. It certainly, subsequently, got back to the Principal. Within a month, creative writing was clustered out of the English department and into health sciences, and the puzzled nurse who ran that cluster found Barry sitting in her meetings, explaining that maybe the Principal had confused "aesthetic" with "anaesthetic" or "circumspection" with "circumcision." Or Barry would point at stains on the carpet and murmur "incontinence," or show the nurses, dental assistants, and lab techs various spots on various parts of his body, or ask them about insomnia, angina, or the early symptoms of prostate cancer.

Barry enjoyed clustering with the nurses.

He mounted a sign on his office door: "Aesthetician."

He devised phoney book lists for his courses and submitted them to the Head Nurse, as he called her, for approval. On these lists, *A Farewell to Arms* became a history of thalidomide and *Moby Dick* a study of hydrocephalus of the penis. Books like *Yeast of Eden*, on minor vaginal infections, also appeared on the list.

Then (or maybe, so) creative writing was cancelled and Barry was back in English teaching a full load of freshman composition. This was a violation of the unwritten rules within the department that heavily enrolled courses (like creative writing) should continue until such time as students don't want them anymore and that instructors should get a balanced load of literature and composition so that the marking is equally shared.

The cancellation of creative writing was, I felt, a direct blow at the sanctum-sanctorum of poetry. I love poetry, though only in the forms that Barry, with pursed lips, condemns as "closed." I accept his judgment. After all, he writes the stuff. Meanwhile, I continue to memorize bits and pieces of the "closed" stuff, especially if it rhymes, and I defend poetry against all comers. I was convinced that the Principal wanted total war.

Realizing that most faculty were hesitant to engage him, I ran for president of our union.

"We must fight this asshole or die," was my slogan.

I lost to my opponent, an economist, by a vote of 90 to 6, but did, as a consolation prize, get to be vice-president. I proceeded to agitate for tougher action. I wanted a fund to hire legal help and managed to get dues increased by 50 percent. I made friends with the chief steward, a brash young psychologist who had been hired just a year previously and was still on probation. His activity in the union was, I kept reminding him, dangerous to his occupational health, but he had a double Ph.D. and was crucial in the criminology and social service programs as well as the usual psychology courses. Also, his "Human Sexuality" course was packed with students. Anyway, he wasn't sure he was going to like college teaching. The psychologist knew a brash young labour lawyer in Vancouver who agreed to represent us.

The lawyer, it turned out, knew all about our new Principal. "Your guy is a hired gun," he informed us. "Don't you academics know anything? Don't you do any research? He did a job in Windsor for the school district there and was paid six figures to leave. You're in for it and don't ever say I didn't tell you."

But not to worry. The lawyer would give us training in labour law and organizing. Cheap.

Most members of the union executive were nervous enough about the Principal to vote the money; they wanted a fallback position in case things got worse. Our union president, convinced that he had a special relationship with the Principal that would save the day if anything drastic was threatened, was amused by our new-found radicalism.

"Chuck is under a lot of pressure," our president would explain. He liked to use the Principal's first name.

"What kind of pressure?"

"The college board wants change. The government wants change. Chuck isn't so sure. In fact, he's assured me that present programs will remain essentially unchanged. But he has to make a show at least of doing something."

So the training sessions went on and included (but secretly) strike organization and tactics.

Our union president got nowhere. His special relationship, involving numerous "working lunches" of soup and coffee and "working dinners" of lobster and wine, resulted in nothing but verbal agreements which, it became more and more evident, meant nothing. Mostly, it seemed, the Principal liked when he ate to tell stories about his past and to weave scenarios for the future. He needed an audience and our president was always an agreeable one.

Everyone knew that the real action took place at about 6 a.m. during the regular "working breakfasts." The menu at these breakfasts was, Barry speculated, warmed-over haggis or fried oatmeal, served to the skirl of the pipes and recitations of Robbie Burns. The managers painted their faces green. Kilts were mandatory. The Principal groped everyone to make sure they weren't wearing underpants.

Our union president was never invited to these breakfasts — luckily for him, Barry figured.

One by one we union executives got sick of all this futile eating and drinking, and declined our president's pleas that we accompany him to the lunches and dinners. "Just get something in writing," we told him. "Don't worry if there's some gravy on it." But he never did get anything in writing. So we began writing a series of increasingly hefty cheques to our lawyer and sitting through the seminars provided by Donna, our lawyer's assistant.

Donna was a professional negotiator. She liked telling "war stories" and talking about her "battle scars." She was in her early fifties. Our psychologist chief-steward was soon on more than professional terms with her, though he refused to tell Barry if she really did have any battle scars.

"I've got a thing about older women," he explained to me.

"I thought maybe it was some kind of research project."

"You should have that vein of cynicism examined by a professional," he replied. "Unfortunately, I can't help you. Cynicism is not my specialty."

Our seminars with Donna paid off in other ways. That November, Barry was laid off, effective the end of August. The reasons given were that creative writing had been cancelled and so Barry's particular expertise was no longer required by the college. This was a violation of the unwritten "first hired, last fired" rule: if you were qualified to teach other courses (in Barry's case, freshman composition and literature) and had seniority, you should be kept on and newer faculty should walk or not be hired. Philosophy,

Spanish, French, music, and history were also cancelled, and their instructors, all of whom had signed on during the college's first year, were laid off without regard to qualifications or seniority.

The Principal had a rationale for this drastic step. "We've gone too far in the direction of the aery-fairy," he told the local media. "What this town needs, what northerners really want, is practical training for jobs. They want a polytechnic."

"What do you say in reply to statements that enrollments in your vocational programs are already dangerously low?"

"I say that the faculty who told you that are a bunch of skunks. If these enrollments are low, in some programs it's due to ineffective instruction. Most of these courses could be taught by interactive television and other more efficient methods."

The Principal had solid support among the public and the media. Most people didn't know what a polytechnic was — they thought they were going to be able to watch TV and get engineering degrees in welding and auto mechanics and make as much money as doctors or lawyers. Attempts on the part of faculty to enlighten the public through over-long letters to the editor were futile. Members of city council, the chamber of Commerce, the school board, and the college board, most of them businesspersons, doctors, dentists, and lawyers, told the newspapers and radio stations that welding certificates were better than university degrees. University training is, they argued, for most people, debilitating. It erodes their values and will to compete and conveys seditious ideas that people of average intelligence sometimes accept without thinking.

Though the doctors, dentists, and lawyers all had university degrees, they were ashamed of them. Sure they had them and even displayed them prominently on the walls of their offices, but they were forced into this by arcane conventions.

A dentist on city council raged (in the presence of a newspaper reporter) at the Shakespeare play he had had to study in his required English course.

"Tell me what this has to do with pulling teeth," he said. "For years I was turned off reading. Even the stock market reports made me sick."

Next, a lawyer on school board attacked his compulsory calculus course, arguing that it had nothing to do with income tax calculations or reading the stock reports. A doctor on the college board revealed that enforced studies of Kant's categorical imperative as a part of his "Medical Ethics" course had turned him off ethics altogether.

Northerners, the local notables all felt, needed a northern education that suited their pioneer mentality. The only way to achieve this was to break the academic old boys' monopoly on university education that encouraged the teaching of "abstract" subjects like philosophy, history, music, poetry, algebra, and foreign languages.

Luckily for me, the college's student association published a newspaper on which I traditionally worked as faculty advisor and columnist. My byline was Saran Awrap, Ph.D., devoted follower of the Mahat Mahcoat. I appeared in an accompanying photo, disguised by a turban and fake beard. My role was that of an avuncular guru, with romantic notions of the academy derived from extensive studies of Shakespeare at the University of Marrakesh.

In this guise, I now ran surveys showing how many local doctors, lawyers, and accountants had kids who were welders, electricians, or mechanics (none), and how many former college board members loved the north enough to stay in it when they retired (5 percent over twenty years). I speculated humourously on the likely "northern" components of programs in medicine, engineering, and commerce — identifying, respectively, alcoholism, venereal disease, frost heaves, and creative bankruptcy as crucial.

Barry said nothing in public. "You don't fight these people on their own turf," he said, "and I don't do journalism." He contacted his poet friends in Vancouver and they launched a cross-country letter-writing and phone-in campaign to save his job.

Faculty were shocked by the layoffs and even more shocked by the comments of local officials, some of whom they had sat beside at service club meetings or even entertained in their homes. Faculty realized that their verbal agreements and understandings, and even their work in the community performing with the symphony or amateur theatre, singing in the choir, organizing astronomy, French, film, and debating clubs, serving pancake breakfasts for charity, judging high school math and poetry contests, and sitting on community service boards, meant nothing. Faculty realized that they were now, in the view of community leaders, irreversibly tainted. They were eggheads, dreamers, and perverts — parchment-packing members of the university old boys' network based in the south. They were not real northerners.

In the course of various shouting matches at subsequent union meetings, it became clear that faculty were now evenly split on whether to appease or fight the Principal.

The psychologist and I increased our pressure on the union president to do something about the layoffs. We phoned our lawyer and described the situation.

"What are you waiting for?" he asked. "The ovens?"

Donna pointed out that the layoffs were in violation of "common practice" as described in the Labour Code. Even though we did not have layoff procedures specified in our contract, the Principal would still have to show some cause for getting rid of only the most senior instructors and hiring new people to do work that the senior instructors were qualified to do. So the psychologist and I threatened to propose a motion to the membership that the layoffs be grieved immediately. Our president said this would make the Principal really angry and asked for a few days' grace so he could consume more lobster and wine in an attempt to arrive at a compromise. He got nowhere. Finally, just before the Christmas AGM, at which we were planning to present our motion, he resigned from the union and took a job in management.

"I'll be able to work more effectively for you now that I'll be attending the working breakfasts," he said in his resignation speech.

In honour of his service to the union, the members of the executive presented him with a baby's spoon and a plastic bib.

So I became union president. Barry figured this was good. At the very least, my job would be safe; the Principal was unlikely to do anything so outrageous as fire the union president. I wasn't so sure, but it was a comforting thought. We launched a grievance — something we had never done before in the ten-year history of our union. Our grounds were that most of the laid-off instructors, like Barry, had the qualifications to teach in other areas. The most important such area was the new Developmental Studies Centre, which used packaged, self-paced, computerized lessons — what Barry called the TWAT (Teaching Without a Teacher) technique — to teach students with learning problems or adults trying to pick up high-school graduation. The DSC had figured prominently in college promotional material as the first of many changes initiated by the Principal to make education more efficient and accessible.

The Principal refused to listen to our arguments, claiming that he was not going to turn the DSC into a dustbin for useless academics who, because of their elitist training, would never enter into the true spirit of developmental studies. And so, as stipulated in the contract, an arbitrator was brought in.

During the arbitration, the psychologist and I had to spell one another off in the conference rooms of the hotel just down the highway, where we drank rancid coffee while keeping notes and providing background information for our lawyer. We were, at first, dismayed to find that the proceedings were complicated and drawn-out. For one thing, arbitrations are like travelling circuses: the arbitrator and his staff come to town for a week or two, then adjourn without rendering a decision to go to another town to deal with some other case. We expected a hearing and then a decision. Second, arbitrators are lawyers and so concerned mainly with precedents; we learned more about the problems of some miners' union in the Okanagan and some woodworkers' union in New Westminster than we ever wanted to know. Third, arbitrators are obligated to ensure that anyone likely to be affected by their judgments should be fairly represented. In fact, most of the first months of the arbitration dealt with approving interventions by other colleges and their faculty unions. This was the first time in the entire college system that a grievance had actually gone as far as arbitration. By the time the arbitrator got to our actual griev-ance, two straight weeks of hearings had passed. When the hear-ings resumed a month later, about forty lawyers and representatives from other organizations were present. We were proud of the stir we'd created, but every hour of the arbitration had to be paid for and all costs had to be justified to an increas-ingly confused and worried faculty.

"Don't worry," said our lawyer. "This is exactly what I expected. Complexity can only help us. The college lawyers are all morons."

"All four of them?"

"Rubes. Their specialty is corporate, not labour, law. Now they're too proud to pull out. We've got them by the short ones."

Our lawyer also pointed out that if we ran out of money, the intervening unions would give us some. "You lose, they lose," he said.

Finally, according to our lawyer, the more complexities and fuck-ups there were, the more likely it was that the arbitrator would opt for a compromise solution and give us something, whereas at the time all we had for sure were six laid-off instruc-tors.

Our lawyer was right. As the arbitration proceeded, it became clear that the college's team of lawyers was not clear in its objec-tives. Nor were they well informed. This was partly the Principal's fault. The few times he spoke at the hearings were embarrassing for the college. He was too much of a politician. He tried to turn everything from a legal into a political if not personal issue, mainly along the lines that he was an ordinary guy taking on the "professional mafia." Lawyers don't like metaphors like that. Also, the information that the Principal gave to the arbitrator, as well as what he fed his lawyers, was often incomplete or even contradictory, so the college lawyers had to withdraw previous statements of fact or ask for adjournments so they could clarify points with the Principal, who was often busy or out of town. This clearly irritated the arbitrator.

It started to dawn on various board members that things might not go their way and that, if the arbitration were lost, dangerous precedents could be set and lots of money lost. For example, if salaries had to be paid retroactively to a significant number of laid-off faculty, the college's yearly budget would have to be rewritten. Board members would ease up to me at the urinals in the hotel washroom or sit down with me in the cafe during lunch breaks and say things like "Aren't we losing our sense of perspective? Shouldn't we be more concerned with student needs?"

"Are you saying that Barry isn't an effective teacher?"

"Of creative writing, maybe."

"He's taught basic composition for years. His evaluations are excellent. Check them out. His spelling is not so good, but he does know how to use a dictionary."

"I'm sure he does, but would he like to correct spelling exercises as a full-time job?"

"Instead of welfare? He'd be ecstatic."

The board banned the Principal from the arbitration proceedings and replaced him with the Vice-Principal Financial — a man who saw everything in terms of columns of numbers.

Meanwhile, the letter-writing and phone-in campaign launched by Barry's literary friends was paying off and the chairperson of the college board was fielding (even at home) calls from writers. Letters were pouring into the board office and into the Ministry of Post-Secondary Education down south. The eastern newspapers and TV stations picked the story up and wanted interviews, but the chairperson did not want to appear on national TV in a debate with some voluble writer.

"No comment," was the official college line.

"I feel I should refrain from comment until the decision has been rendered," said the chairperson.

In July, only a month away from his last paycheque, Barry was permanently fortressed in his living room with neighbours, friends, colleagues, students, cases of empties, and piles of letters of support.

"I've got Atwood," he'd say, waving a letter.

"She knows you?"

"I got her out for a reading during the college's first year. She stayed with us. She even helped me drown a couple of puppies that we couldn't give away. I just couldn't do it."

"How about Farley Mowat?"

"No answer, the shithead. Probably out on an icefloe some-where."

"Maybe he heard about those puppies. What about Richler?"

"Sid's getting in touch with him. They got drunk together at some book launching and have been buddies ever since."

In August, Barry was offered a part-time job in one of the col-lege's church-basement campuses in a town two hundred miles north. But Joy was not interested in moving, certainly not for a part-time job.

"I'll get a job," she said.

"That's hard to do these days."

"I'll hang my ass out on Third Avenue. Whatever it takes."

So Barry said no.

A few days later he was offered his full-time contract back, but he would have to teach in a church-basement campus eighty miles south.

"I'm not leaving this house," said Joy.

I agreed with her. Student numbers were always low in the

regions, and lack of enrollment was an unassailable rationale for layoffs. There was nothing in the collective agreement to protect us from it. "It's a set-up," I told Barry. "If you get laid off again, no one's going to start another letter-writing campaign."

So he turned that down too.

Finally, at the beginning of September, just when I was starting to worry (this is the burden of the politician) that I'd maybe helped to finish Barry's career, Barry was offered his contract back ("without prejudice") if he was willing to work in the DSC.

He took it.

Meanwhile, the arbitration ground on. The psychologist and I were tiring, but our lawyer urged us on. "The whole system is watching," he told us. "This is the first major layoff dispute it's ever experienced. And you know what? I think we're going to win big."

So we wrote him another cheque for $5000 and called another meeting to calm down those faculty who objected to the expense and were worried that, if we won, the outcome would be seniority, which was, after all, a shop-floor concept and therefore an affront to their professionalism. The psychologist (who was not as good at democratic meetings as he was at arbitrations) called them faculty prima donnas.

"You're working for a psycho," he'd yell. "Wake up and smell the goddamn coffee."

Fortunately for us, Barry came to all these meetings. His hurt presence tended to shut up all but the most insensitive of objecting faculty. Everyone knew that if you messed with Barry you'd have to put up with a fine and therefore penetrating spray of insinuation coming at all times from all sides, but mostly from the back.

"Fucking scientists," Barry would say in reference to a biologist and physicist who were questioning the arbitration costs. "I thought skepticism was essential to science. No wonder these bozos ended up in this shit-hole."

"But there were hundreds of applicants."

"They hired the biologist only because they wanted his wife, a geologist. She wouldn't come without him. God knows why. She's been doing plenty without him since they got here. As for his buddy, the hippy physicist, if we lose this arbitration he sure as hell won't have that stupid ponytail for long or be walking around the place in a mackinaw and workboots."

It turned out that Barry liked his job in the DSC. There were hardly any students there, so he had lots of time to write. All he had to do was mark a couple of spelling tests each week for students exhibiting symptoms of dyslexia, who could study and take the same tests over and over and get the same grades, and look after Dino, who was brilliant intellectually but had some kind of disease so he slurred his words and dragged his feet. He also had temper tantrums. The manager of the DSC was afraid of Dino because he was "challenged," a type of student for whom the DSC was specifically designed to provide a long-overdue service. It was politic to keep him happy, particularly since the DSC was having trouble attracting students of any sort and for long periods of time was completely empty. Dino sensed his importance. He had already acquired a sensitized cloth keyboard, about the size of a bath towel, for the computers in the centre. He wasn't coordinated or patient enough to use ordinary keyboards without smashing them up. He had a stack of games that the manager had purchased to keep him busy until something valuable could be found for Dino to do.

This was not an easy task. Dino completed the ordinary learning packages in record time and declared them to be "Mickey Mouse." He hated the accompanying instructional materials, mostly videos from the U.S. with a lot of footage of the stars and stripes fluttering in the breeze, and Blacks, Hispanics, and Whites puckering up their faces and attacking complex math and English problems. When he watched these videos he would bawl, "Whattafuckitgottadowi'me!" He'd punch the tape out of the machine, whack it across the table and onto the floor, and lurch around trying to crush it with his feet or crutches. Sometimes it would take the manager and an instructor or two to force him into a chair and calm him down.

Dino could've been a racist or nationalist, but Barry said no, he was the opposite of these, a sensitive and intelligent individual who didn't like being force fed shit.

Since Barry was the only instructor in the DSC who Dino would talk to, Barry became his sitter. They would sit in Barry's office, which was wired with a TV, stereo, and computer, and listen to jazz tapes or watch *Gilligan's Island* or *Beverly Hillbillies* reruns, or pound away on the cloth keyboard playing games. Finally, the manager, all ice, would ask them to please close the door or quiet down, and Dino would demand permission to go out under Barry's supervision. If he didn't get permission he would make a scene or lie down on one of the tables for a "nap." This, Dino had discovered, looked bad for the manager if any politicians or members of the college board or the general public happened to drop around. Dino had overheard the manager instructing the receptionist at the front desk to contact him immediately if anyone inquired about the location of the DSC. The manager spent half of his time with a sheet of paper in his hand (so it looked like he was on his way to the photocopier), patrolling the hallway out to the front entrance just in case any visitors got past the receptionist.

Once Barry figured out Dino's tactic, he took to lying down on the table next to Dino's on the pretext of reading Dino a chapter out of *Jane Eyre*, which was required reading in the English course that Dino was taking. In no time they would both be snoring. So the manager would tell them to go, and Barry and Dino would drive in Barry's truck to the mall or make their way across campus to the Academy Pub for a beer until such time as the Peter

Pan bus appeared and Barry helped the driver load Dino who, when he drank beer, spoke a lot more coherently than usual but became completely incapable of moving his feet.

Finally the arbitrator ruled that the philosophy and Spanish instructors should have their jobs back, on the grounds that they were long-time employees eminently qualified to teach in the DSC. Furthermore, these instructors should be given their wages for the months they had missed. Two of the newly hired instructors in the DSC were laid off. They had to be paid out; so determined had the Principal been to snub his nose at regular faculty that he had placed DSC faculty high on the pay scale and waived their probationary period.

I immediately quit as union president. I had finished the previous president's term and been voted in (near-unanimously) for another year, but I completed only half of that term. My wife had discovered that, in the course of a Nanaimo conference directed at bringing the various college unions together into one provincial federation, I'd spent a night in a hotel room with a colleague from another college.

"Pressure of work," I tried to argue.

I blamed the pressures of union politics, the necessarily close relationship that builds up between cadres until an aura of horniness hangs over meetings. Especially the boring meetings.

I begged my wife not to leave me.

She went to Vancouver to upgrade her nursing degree, assigning me to the care of a shrink and our kids. The kids kept me sane.

While in Vancouver, my wife fell in love. The kids didn't want to move there, so they stayed with me.

The brash young psychologist took over as union president. The reinstated instructors were welcomed back as heroes. The psychologist, the lawyer, and Donna were heroes too, and I was a fallen hero. The prima donnas were silenced — all the more so because the stories told by the reinstated instructors were so frightening. The Spanish instructor had gone through her unemployment insurance and then, seeing no chance of getting another position in Canada, cashed in her pension and moved to a suburb of Mexico City to make the money last as long as possible. The union was demanding that she be allowed to put the money back into the pension plan and carry on from where she left off. The philosophy instructor had taken up selling educational insurance door-to-door, but sales were spotty and he'd ended up renting out his house (at only two-thirds the cost of his mortgage) and taking a basement suite, then giving up on educational insurance altogether, going on UI, and living in his mother's rec room in Vancouver. There he'd spent most of his time in Stanley Park, staring through a locked gate at the Vancouver Yacht Club and brooding on the imminent necessity of taking early retirement. He was convinced that his retirement plans, which included cruising the Caribbean in his own yacht, were, after twenty years of service to the college and contributions to the pension plan, ruined.

Most faculty concluded that seniority, while it might perhaps in rare cases contribute to an erosion of teaching effectiveness, was necessary under the circumstances as a guarantee of academic freedom. We paid our lawyer another $2000 to put the arbitrator's ruling into contract language in preparation for the next round of negotiations.

A year after that there was a staff strike. The Principal had refused to raise the pitiful wages of the secretaries and janitors, so they joined the local pulp mill union and rolled out the burning barrels. Since the college could function with dirty toilets and the managers doing their own typing, the whole affair hinged on whether or not faculty would honour the picket lines. Management threatened cancellation of courses and possible layoff. They advertised the plight of the students, who were rapidly losing their semester, and blamed the whole strike on faculty. But faculty, especially the senior ones, held the line. They knew that if they gave in, they would lose everything they'd gained as well as any chance of getting their photocopying done when they needed it (which was usually right away) or the sandwich wrappers and milk cartons emptied out of their office wastepaper baskets before the smell became unbearable.

Most faculty quickly went broke, but we were helped by interest-free loans provided by the other college unions in the federation. Barry was also a major factor, delivering impassioned speeches around the burning barrels on how, if you went in, you'd have no protection.

"The collective agreement is out here now," he'd say, pointing at the ground. "It's not in there anymore. Remember that."

One day I saw him chasing a biologist who had arrived at the picket lines with his briefcase and started edging away from the burning barrel and towards the building. He took the man to a cafe and talked him down.

"His wife is going nuts," Barry reported to me later. "She can't go shopping because their charge card is over the max. They're talking about selling one of their cars or maybe their boat or trailer. She gets shivering fits at night and he has to put her in a hot bath. Meanwhile, he can't sleep for worrying about whether the managers are taking proper care of his white rats. He dreams about getting phone calls at midnight. 'Ve haff your rats.'"

Finally the secretaries and janitors got a few more dollars out of the college, and the burning barrels and porta-potties were carted off by pulp mill workers. Faculty paraded, arm-in-arm with the secretaries and janitors, back into the building.

The loss of the strike seemed to demoralize the Principal. He withdrew. No longer was he involved in every committee and present at every meeting. No longer were our mailboxes full of initiatives and directives. He allowed the Vice-Principal Financial to fill in at board meetings and public events and allowed his managers to manage (but not, it seemed, innovate). He travelled to New York for a speech by Ivan Illych (over interactive video-phone from Mexico City), to Japan to talk to businesspersons about funding a Japanese language school in our town, to Scandinavia for a conference on "circumpolar education." Between trips he could be seen wandering the halls and reading the bulletin boards or talking to students.

"He's actually got some good ideas," faculty reported.

Barry was worried. He continued his practice of scanning the newspaper for the Principal's name. He phoned friends in colleges down south to get any rumours.

"The canny little fucker is up to something," he said.

He was right. A year later, our Principal was back in the local news with his latest (and last) great idea. He and a group of prominent local businesspersons and professionals (mostly doctors, dentists, and lawyers) announced a campaign to get a university for the northern half of the province. They called themselves the Society for a Northern University (SNU) and advertised "contributory" memberships in the society for five dollars each and "executory" ones for fifty dollars.

The idea was very popular and the memberships sold like hotcakes. In most towns, in fact, they sold *with* hotcakes. Town councils and Chambers of Commerce all over the north voiced support and launched their own campaigns. Local politicians of all possible stripes tested the wind, found it strong and steady in the university direction, and ran before it. Within a few months, SNU had the money to commission an expert named Igurd Sigmund Ragmussen to produce a report describing a model university for the north.

We researched Ragmussen but found nothing.

He was seen everywhere, usually with our Principal, arm-in-arm, heading for the cafeteria or a conference or seminar rooms.

"They must have met after the Illych seminar, in the lounge at LaGuardia," said Barry. "The entire plan for the university is written on a placemat which is framed and will hang on a wall of one of the executive offices at SNU. Ragmussen is, in actual fact, a terrorist hired by the Swedish government as part of a plan to spread socialistic and anti-Christian concepts like free love, universal day-care, and unisex saunas and washrooms all over the world. The new university will have a medical school specializing in sex-change operations."

Ragmussen's report, when it appeared, described no ordinary university. First it stated that the university had to be an "engine of economic growth." It would be no "ivory tower" but would work hand-in-hand with local industry to stimulate the economy and train students.

This was an attractive idea. After almost ten years of minimal growth, the town needed something to hope for. The coal mine megaproject up north was dead and the proposed aluminum smelter out west had been put on hold for an environmental review. Smaller and more localized projects like a chopstick factory, a computer-assisted manufacturing facility (another of our Principal's innovations), a reindeer farm, and a convention centre had also failed. It turned out that three billion Asians didn't need fresh sets of chopsticks three times a day (not counting snacks) so that every aspen for hundreds of miles would have to be logged. Besides, the chopstick manufacturer, after landing (with the help of local politicians including our Principal, who was at that time heading up the Chamber of Commerce) citizenship for himself and his extended family, and after collecting a pile of government incentive grants, couldn't figure out how to keep the aspen from cracking while it was being dried, so his customers were getting slivers in their tongues and lips.

The reindeer, after being herded all the way from the Northwest Territories by colourful Laplanders in felt boots and over-sized fur hats (the newspaper ran regular features on their progress), picked up anthrax when they got involved with a herd of buffalo in Athabasca. Those few that made it to town arrived much later in the form of bags of dried dogfood.

The huge corporations in the south were not, despite extensive and expensive lobbying (at college expense) by our Principal in airport lounges all over the world, interested in rushing into town to share our computer expertise. Businesspeople from the south did not want to breathe sulphur, drink dioxins, and watch the sun set colourfully behind columns of smoke from the mills while they made decisions in our new convention centre.

To maximize the university's economic potential, the Ragmussen plan put the main campus downtown where it would "rejuvenate the core." University programming would emphasize resource studies, as was appropriate in a town that lived off logging and mining. Finally, the university would have high-tech labs and a faculty hired largely out of industry on the basis of expertise rather than intangible academic credentials. In this way, the university would attract the financial support of the huge, foreign-owned corporations that dominated the town's economy.

Besides being an "engine of growth," the university had to be designed so that it would interest people in all ten ridings of the north, some quarter of a million voters, most living in pit-stop towns up to 1500 miles apart. To appeal to all these people, the new university would be "networked" in a string of campuses across the north, with the main campus in our town. It would make extensive use of interactive TV — possibly, Ragmussen speculated, buying into a communications satellite that could pay for itself by carrying entertainment channels as well as educational ones.

"Oh boy," Barry said. "Swedish porn."

My colleagues, many of whom (ever the optimists) had, in the initial stages of local enthusiasm for the project, laid out their $5 and joined SNU, were puzzled by the Ragmussen report. No one believed that such a university would work. Science and technology could not be taught on TV; you had to have labs. And how could you have sophisticated equipment and specialized faculty scattered throughout a dozen small towns? How would you find first-rate faculty who would be willing to spend a lot of their time driving thousands of miles of winter road or flying in small planes into remote outposts? There was even the question of whether the hewers of wood and drawers of water in the north really did want technical courses and not those same literature, math, film, history, science, psychology, and creative writing courses that had survived two decades of long, cold winters in the college's church-basement campuses across the north.

Faculty concluded that the university idea should be worked out realistically and responsibly or it would fail, just as the computer centre, chopstick factory, and reindeer farm had failed. They made the mistake of saying all of these things publicly, as individuals, in seminars and in overlong letters to the editor. Then, when nobody listened, they made the even bigger mistake of saying them as a union, through press releases and paid advertisements in the newspaper.

Faculty were quickly buried under accusations of "negativity" or, as one city councillor more aptly put it, "premature objectivity." They lacked vision. They were, as another councillor put it, "Johnnie Come Latelies" who liked to pick apart all the positive initiatives that came up. It was suggested, too, that they merely feared for their jobs. They were advised to relax and let the local politicians handle things. Later, when it came time to "dot the i's and cross the t's," their expertise would be needed and maybe they would even be hired to work at the university. Right now the idea was to do a good selling job so that the north was solidly behind the university and the southern politicians couldn't kill it as the bastards did everything else that happened up here. Local politicians assured faculty that the university would not threaten the university program at the college; the two institutions, working together, would generate more students for one another by increasing the (scandalously low) northern participation rate in post-secondary education.

Meanwhile, Ragmussen came up with an answer to all of the objections of college faculty. The answer was consistent with the major recommendations in his report. The university, he said, would be modelled on a couple of highly successful universities in northern Sweden. These universities had lots of branch campuses scattered through the north of that country and were technology oriented.

Guided by Ragmussen and our Principal, various dignitaries from SNU, city council, the Chamber of Commerce, and the college board, along with a reporter-photographer from the local paper, went to Sweden to visit the network universities. They returned with body rubs and glowing reports that the network system worked just fine. The newspapers published photos of happy, young, blonde, blue-eyed Swedes cavorting in swimming pools and talking, colourfully sweatered, under glass roofs by potted palms. The photos and the accompanying report filled the entire front page of the newspaper and a special six o'clock feature on local TV. The town's imagination caught fire. Faculty were silenced.

Except for Barry.

"Nobel Prize-winning scientists studying the effects of sex-change operations on clear-cut logging and local Stihl sales," he speculated. "A music department run by ABBA or some other equally mediocre Swedish rock band. A faculty club with a unisex sauna, with faculty running out onto campus nude to roll in the snow and whap one another with peeled willow branches before settling in the faculty lounge with a Tuborg or four to watch the sun set behind columns of smoke from the pulp mills."

"You're too smart by half," I said. "Even that sounds better than what we've got now."

We waited and watched. We assumed that the government would bring the locals back to their senses. Who would give hundreds of millions of dollars to people like Ragmussen and our Principal?

For awhile, it looked like we were right. The premier, on one of his tours through the province, was evasive. The prime minister, on one of his tours, seemed completely unaware of the northern university. The Queen and Prince Philip toured Vancouver without coming north to ask when they would be officiating at the opening.

Following events such as these, city officials and SNU filled the newspaper and the media with outrage, pleas, and threats.

Eventually the Minister of Advanced Education arrived in town to see what all the fuss was about. In a conference room in a downtown hotel, he spoke about the university concept. Barry and I made a point of attending. Five hundred people turned up, so everyone had to be moved to the ballroom and even there people were standing around the walls. The minister, perhaps not noticing the mood of the crowd, or perhaps attributing its size and enthusiasm mainly to his own presence, congratulated the town on its initiative and then questioned the concept. He was familiar, he said, with the Swedish model. In fact, he was originally from Sweden and though he had immigrated to Canada when he was four and was forcibly settled by his parents in Vancouver, the same red northern blood coursed through his veins as coursed through the veins of everyone in the audience. But the Swedish network university, he pointed out, was not a university in North American terms but a combination "university-college," incorporating career as well as degree programs. Undoubtedly, he concluded, the most efficient plan would be to expand the present college, capitalizing on its already-established and very successful (Barry and I cheered and wrote the minister's exact words into our notepads) university program, allowing it to offer degrees, perhaps at first through the three universities in the south (whose degrees were well-known and very credible), but later, if the experiment succeeded, on its own. The present college building, he pointed out, could be built up two more stories, and there was space for a residence building for out-of-town students and a solarium to house the potted palms. He speculated that the changes could mean some twenty-five million dollars worth of contracts for local builders and suppliers.

I was captivated. I saw myself, briar pipe in hand, a senior prof in the new university-college, sauntering across the campus to my seminar on Swedish suicides in the Canadian prairie novel and then (finding the room empty?) repairing to the faculty club for a sauna with, possibly, some bare-breasted and aromatically sweating member of the Swedish nursing faculty who would listen sympathetically to my list of medical complaints and then join me in the lounge for a therapeutic Tuborg or four and a magnificent view (from the newly completed fourth floor) of the sun setting behind the columns of smoke from the pulp mills.

When the minister finished, he looked up through his shiny, wire-frame glasses, evidently expecting rapturous applause. But the only applause he got was from Barry and me and some dozen other college faculty scattered around the room. We cheered and clapped as long as we possibly could, but this clearly did not comfort the minister. Confused, he backed away from the microphone and our Principal took it.

The Principal was hurt and angry. He said he couldn't bring himself, under the circumstances, to talk for long. He wanted to point out only that, despite the minister's speech and the support of some government "lackeys" planted in the audience, the town was "adamant" that a "free-standing" and "distinctive" university be built here for the benefit of all northerners, and that anything less was unacceptable.

There was a thunderous standing ovation. Real estate agents cheered and whistled. Contractors and retailers started to chant the Principal's name and the chant was taken up all over the room. Barry and I sat clutching our notepads, while the minister and his staff made for the rear door.

The next day the college board (all of whom had been appointed by the minister) voted unanimously to reject any offer from the minister to expand the college. Faculty were stunned.

"Aren't they supposed to be *for* the College?" they asked one another in the hallways and the mail room.

"How can they vote to *reject* a major expansion? They've been asking for one for years!"

There was some talk about calling a meeting and moving a

motion of nonconfidence in the board, but it wasn't clear what the implications of that would be. Would we, in good conscience, be able to cash our paycheques, every last one of which was signed by the chairperson?

Barry and I grabbed this opportunity. We did a satire, a series of multiple-choice questions (mostly concerning sex-change operations and Tuborg) about what Barry termed the "Björne-Again University," and published it under my by-line in the student paper. It was a big hit. Students were seen laughing over it in the cafeteria, and faculty clipped it and posted it on their office walls.

But the morning after it appeared, we found an anonymous message in our mailboxes. It was a picture of Einstein, his hair wild. Underneath it, in bold letters, were the words "large ideas are always opposed by small minds." There was nothing on it to identify the sender.

"They're onto us," I murmured as darkly as I could.

"If Einstein said that," said Barry, tossing the message into the garbage, "he should have stuck to physics."

My neighbour Carl, while he enjoyed the satire, informed me that if I read the label on the bottles I would find that Tuborg was actually a product of his native Denmark, not of Sweden. He also said that, in his opinion, the university could do some good so long as it taught young people to appreciate the classics and live off the land, talents that the college (and here he looked at me piercingly over the rump of a pregnant cow) sure hadn't succeeded in teaching.

A few weeks later the minister, obviously subdued, gave SNU a hundred thousand dollars to operate for another year and do a more detailed study of the Swedish concept.

This was a major victory for our Principal, but he had no chance to savour it. Past events were catching up to him. The same issue of the paper that announced the new funding (on page one) also announced (on page four) that the Principal was taking a temporary leave of absence from the college and resigning as chairperson of SNU. It seemed that the police were on the verge of laying charges against three senior managers at the college in connection with the awarding of college contracts to a local, private, trades school owned by these same managers. The contracts had been awarded through an educational consulting firm that was also owned by the three managers. Also, it seemed that certain pieces of college equipment had been leased by these managers to their private school for no charge, without the college knowing about it. The college had actually reported some of this equipment stolen and collected insurance on it.

At the preliminary hearing, which started a month later and was attended, at first, by some local reporters and the chief steward of our union, it came out that most of these activities were in connection with an Indian reservation in the far north. The government had agreed to build a new band office for the Indians, and the Indians, under the leadership of the local priest, who'd had experience some decades earlier building a mud chapel in Somalia, decided that they would benefit most if they built the office themselves. The government agreed, on condition that the Indians get the assistance of the college, which could supervise the construction as part of trades courses in carpentry, plumbing, electricity, welding, and heavy equipment operating. Our Principal went north and was photographed shaking hands with Indian leaders and visiting shacks containing ragged-looking Indian children who, he said, faced a promising future if cooperation between the band council, college, and government could continue on a permanent basis. He returned to town and announced that the college would, due to lack of appropriate faculty expertise in building requirements and regulations in the far north, contract the project out to a private trades school.

From time to time, the newspaper published pictures of the happy Indians. They were wearing hard hats and sitting in bulldozers and bucket loaders, or standing on the roof of their new band office brandishing hammers and power saws.

This had all ended when the inspectors turned up to look at the near-finished building. They found that some of the windows and doors were on upside down and/or inside out, that some staircases led nowhere, that parts of the foundation were crumbling, that much of the wiring and plumbing was exposed, and that the building was a thousand square feet smaller than the original plans called for. The inspectors concluded that the building would have to be torn down and rebuilt. The police were called in to investigate.

The preliminary hearing lasted all through that June and July, and the trial was in August. Most of the managers at the college had to testify. Basically, the Principal and his group blamed it on the Vice-Principal Financial and his group for not keeping track of things and for putting in false insurance claims. The Vice-Principal Financial accused the Principal of using contracting-out to hide information that was the Vice-Principal Financial's by right of his duty to oversee all college spending.

The rest of us, that summer, went on holidays. No reporters showed up at the trial. Only Barry sat through all of the proceedings, notebook in hand. Joy tried to get him to go fishing or take the kids to Disneyland, but it was no use. Finally she went off without him.

"I have to see this through," Barry explained. "These are the guys who canned me because creative writing was a waste of money. One of those fuckers even ripped open a bunch of my mail once to see if it was all on college business. He dicked me thirty cents for a letter to my mom."

"It wasn't college business?"

"If more people regularly checked with their mothers, the world would be a better place."

Barry got the union to provide secretarial help so that all of his notes were typed up and saved on the computer. The union felt that the information could be useful in future dealings with the board.

At first, Barry said, the college lawyers tried to intimidate him. They took him aside and asked who he was and why he was taking notes. Then the prosecution took him aside, telling him he had a perfect right as a citizen to attend and take notes but that he'd better not talk to any of the witnesses or the media or the case could be lost. He was also advised to stand up and bow whenever the judge came in and went out or he'd be kicked out and maybe prejudice the case.

By the time summer came to an end, Barry was an acknowledged part of the proceedings and most of the prosecution lawyers had become regulars in his living room. The coffee table was cluttered with empties and books of statutes and precedents.

Faculty wanted to see the Principal convicted, but Barry wasn't expecting that. "He's not greedy for money," Barry explained to Vivien and me when we returned from the summer's hiking in Peru. "He simply needs power and attention, which he gets by pitting people against one another. His managers took advantage of his hatred of faculty and put one over on him."

It turned out that the teacher sent by the private school owned by the managers had hung around the reserve for only a week, just long enough to deliver truckloads of college equipment and building supplies and to collect his money, paid by the government through the college to the private school. The teacher told the judge that he'd been told by the priest and the chief that his services weren't really needed. The teacher had paid the priest to teach the course and had the cancelled cheque to prove it. The priest admitted that he'd cashed such a cheque but regarded it more as a donation. Anyway, he'd used it to pay salaries to the half-dozen Indians who had rallied around him in the spirit of Christian fraternity to complete the building after the teacher disappeared and the other Indians, originally registered as students, had dropped out. These payments had been made in cash, the priest admitted apologetically, an error that, he implied, was more a testament to his excessive trust in human nature than to any dishonesty. The faithful Indians, however, couldn't remember ever being paid. That was why they'd finally quit working on the band office and made off with tools, wood, and heavy equipment that investigating RCMP had found hidden in various locations on the reservation.

In the end, the three administrators were found guilty of falsifying contracts and possessing stolen goods. One went to jail for six months and paid a $20,000 fine; the other two paid $10,000 fines. The church returned the money paid to the priest and sent him back to Somalia. Three truckloads of equipment were returned to the college. The college board fired the Principal, who left for retirement in the Gulf Islands, still maintaining that it was all the Vice-Principal Financial's fault and threatening to sue. The Vice-Principal Financial took over the college.

The trial results were reported in the newspaper, but near the back and not in any detail. The Principal, before he left town, was interviewed, but his statements were nearly incoherent, the result, it seemed, of rage (which tended to thicken the Principal's burr) and heavy editing. Mainly the Principal railed against the local politicians who had once called him friend and even tried to conscript him as a candidate, but who had in the end stabbed him in the back.

"As for the college," he said, "I wash my hands of it. It's owned and operated by the faculty union. I hope the new university will prove more worthy of public support."

The vice-president of SNU, a lawyer and close confidante of the Principal, took over SNU and, in a short time, released a second report that drew attention from the college and its problems. This report, also written by Ragmussen, was entitled "Circumpolar Universities: An Idea Whose Time Has Come." It expanded on the original SNU concept. Once the main campus was built, said the report, ten other towns with populations of 5000 people or more would each get a branch campus. Ultimately each campus would specialize in one field in which it would offer graduate degrees. Towns along the coast would get marine biology, Asian studies, and Japanese and Chinese language studies; towns in the north would get Native studies and mining; towns in the Peace River region would get agriculture and natural gas technology; the main campus would get forestry, business, and (as Barry had predicted) medicine. Both the high-tech labs and the faculty would be itinerant. Each professor would teach his or her course in concentrated sessions of six weeks, repeated five times, in five different towns, during the school year. This was called "block scheduling" and Ragmussen had found a model of it at a college in Colorado. He took the mayor, some dignitaries from SNU and the Chamber of Commerce, and a reporter-photographer to see the Colorado experiment first hand. They returned with tans, body rubs, glowing reports, and footage of students cavorting in pools and conversing, colourfully sweatered, in a solarium.

SNU also unveiled an oil painting by a local artist which showed our ex-Principal, an inscrutable smile on his face, pondering the intricacies of the wooden model of the university that had, as part of the SNU membership drive, been on display at various shopping malls throughout the north. He looked, Barry said, like a leering Santa Claus.

Barry and I decided that it was time to grab local headlines by breaking into the southern newspapers. This was often a decisive tactic in battles like these. We packaged a selection of clippings on the university with some of our Swedish satires, and sent the package to two of our literary friends: Stan at the Vancouver *Sun* and Ian at the Victoria *Times-Colonist*. We summarized the story, pushing the idea that the planning for the university was out of control and that the university project compared in expense and likelihood of success to a number of megaprojects, like the coal mines, that had failed in the past ten years.

Ian called the university plan a "Northern Boondoggle," compared it to the failed megaprojects, and used our Swedish jokes about ABBA and Tuborg. Stan speculated that the university was a Conservative trap lying in wait for the Socialists, who would win the next election. "This university," Stan said, "will blow the Socialist education budget out of the water." Stan also used our Swedish jokes, preferring the sex-change ones and the image of nude faculty running out of a sauna and rolling in the snow.

Both Stan and Ian mentioned Barry and me as sources, so a few days after their articles appeared, a television crew from the six o'clock provincial news came up to interview some SNU officials and us. Barry disappeared, so they filmed me in my computer lab with my business students and then set me up in Barry's office. They were disappointed with my office because I keep no books there. Books were needed, the crew said, for an appropriate background. So with *The Collected Works of William Carlos Williams* prominent behind me, I told the public that the university was wildly ambitious and that if it were actually approved by the government, the southern taxpayer would pay through the nose.

The interview was broadcast the following evening and my mother phoned to say that I looked very professorial, that my voice was nice, that she'd always thought I'd make a good anchorman on the CBC, that Knowlton Nash had retired and was writing cookbooks and doing good work for charity so maybe they were looking for someone, that it was too bad the man who'd interviewed me had suggested that my cause might be "sour grapes," that she was going to write a letter of complaint, and that there was a box of jam in the mail for me.

Local TV replayed the interview and in the weeks that followed, editorials and letters in the local newspaper accused Barry and me of everything from faulty scholarship and plagiarism to perversion.

And then, finally, just when it was all turning into real fun, the inevitable happened. Marcus Vingaard, a member of our union executive who was also the Socialist candidate in the region, informed a meeting of the union that his contacts had told him the government was going to proceed with legislation to set up a new university in the north.

"Draft copies are being distributed to all MLA's. After the legislation passes, SNU will be given money to hire a president and some other officials, to rent a temporary building, and to start drawing up an operating plan."

"What happened to the minister?"

"He's been moved into a very, very unimportant ministry."

"Who takes over?"

"Our local MLA."

"He's a backbencher! He's never been to university! He hates the college!"

"All of which is irrelevant. He's *for* the university. Anyone who isn't *for* the university, and that includes me and maybe even you, is finished. But not to worry. Once we Socialists get in, we'll make sure no one gets hurt during the transition period."

"Did someone just open a window?" whispered Barry. "I feel cold all of a sudden. Hey! Put your hand here! My balls have retracted! Do you think it could be permanent?"

After a decent lapse of time, the union passed a motion calling for cooperation "among all existing institutions, including the new university, in providing integrated post-secondary opportunities in the north."

Vingaard thought it politic that the motion pass with no dissent, so there was none except for the gagging noises that Barry and I made from the back of the room.

Since then, Barry's been watching the new university for any signs that the "Loch Ness monster" still has a hand in it. Recently he started a poem sequence about his time in the Developmental Studies Centre.

A few days ago we were in his living room, drinking beer and looking over the first draft of the poem.

"As I see it, you're starting an epic. The trouble is, the Principal doesn't appear in it at all. At the very centre of the Centre is nothing. A big zero."

Barry took a long draw on his beer.

"Exactly," he said.

Leave

To go away, depart from. To give up, abandon. As a noun: liberty, permission, and (in particular) a short period of rest and recuperation, originally in the military sense, away from the front, but now generally away from any duty or work.

Barry and I are experts on leave. Without leave to hope for and dream of, feelings of futility and self-disgust would soon overpower us. Even with the dream, we are plagued by migraines, colds, depressions, and other psychosomatic ailments. We are subjected to long bouts of sexual impotence during which we dream of random fucks with adjacent women who are similarly cynical and depressed. We gossip viciously about our colleagues and bosses, and whine incessantly about our workloads and timetables.

To make matters worse, Barry and I believe that we have important work to do above and beyond our jobs. Slim books of (in my case) stories and critical essays and (in Barry's case) poetry have appeared and been moderately well received.

"A promising debut," said one critic about Barry's fifth volume of verse.

"Future works of his will undoubtedly be included in Canadian literature survey courses," said another critic about my collection of stories.

Promising? Barry and I should, at fifty years of age, be well beyond that. Future? If my present works don't deserve even the dubious honour of inclusion in survey courses, what are my chances now of producing new ones that will earn me real fame? As the years pass, Barry and I feel with growing urgency that if only we had more time to write, we would quickly be famous, gone from our jobs and doing something more suitable to our natures and important to civilization.

For example, I've long been convinced that the world would be a better place if Jane Fonda enjoyed an intimate friendship with me. Barry believes that any Nobel Prize acceptance speech by him would be a watershed in the history of literature. He recently told me that this year, if he wins, he will give advice to poets.

"Such as?" I asked him.

"Always wear dark ginch."

"Your reason?"

"Doesn't show the stains."

Of course we could just quit our jobs right now and commit ourselves to writing. Many people, from our spouses and kids to our most casual acquaintances, have suggested that option to us. Barry's wife Joy is the most persistent.

"Why don't you just fucking quit if you're so fucking unhappy?" she often asks as she breezes past us in her living room or leaves us for a different table at the bar.

Joy's question haunts us. After twenty-five years of work, the chain that binds us to our jobs is coruscated with obscurity. We know that when we were idealistic young writers, teaching attracted us with its promise of time to think and study and of sensitive colleagues and idealistic students to talk to and impress. The physical appearance of the academy, with its manicured gardens, expansive lawns, and sedate architecture, seemed like an earthly paradise.

During our first decade at work, we believed that we were among the lesser gods — having arrived there by a state-sanctioned shortcut opened unto us by virtue of our obvious potential. We acted like real writers, treating important topics like sex, death, nature, and childhood. These are topics that could, it seemed to us at the time, be developed with a minimum of personal experience and a lot of book knowledge, supplemented by funded trips to culturally significant places that happen to be near beaches. We even taught people, who were only slightly younger than ourselves, how to treat these same topics, and we established magazines and publishing concerns in order to find an audience for this writing.

However, our work never gained us the attention we expected. For no reason apparent to us, many of our fellow teacher-writers got more publications, readings, and leaves than we did. They became famous, their names on awards lists, their books reviewed in the big magazines.

Out of sheer jealousy, I began to write critical reviews trashing the writings of these people. I found it surprisingly easy to get these reviews published. Barry, impressed by my abilities and suspecting that literary criticism could be my real forte, fed me topics. He would come into my office and drop a book or magazine on my desk, the pages opened to some story or poem:

Might as well bungie-dive, you
and I into

the canyon. Real live
Houdinis of the tomb.
Our block and tackle
of resurrection. Wind-sheer
working the oyster dream, a placid eye
for its opalescence. Beyond the veil
no shuck, no jive.

And here come the words to the hum-along.
In a good song it's not

till the hook they gore

your disappointment. Claw-
back of the metaphor.
It's all about love again after all.

"What do you think?" Barry would ask after giving me a moment to read.

"Give me a clue."

"An old McGill friend of yours. Now a prof at Toronto. This was in a magazine ad for his new book. If you tell me what it means, I'll buy you a copy of the book."

"It's a riddle, as Aristotle puts it in the *Poetics,* metaphor enclosing metaphor. Just when we despair of deciphering it and start to dream about shitkicking the poet, the poet withdraws the entire poem except its topic which is, simply, love. Warmed by this topic and our relief that we don't after all have to decipher the riddle, and feeling guilty about our initial urge to shitkick the poet, our final attitude to the poet is one of appreciation for his charming awareness of his own incompetency and sentimentality."

"You're saying that the poem is a good illustration of bad poetry?"

"Exactly. When do I get the book?"

Barry himself, during that first decade, lived a number of literary lives. He was the romantic poet, swimming in sentiment. He was also the energetic publisher of friends and colleagues, smelling of ink, machine oil, blanket wash, encouragement, and honest sweat. And underneath all this, he was a satirist, parodying (in some cases) the very work he wrote and published. As Rick Torch he produced prose-romance masterpieces like *Lust Lodge,* self-published in a Coles Notes edition. And he was Yu Noh Hu, translator (and modernizer) of the ancient Chinese poet Tu Fat (800 B.C.):

together, a video we watch, and it's night
when our children snore custard-clotted dreams

of england or the ripple sea
scant miles away

(we got the grant!)

two girls fucking a man, is on the screen. are your
panties as wet as mine?

All of these activities were fun and gained us some badly needed attention. However, as we drifted into our second decade of teaching, Barry and I began to worry. First, our early work embarrassed even ourselves. We thanked the real gods that it had never been recognized. Second, we knew that cynicism and envy, the dominant forces behind our best writing, produced at best satire and invective — the more cerebral and therefore limited of the genres. What about comedy and tragedy?

So we gradually turned for material to the circumstances of our jobs. Realists by nature, what other choice did we have? Here we encountered another problem. The manicured shrubbery and expansive hallways of the academy are, while safe and attractive, heavily regimented places, and students are as homogenized and predictable as domestic rabbits. In the twenty-five-year history of our college, the high point of violence occurred when a student was seen in the college parking lot letting the air out of an instructor's tires. The height of drama was when a colleague — stressed by marital problems and reacting badly to his medication — freaked over a missing comma in a student's bibliographical citation and ran screaming through the library, uprooting the potted plants and baptizing himself with dirt. This is not promising material for literature.

But it was all we had, and by the end of our second decade of teaching we were attached to it. In our writings we broached the theme of bureaucracy, describing the pitiful feelings, sad aspirations, and laughable struggles of officials, among whom we daringly and disarmingly included ourselves.

These stories and poems, we found, went over well in readings at colleges and universities. Encouraged, we rationalized that the bureaucracy as we experienced it was a paradigm of contemporary human experience. We celebrated Kafka, Conrad, Atwood, Wayman, and others who wrote about jobs. We rationalized further that other themes were sentimental, indicating a reversion to the primitive that was increasingly irrelevant.

We seemed to see this reversion in the writers that we brought to the college to read or to teach creative-writing workshops. These writers, engaged full time on their writing but still without a public and therefore state-supported through the Arts Council, made up a veritable parade of eccentricities.

Some of them came to our classes clad in buckskin, foreheads streaked with the blood of some noble moose or elk that had given its life to them.

"I come in peace," they informed our students. "Make a circle and hold hands. What you're about to experience is an ancient Blackfoot dreambed ceremony. The voice you will hear will be mine, but the words will be those of your ancestors."

"Is this going to be on the test?"

"Ai-yi-hi-yi . . . ."

Others came in ethnic garb: feathers, kilts, chadors or yarmulkes, babbling about Culloden, Belsen, Hiroshima, Greenwood, or Wounded Knee. Peddlers of lost causes, these writers in particular focussed their anger on me and Barry, ignoring all the paperwork and organizing that we had done on their behalf.

"What have your teachers told you about Belsen and Treblinka?"

"Sir, they're not on the reading list."

"What *is* on the reading list?"

"Atwood and Richler."

"Sir, in your opinion is Richler an anti-semite?"

"In my opinion Richler is nothing. You are studying a zero. Two zeros if you include Atwood. Two purveyors of bourgeois, Christian-humanist values that cannot sustain us in the age of Stalin and Hitler. You are studying eunuchs and parasites! Put that on your test."

"Right on!"

"What's a eunuch?"

Or the writers wore dirty jeans, workboots, and caps festooned with union buttons; they talked about the proletariat and shed bitter tears over the betrayal of socialism in the Soviet Union. Others had pins stuck through sensitive parts of their bodies and were sheeted in leather. They affirmed that language had been used for so long by white males as a tool of oppression that it was totally untrustworthy. Then they enquired as to the location of the washroom or when they could expect their Arts Council cheque.

Many, gentler souls, arrived half-drunk and immediately asked to be taken to the nearest bar. Sipping their whiskey, they muttered darkly about corporate takeover, government by World Bank, and the death of the Arts Council.

"It's the end for me, I'm afraid. My publisher's in receivership. A thousand copies of my latest book are heading for the shredder even as reviewers are praising the book and bookstores across the country are crying out for copies. Of course, if someone bought them all they would be saved. Perhaps your English Department would consider it; I've noticed that you advertise a freshman course on the modern short story."

"The department is committed to the New and Messenger book."

"Ah yes. Fellow academics. I suppose charity *is* supposed to begin at home."

Almost invariably, the college's beat-up, piss-smelling washrooms, its offices stuffed with dusty rhetoric books, unmarked papers, and coffee-stained cups, and its overheated classrooms, depressed these writers. They withdrew even further into their causes, grievances, theories, and pasts.

Sometimes, at the day's end, we had to carry our visiting writers to their hotels.

Once, a Montreal short-story writer tried to stab me. Barry and I had dragged him out of a classroom after he started careening from wall to wall and shouting curses at the audience who were trying to applaud politely and leave. We drove him to his hotel, carried him into his room, and laid him on his bed. I was busy removing his shoes while Barry found the writer's liquor supply to pour us each a drink.

"Do you think that's a good idea?"

"Obviously we need it more than he does. How are we going to explain this to our students tomorrow?"

"All great artists are manic-depressive."

"Besides, we're going to have to stick around for awhile to make sure he stays in the survival position. Otherwise, he could choke on his own vomit."

"Good thinking. We'd get the blame, like the academics who chaperoned Dylan Thomas during his last tour."

"In this particular case, blame might be tempered by appreciation."

I found a movie on TV and we were just settling into it when suddenly the writer, suffering a spasm perhaps, or hearing the TV, or achieving consciousness due to the sharp sound of bottles clinking on glasses, reached over to the bedside table, seized the TV remote, and plunged it at my back. I disarmed him and he sobbed in my arms for a few minutes before passing out once again.

"The horror," he sobbed. "The horror."

As the years went by, Barry and I started inviting only those writers that were still reputedly rational. Mostly, these writers were fellow academics. Dealing with them was much less trouble and had the added benefit of obliging them to invite us to their institutions.

But still we hate to see our fellow artists — especially those with the courage to dedicate themselves entirely to literature — falling along the wayside in the forced march of civilization. We feel that by sticking with our jobs *and* excelling at our writing, we can gradually demonstrate the value to civilization of more formally recognizing and providing for artists. By sticking to our theme of bureaucracy, we can parent a new literary school, creating our own audience. Perhaps, ultimately, we can inaugurate and be the shining lights of a new age of patronage, a neoclassic age, a new version of Chou Dynasty China or of Byzantium:

> *Where blood-begotten spirits come*
> *And all complexities of fury leave,*
> *Dying into a dance,*
> *An agony of trance*
> *An agony of flame that cannot singe a sleeve.*

In every way possible, we will teach the arts how to flourish within the huge and intricate institutions that, many theorists say, will characterize civilization in the future.

We will refine leave into a vehicle for art.

Sears cafeteria, situated deep in the basement of Spruce Centre Mall, is a favourite spot for planning our strategy. There, a short distance away from the college but, in reality, in another dimension, we are undisturbed. The only other customers are Sears staff and young mothers in baggy windbreakers and stretch-tight lycra pants. The young mothers are all built like either sticks or blimps. They team up in large groups to steer convoys of shopping carts full of children and baled diapers through the mall. The mothers and Sears staff are not interested in us. Also, all of the staff and most of the mothers smoke and so sit squashed together at the other end of the cafeteria. Except for the odd toddler who drifts over to our table to stare at us through big, unblinking eyes, probably wondering why there is no smoke coming out of our mouths, no one comes near us.

A final attraction of Sears is cost; meals are "cheaper than dog-food," as Barry puts it. This adds to our feeling of security. A breakfast consisting of two eggs any style, hashbrowns, toast, and coffee costs only $3.87, *minus* 10 percent. As members of the Sears "Mature Outlook Club," Barry and I have cards that entitle us, at a cost of only $9.95 per year, to 10 percent off any food and non-alcoholic beverage at any Sears cafeteria. We also get $100 of Sears money coupons, but these, we quickly discovered, cannot be spent in the cafeteria. Usually we use these coupons to buy the Harris tweed sportscoats that have become a kind of uniform.

We also discuss leave in various hotel lounges around town and in the Other Art Gallery and Coffee House. But these places are not as close as Sears and can be dangerous. They are frequented by professionals, most of whom are actively seeking social intercourse of one kind or another. These professionals gravitate to Barry and me. With our tweed sportscoats, spectacles, carefully trimmed mustaches, moderately portly figures, greying hair, and minor reputations as writers, we exude a cosy atmosphere of sensitivity and intelligence. Also, we are well known among local professionals. We have both been around our little town for over two decades. As college instructors, we have processed thousands of students — young people who encountered us at an impressionable age. Many of these students stayed in town after graduating or took university degrees in the south and returned. Among these former students who regularly sit with us in lounges and Other Art are my doctor, Barry's financial advisor, and Harvey.

The trouble with all of these people is that, even though Barry and I are on friendly, even affectionate, terms with most of them, none of them want to hear us talk about leave any more than they want to hear us complain about our jobs. Mr. Chips never complained, and aging professionals like to view their university years through a glass amberly.

Most wonder why we can't just be happy with our relatively soft jobs and stop trying to escape them.

Why can't we, in sum (as Vivien most succinctly puts it), shut the fuck up about our so-called problems in finding time from our so-called work to pursue our so-called art?

It's not easy to be leaders, to spread the gospel of leave, but Barry and I have learned to accept our evangelical calling with the resignation of true saints.

Thanks to Harvey, we are safer in Other Art than in the lounges or in any of the other coffee houses in town. This makes Other Art a welcome break from Sears cafeteria which, in our town, doesn't serve alcohol and cooks its coffee in a giant stainless steel urn.

Lilla, Harvey's partner, lets him out of his studio only when she's certain it's safe. She knows he's safe with us. In fact, she knows that, for us, he's a major attraction. Regarding us as legitimate artists, if only barely so, Harvey likes to advise us about our careers. His mere presence drives away any of our other friends, most of whom find Harvey to be a morose, aggressive, self-righteous prick. Harvey hates our colleagues and most of our friends. His attitude to professionals is that they are all sellouts who have abandoned their ideals and even disciplines in the quest for security. As a result, their self-esteem depends entirely on the immediate gratification of minor purchases, a daily calculation of the value of their houses and pension plans, and the harassing of any quivering, mini-skirted waitress who serves them lukewarm coffee or messes up their orders.

But if Harvey's mere presence is usually protection enough, Harvey will also, at times, go out of his way to protect us.

"Don't talk to Brent anymore," Harvey will say. "You really pissed him off last night. Luckily for you, he still regards you as authority figures, but if I were you I wouldn't push it. He's been selling houses for ten years and still isn't doing very well. All that stuff about your pensions, sabbaticals, RRSPs, and four months of paid vacation got to him. He regards such things as a burden on society — on himself, in other words. Especially don't talk to him about Arts Council grants. I don't want to have to protect you from the shitkicking that you so richly deserve."

"But Brent doesn't need a pension," says Barry. "His father owns the real estate company."

"I guess you weren't listening, as usual. It seems the company isn't worth much, and maybe Brent won't end up getting it anyway. He told me that he cleared only about $30,000 last year, and his old man's taken to snarling at him. The old man hired a 25-year-old woman out of the program at the college, and she made $30,000 in her first six months. I suspect she's fucking the old man, too, but Brent didn't say that in so many words. It's a tough world out there."

Regarding leave, Harvey is as impatient as our other friends with our constant speculations on it. He advises us to abandon any faith in it. His theory is that suffering is essential to art. He knows from his own college experience that our jobs, teaching young people to weed all traces of figurative language from their writing and to read literature for its socially redeeming merits, are extremely boring. But boredom is a form of suffering. Instead of trying to escape our job-related boredom by getting leaves, Harvey feels that we should actually embrace it in the same way that he, for example, has embraced debt in order to create the unusual experience of Other Art.

"Immerse yourself in the destructive element," Harvey advises us.

He further postulates that boredom could be, at present, the single most important source of art and therefore its major theme. It is, after all, the most common form of suffering in advanced societies.

"Primitive life," says Harvey, "is nasty, brutish, and short. Civilized life is nasty, brutish, and interminable."

"But how can boredom be entertaining?"

"I'm counting on you two to figure that out for me, but probably you're just another of my futile experiments."

Barry and I do, naturally, agree with Harvey that our jobs are important parts of our lives and therefore must be our subject matter. But we don't believe in succumbing to any kind of suffering, including boredom, in the expectation that we will be driven to desperate acts of creation. Harvey wants to see us explode — rip off our tweed sportscoats and expose our shrunken chests. Surely that is, in reality, just another romantic dream, another reversion to primitivism. Surely, in the creation of great art, emotion, even such an emotion as boredom, must be "recollected in tranquillity" as Wordsworth said.

Surely we need leave.

So we turn from the advice of Harvey and our other friends to section six of our college contract, the section that describes leave. Section six is our Bible, drawing us into prolonged bouts of hopeful speculation. As a kind of commentary on section six, we keep files of documents pertaining to the experiences of various faculty members who have been on leave.

Our files on most varieties of what section six calls "personal leave" are slim. Almost alone among these varieties, it is sick leave, the manipulation of which is rife among the inmates of any bureaucracy, that really concerns us. And beyond sick leave lies the mysterious and seductive world of permanent disability.

The sad fact about sick leave, though, is that both Barry and I are still incredibly healthy. We're good for, at best, a day or two of sick leave each semester. This is at least partially due to the excellent benefits package provided by the college — benefits that keep us, free of charge, in spectacles, dental fixtures, psychiatric services, and pharmaceuticals. Barry's frequent migraines sometimes result in double vision so that he bumps into doors and walls and has to stay at home for an afternoon. I acquire at least two psychosomatic colds every semester, always at times when my marking load is driving me to distraction. Once the marking is done (and I do a more effective job when my mind is partially numbed by certain kinds of antihistamines), I get better.

Barry and I hope that by the time we reach our sixties, our systems will be weakened sufficiently to get us plenty of sick leave.

Barry, as is appropriate to a poet, does suffer from long periods of profound depression. Depression has potential as a basis for sick leave and disability, but only if it manifests itself in tangible symptoms or is produced by a tangible condition. This actually seemed to be the case with Barry a couple of years ago during his second sabbatical from the college. He became depressed in January, as he always does, at the thought of the imminence of September, but this time his depression was aggravated by the thought that he was on sabbatical and thus wasting his *own* time being depressed. He was incapable of working on his sabbatical project or even (on some days) of getting out of bed. He dragged himself to the doctor, expecting to be sent back to his shrink as usual, but this time the doctor, to Barry's delight, discovered an irregularity in Barry's heartbeat. Unfortunately, subsequent tests demonstrated that Barry's depression was not caused by his arrythmic heart or vice versa, though his arrythmia could possibly explain his interest in jazz and the poetry of Robert Creeley.

Barry was once again left alone with his shrink and with no clear reason for being depressed. Worse, he had no excuse for not continuing with his sabbatical project.

He summoned me to a lounge to discuss this impasse.

"You're my shop steward," he said to me. "What should I do?"

I hauled out my pen and pulled over the nearest napkin. "You can't get any work done on your project?"

"None. It seems so infantile. It nauseates me. I'm writing, though."

"Writing?"

"A series of poems, I think. Yes, that's what it feels like. Maybe it's prose. I spent all yesterday at it. The working title is *Arrythmia Suite*. What do you think?"

"Maybe you should call it *Biofeed-Backfire*."

"I mean, what do you think I should do about my sabbatical?"

"Are you supposed to be writing poems?"

"Hell no. I didn't dare propose it as a sabbatical project. Before yesterday, I hadn't written a line for over two years."

Barry went on to explain that he was supposed to be producing a book of interviews with fellow poets who had started small presses and magazines. He'd done all the interviews, driving from B.C. to California on an Arts Council travel grant. To save money, he'd stayed in interviewees' homes and camped along the road instead of booking into the motels he'd budgeted for in his grant application. All he had to do now was transcribe the tapes he'd made.

"Another problem is that I interviewed only guys. You can guess what'll happen when the feminist critics see the book."

"Why didn't you interview Sharon or Daphne?"

"Are you kidding? I can't stay with them. Joy would go nuts."

It occurred to me that Barry could try to get sick leave. The college would then know, formally, that he wouldn't necessarily be able to finish his project. He would be free to work on his poems.

"You're saying that I should go on leave *while* I'm on leave?"

"It could be a useful precedent."

Barry was pleased with this tactic. It had, he said, a sort of poetic resonance. He enquired as to whether or not being on leave from leave meant that he would be, in effect, *at work,* in the sense that two negatives make a positive. And if this were the case, Barry continued, would he not then be entitled to his full working salary rather than merely the two-thirds salary paid on sabbatical?

"Sorry," I told him. "Sabbatical time, like vacation time, is fixed between specific dates in the contract. You definitely would not be working when on leave from leave, any more than you would be working if you got sick on your vacation."

"Too bad. Being on two-thirds salary is killing me. My charge cards are both at max. So are Joy's, apparently, and I don't even want to know how many cards she has. It's depressing."

"What about the travel grant money that you didn't spend?"

"The kid just turned sixteen. He wanted a truck."

"I suppose that is a kind of travel expense. Didn't you also budget for someone to transcribe the tapes?"

"He wanted a *nice* truck."

However, even if Barry had to remain broke for the rest of his sabbatical, our basic tactic was sound. After some consultation with the union, management did give Barry sick leave, without prejudice to other agreements past or pending. The due date for Barry's sabbatical project was postponed indefinitely. Barry was free to write poetry.

Thus, Barry himself attained a place of honour in our "leave" file.

But while sick leave and disability offer increasing promise of release as we advance into old age, the broad category of "professional leave" remains most relevant to us at this stage of our lives. Sabbatical Leave, which Barry has enjoyed twice in his long career, and upon which I hope to embark, for my second time, in about eight months, is the most important of all the kinds of professional leave. It is the pot of gold at the end of the rainbow, the payoff, the chance, if you plan carefully, to do more or less what you want *and* get paid for it.

The key to planning for sabbatical is the seniority list, on which the dispensation of sabbatical is based, with the complication that faculty are permitted to defer sabbatical and yet retain their place on the list. They defer because they get sick, are close to retirement, are in debt, or are so far out of touch with their teaching disciplines that they cannot think of credible projects. When these faculty defer, faculty further down the list can suddenly be catapulted upwards to take their places. But of course you have to be in a constant state of readiness, like an airline passenger on standby.

Back in September, after only eight years on the list, I was catapulted upward and offered a sabbatical.

I was ready. Because of the deferment policy, Barry and I have modified the eligibility list so we can tell at a glance who is closing in on retirement (symbolized by a watch), who looks like an imminent stroke or heart-attack candidate (a skull and crossbones), who is teetering on marriage breakdown (a cracked heart), and who is so far in debt that any cut in salary would mean prison (a reversed dollar sign). We meet regularly to keep the list up-to-date.

For example, Barry will come into my office and say, "I was just over in the shop getting my snow shovel welded. Martin looks awful. He's red in the face and puffs all the time."

"Is he still smoking?" I'll ask, recognizing instantly the importance of Barry's information. Martin is on the very top of the eligibility list. He already has a watch by his name, indicating that he could take early retirement at any time.

"Yeah. He says he might as well smoke. He breathes fumes all the time anyway. He estimates that each week of aluminum welding is the equivalent of inhaling one beer can. He's been teaching for thirty years, with eight weeks per year devoted to aluminum welding, so he figures he's inhaled enough aluminum to build a thirty-foot riverboat. What difference will a few drags on a few cigarettes make?"

So I'll draw a skull and crossbones beside the watch beside Martin's name on the list.

Thanks to this sort of careful preparation, my proposal to the college committee that grants sabbaticals and my application to the Arts Council for travel money were completed and neatly typed long before I received notification of eligibility for sabbatical.

My proposal is to go to Guatemala and write a novel about the college. All I have to do in the coming months is convince both the Arts Council and the committee that travel will be beneficial — that a serious novelist, in order to tackle the really big themes, even (nay, *especially*) if these themes are to be portrayed in a story about the very place that he or she customarily inhabits, needs a grass shack on the beach, insufferable heat, tequila, and the proximity of scorpions and armed insurgents. I plan to show that it's a matter of perspective, of stepping aside to view things in a larger context.

As for proposing a novel as a project, Barry and I agreed that I had no other option. First, I have some credibility as a writer of fiction due to my slim book of short stories. The book by some fluke landed on the bottom of the provincial bestseller listing for a single week in the Vancouver papers, a fact that a manager at the college brought to my attention one morning, running all the way down from his spacious third-floor office to my basement hole with the newspaper in his hand and his eyes wide.

"Is this you?" he asked, shoving the paper between my face and the grammar exercise I was trying to mark.

"Are you paid to read the paper?" I asked.

This sort of recognition in the big city, no matter how minor it really is, is regarded with mystical awe in our town. Word about my book spread through the college like a spring virus. Even board members, most of whom like to be regarded as too practical to be more than barely literate, were seen sneaking my book out of the library. Subsequent reviews of the book, one in a well-known Toronto magazine, were decent.

It would seem only natural, then, that I would now be reaching for that jewel in any writer's crown, the successful novel.

Second and more importantly, I have in a box somewhere a novel-in-progress about my years of college teaching. This novel is the product of a sudden impulse a few years back when I sold the timber off my acreage and spent a fall semester on unpaid leave, watching the leaves turn and the snow fall. The novel is, at least so far as weight is concerned, done, featuring a title (*Upstream Orpheus*) and some two-hundred pages (double-spaced) of neat typing. It lacks only a plot, convincing characters, and an engaging style. I mean to come up with these features during my sabbatical.

If I don't, I can at least present a bulky manuscript and argue its socially redeeming merits.

I could also, like Barry, go on leave from leave.

Barry has already begun to prepare me for this possibility. Yesterday, at Other Art, he advised me to strengthen my medical dossier in the coming semester, "just in case." He argued that being prepared to make a good case for leave from leave would, if nothing else, ease the pressure caused by the anticipation of failure — a failure which, in my case, is almost certain.

"Face it," said Barry, "writing a novel is a complex undertaking and you're inexperienced. So far, all you've got on your hands is that tortured pile of shit that your trees paid for with their lives. And I'm not saying that just because the book is really a thinly disguised satire of me. You'll need a backup plan in case you fail. When did you see Gurmit last?"

"Just a couple of nights ago."

"Not in the bar. In his office."

"Last year. My prostate was acting up. Believe me, dropping your pants in front of a former student is not easy."

"In the mood he's usually in, you're lucky he didn't stick the rubber gloves in the fridge before he probed your ass. But then you did give him an A. You made a real friend there. If I remember, he couldn't even speak English then, let alone read or write it."

"He wanted into medicine and I knew he was smart. He started an 'I Hate Yeats Club' in the back of my class."

"Do you really have prostate problems? That could be convenient."

"It's becoming all the rage among men. My theory is that men with faulty prostates are actually higher on the evolutionary scale than other men. They slept lightly and kept their fires going at night, so their families had a better chance at survival. I'm thinking of writing a book about it called *Urine John*. What do you think?"

"What else have you got wrong with you?"

"A hemorrhoid."

Barry wrinkled his nose. "You could arrange to get either the prostate or the hemorrhoid hacked out, I suppose, as soon as you get back from Guatemala or maybe even *in* Guatemala. That would be a perfect excuse for going on sick leave."

"I don't want to get them hacked out right now. I want to write about them."

"Suit yourself. Anyway, prostates and hemorrhoids are too tangible. You don't want anything that a doctor can actually poke. Why don't you go to Gurmit right away for something intangible like insomnia? Get some pills. You can give them to me if you don't want them. Try to get the kind with pentobarbital in them. Do you want me to write that down for you?"

"No."

"It's great stuff, especially if you take it with any kind of alcohol. For variety, you can administer it by suppository. Having hemorrhoids, you'd probably get an extra kick out of it. Anyway, once you get the pills, book in sick for a couple of days. Then, in a month, go for something else and book in sick again. Do you get headaches? Stomach aches?"

"Unfortunately, no."

"How about depression?"

"I *am* starting to feel depressed, now that you mention it."

"So am I," said Harvey, who had been twiddling his thumbs through our conversation and staring stonily first at one of us and then at the other. This is a familiar indication that Harvey is bored. "Let me get this straight," he continued. "You're preparing to go on sick leave while you're on sabbatical leave?"

"Barry did it a couple of years ago."

"It saved me," said Barry. "That's when I wrote *Arrythmia*. I owe that poem to John here. It was a brilliant tactic."

"But it's been done," I said. "What if they notice?"

"Nobody's done it since."

"What do you think, Harvey?" I asked.

"I think you should do it. You two are probably the first people on this planet to spin variations on leave from leave. You *must* be sick."

Having said that, Harvey got up and returned to his studio.

Barry and I watched him go. Barry sighed. "I had hopes for him, but he still doesn't quite understand what we're doing. His comment is a kind of compliment, though. I think we're getting somewhere with leave from leave. I think it could be the breakthrough we've been looking for."

"Maybe he's right. Maybe we *are* crazy."

"If so, we get permanent disability. Meanwhile, what about those messy colds you always get? Think you could stay off for a week instead of a couple of days, then go see Gurmit?"

"Maybe I'll just take the extra days."

So I put Barry off. It's dawning on me that our tactics need fine-tuning. There's nothing wrong with planning for failure. There's nothing wrong with security.

Unless you've got a novel to think about.

Chris
From Alberta

We heard about him before we met him, while sitting at breakfast, outdoors, at the Unica Deli in Panajachel on Lake Atitlan. We were with Gene, from home, and Avital, from Israel. We were doing what all travellers do, telling stories of our adventures and listening for any useful pieces of information. We were eating bowls of granola, fruit, honey, and yogurt, with stacks of multi-grained bread with more honey, and sipping, greedily, good Guatemalan coffee, the stuff generally exported and usually found only at the airport or the chain hotels. After weeks in the Guatemalan hinterland, we were back on what the locals call the "Gringo Trail," cleaning up, resting up, and planning future exploits.

Gene started telling us about his hike around Lake Atitlan. "I'd come off a twenty-hour bus trip from Tikal," he explained. "I'd been hauled off the bus twice by the army, made to go spread-eagle at gun point, felt up, and then billed for the experience. I was tired and fed up. I got here and slept and ate for two days and then decided to hike around the lake to San Pedro, lay on the beach for a day, and then take the boat back here and sleep and eat some more."

Vivien and I were all ears. We love hiking. Vivien was gathering information for her travel book, and I was interested in deflecting her for as long as possible from our next chickenbus trip. I badly needed to stretch my legs and be alone with Vivien in the comforting if snake-infested bush, away from all the noise of the buses — the incomprehensible chatter, the yelling, and (especially) the taped marimba music.

As it happened, though, we didn't learn much about Gene's hike. His narration, and the ensuing discussion, went elsewhere. This was because, on the first day of the hike, on the boat trip to trailhead at Santa Cruz, he met Chris from Alberta.

"It got strange the minute we got to Santa Cruz," said Gene. "There was only one hotel with only one room, so we agreed to share. Settling in, I noticed that he smoked nonstop, viciously, like he was trying to suck the tobacco out of the cigarette. Between puffs he chewed his fingernails, which were already chewed to nothing. And he talked. Endlessly! Mostly it was about his trip, where he'd been and when, accurately remembered and impeccably planned, it seemed, but always involving some screwup. He was robbed, cheated, or taken to the wrong place and abandoned. The obvious explanation, the one he never seemed to consider, was that he was stoned half the time. I got tired of the inconsequential chatter and decided to explore the town. But he tagged along, talking and smoking. He was convinced that we were being followed. Hadn't that guy, in front of the cantina, also been in front of a cantina when we left Panajachel? And hadn't those two guys been following us since we left the hotel and shouldn't we maybe duck down the alley? Soon I was steaming along, and I'm a fast walker, but he was right at my elbow, smoking and talking. I wasn't seeing anything of Santa Cruz, so there was nothing to do but go back to the hotel and try to sleep."

Gene looked up appreciatively as the *muchacha* filled his coffee cup. He stirred more honey into his fruit and granola and continued.

"But sleeping wasn't easy either. So far as I could tell, Chris didn't sleep all night. So far as I could tell, he didn't even get into bed. I'd doze, then hear him go out the door or come in the door or open the window or close it. He shook me awake at some point to look out the window. The two guys (or was it the guy from Panajachel?) were supposedly out there. All I could see were shadows. Once I got up to go to the *baño* and he was gone, his bed stripped bare though his pack was still on the floor. Later, he came banging in, barricaded the door with a chair, sat down on his bare mattress, and lit another cigarette. I snuck a look at my watch. It was 4 a.m. and I was wide awake but didn't dare get up or say anything for fear of setting him off talking again. I concentrated on thinking about home — the state of my bank account, the probable weather, what my ex-wife might be up to ... anything. Finally the sun popped up and the *muchacho* started chopping wood. Chris was outside, checking the garden for footprints. The *muchacho* was trying to control himself, but he was angry. Just about every plant in the garden was flattened, and Chris's bedding was still out in the dirt under a tree."

Vivien and I forgot all about Gene's hike in the ensuing conversation. We agreed that Chris must've been coming off something, like cocaine. We expressed our amazement and dismay at all the druggies who'd suddenly turned up in Panajachel over the past few years and who you could see wandering around town half-dressed or sitting stoned and silent in front of their hotels.

"The place is spoiled," said Vivien.

Suddenly it was noon and Gene, wishing us a quick *"bien viaje,"* rushed off to clear out of his hotel and catch a bus.

So the next day we had to start hiking with almost none of the information we needed. We didn't, for example, know why Gene had taken the boat to Santa Cruz; judging by our tourist-office map, you could walk there. A couple of Indians that we met on the highway just out of town were encouraging. They directed us onto the road that went past the luxury hotels and over to two highrise towers that seemed to have been abandoned, slightly before completion, some time ago. The guard at the towers, who had his straw mattress, table, chair, dog, and radio (tuned to marimba music) neatly arranged in a corner of the chandeliered and glittering foyer of the first tower, put us onto a trail around the first bluff.

The trail hung precariously over the water, and we had to scramble in places, holding onto vines, branches, and bunches of dried grass. Then we crossed a grassy flats with a river down the centre, which we forded where it ran into the lake. Then we hit another bluff, much bigger than the first one, and couldn't find a trail. We woke up a lone Indian man, asleep in his mud-brick hacienda with the radio playing marimba music. He called his dogs off us and told us that there was a trail but it was obscure and very dangerous. *"Muy peligroso,"* he said, rolling his eyes and indicating with gestures that the trail was steep and close to the edge of the bluff. We saw he had a boat and asked if we could hire him to row us around the bluff, but that too was *"peligroso."* So he started us on a short-cut across the flats to San Jorge, which was near the highway that ran down to Panajachel.

Two hours later, after fording the river again and getting completely lost in the high bush, we stumbled onto a farm road that led to San Jorge. There we bought and ate a large bag of mandarin oranges and watched a football game. An hour later we dragged ourselves up to the highway and began the walk down to Panajachel. It was dark when we arrived. Luckily there was a room left in one of the smaller hotels.

Late the next morning, after a three-course breakfast at the Unica, we got on the first boat we could, which was going to San Pedro with a single stop on the way to drop a load of freight. We figured we'd start at San Pedro, walk to San Sebastian, double back to Santa Cruz, and then pick up a trail from that side of the bluff and make our way back into San Jorge again.

The boat was almost empty. There were a couple of Indians

with chickens. There was a Canadian, Danny, an exporter, who was going to rest on the beach for a week. He looked tired alright, pale and ragged. He explained this was due to a rough trip up north buying blankets and (he confessed) to the ridiculously low price of beer, which was just too much of a temptation for a Saskatchewan boy. He told us about his business and where in Vancouver we could find his stuff.

And there was Rafael, drunk or high, a graduate, he told us in broken English, of Tegucigalpa University in Honduras. A mestizo, he proudly proclaimed, pounding his chest and belching in my face. He had an English book about Marcus Garvey, Haile Selassie, Malcolm X, and Jimmy Cliff, and he went through it, showing me every picture and getting me to read the captions to him. Then he staggered over to Danny, who immediately told him to fuck off. So he sat beside the Indians who didn't speak much Spanish and were scared of him and tried to pretend he was invisible. Finally he went up onto the roof of the boat, where he passed out in the sun.

At the freight stop just out of San Pedro, on a wobbly plank pier, with nothing visible on shore but a grass shack and a path winding off into the bush, we picked up a couple more Indians and Larry, a short, slightly overweight American with Coke-bottle glasses and a torn straw hat. He wanted to sell us some cocaine. Danny waved him off, which Larry didn't seem to mind at all. He settled in beside us anyway and explained that he was out of cash.

"I couldn't pay my hotel bill in San Pedro," he said, "so the owner took my passport and most of my stuff and kicked me out. Now I can't leave the area. I walked over here yesterday and slept in the hut. One of those Indians bought my watch for twenty quetzales and this bag of carrots, so I'm going to get my room back and have a shower. Need any carrots?"

When we got to San Pedro, Danny and Larry led us through a maze of coffee fields and gardens to the best hotel, the one that Larry had been thrown out of. We all signed in, Danny and the *muchacha* at the desk bantering back and forth in Spanish. Then we sat in the thatched-roof cafe with some beer and delicious banana pancakes with chocolate syrup, the only thing on the elaborate menu that the *muchachas* in the kitchen were willing to cook.

While we ate, we watched Rafael, who must've finally awakened on the beach where the boat crew dumped him. He was trying to get to the hotel. He'd appear in an open space between the beach and the hotel, and Danny and Larry would shout at him. He'd look up and fall on his face and stand up and wave and stagger towards us and disappear behind some trees or bush and then appear again on some other path or in some garden, staggering back to the beach again. Danny and Larry would shout and the whole process would start over. Danny and Larry made no move to get Rafael, and Vivien said that if we were lucky he'd maybe die of sunstroke before he made it to the hotel.

At breakfast next morning, the *muchachas* proudly produced a jar of instant coffee and some almost hot water. Banana pancakes were still the only available food on the menu. Danny was at one table, hunched over a coffee and seriously contemplating, as he put it, "going home to Mom." Larry, at another table, was drinking straight from a giant bottle of beer and eating his carrots. He talked at us while we ate. He was an anthropologist and had had some part in creating a computer catalogue of Guatemalan antiquities.

He was also selling — with the permission of the hotel owner — his possessions. They were arranged neatly on his table, each with a scrap of paper on top, with the price written on the scrap of paper.

One of the books was a biography of Mussolini. When I paused over it, Larry told me that it was very informative.

"It seems he didn't have advanced VD after all," Larry explained. "He was just plain loonie-tunes."

Vivien pulled me away. "If you help those people out, you just encourage them," she whispered.

So we ignored Larry, finished eating, and went off to explore San Pedro. We thought we might hike to Santiago in the afternoon, but the hotel owner warned us that the army was there. We then decided to walk to Santa Cruz. Over banana pancakes at lunch, however, Larry, still at his table selling things and drinking beer, told us that Rafael had set out in that direction just an hour before.

"All he has is his book, a pair of jeans, a staff, and a shoulder bag full of whatever he's on," Larry explained. "He thinks he's Gandhi, out to unite all the coloured races of Central America so they can exploit the whites instead of vice versa. But I don't think we need to head for the hills. In fact, any army that he raises I could beat back with a towel. With enemies like Rafael, who needs friends?"

Vivien didn't want to encounter Rafael again, so we decided to give up any idea of hiking and head back to Panajachel on the afternoon boat.

While Vivien took a shower, I bought the Mussolini from Larry and hid it in my pack. He couldn't make change and pressed me to take the underpants.

"Near new," he said, picking them up and stretching the elastic. "Don't worry. I got the *muchacha* in the laundry to wash them. You can try them on if you want."

I told him to keep the change.

On the boat, Vivien wrote up the notes for her book, pronouncing San Pedro "spoiled."

Two weeks later, after an excursion to Livingston on the Caribbean, we were at the Canadian Consulate in Guatemala City, looking for mail from our kids and reading the Globe and Mail on fax. We'd been in the city for three days, staying in a cheap hotel downtown and hiking five miles each morning out to

Zonas 9 and 10, where I'd discovered the Conquistador Sheraton, the Camino Real, and other chain hotel wonders with their quiet cafes and lounges and well-stocked washrooms. The consulate was nearby, and we'd taken to going there for news. This was our last visit before we left again for the hinterland.

A tall, blonde guy came in and told the trilingual Guatemalan in the shatter-proof cage that he needed help. He'd been robbed at the market of everything except his passport, which he'd fortunately left with his hotel manager. He needed money. The Guatemalan told him that it would take a day or two, and the blonde guy got upset. He would pay whatever it cost. He had thousands in his bank in Calgary. He'd sold his house in order to finance his trip. He had to pay his hotel bill because the manager was threatening to call the police.

We were listening to all this because we wondered what the consulate could do. It turned out to be simple. The stranded tourist fills out a form that includes the name, address, and phone number of someone in Canada who can go to any chartered bank and put a small amount of money in the consulate's Canadian account. The consulate contacts this person and then, a day later, phones its bank to verify the person made the deposit. Then it turns the equivalent in Guatemalan currency over to the stranded tourist. Meanwhile, the tourist can go to the Bank of Guatemala and arrange for money to be wired in. This takes a week or more because there are no computer hook-ups or special connections between any Canadian and Guatemalan banks.

But this simple arrangement didn't satisfy the blonde guy. He couldn't think of anyone in Canada who could put fifteen or twenty dollars in the consulate's account. He didn't want to worry his parents, who were old. He was a good friend of the manager of the Calgary branch where he kept his money, but that manager had recently moved on to some other branch.

The trilingual Guatemalan listened blankly, having already

explained the process and shoved the necessary forms under the glass. The blonde guy finally stopped talking, picked up the forms, and sat down at a table near us.

Vivien whispered to me, "Maybe we should help him out."

"Sure," I said.

She turned to him. "Having trouble?"

"I can't believe there are no computer hook-ups," he said, shaking his head.

Vivien went to the window and asked the woman, in Spanish, for a list of banks that might do business with Canada. She wrote the names of three on a piece of paper, with their addresses. She was doubtful that they could produce any money very quickly but, as she said with a smile, "Things are improving all the time, even in Guatemala." We then arranged to meet the blonde guy, after he'd finished filling out the forms, in the cafe across the street. Before we left, we introduced ourselves and shook hands. He told us that his name was Chris.

We'd picked up our bags from the armed security guard outside the room and were in the elevator when it struck me. I turned to Vivien. "It's Chris from Alberta," I said. "Gene. Santa Cruz. Remember?"

She thought for a moment and then her eyes widened. "How do you know?"

"How many guys named Chris can there be wandering around here? He's from Calgary. He's tall. He talks. He doesn't have fingernails. It was like shaking hands with a chimpanzee."

Vivien was doubtful. She has (and justifiably, too) some confidence in her instincts. She couldn't believe that she'd just volunteered to help a druggie. But when Chris arrived at the cafe and sat down and lit a cigarette and started talking, she eased him around to telling us where he'd been, and finally the story came out about Santa Cruz and how he'd shared a room there with a guy from British Columbia who was going hiking.

He also revealed that he knew where we were staying. He'd checked us out in the registry at the entrance to the consulate.

It wasn't easy to dump Chris. We walked to two of the banks, one over in another zone, where Chris would blather out his story, in English, to bank officials who didn't understand a word. Vivien would step in and ask in Spanish what could be done, and the officials would all shake their heads. Vivien and I would say *"gracias"* and head for the door. Then Chris would talk at them again in English while we waited outside.

Halfway to the third bank, I was tired of all the walking and talking, mainly the talking. I told Chris that we really had to get off on our tour of the local museums. "You know where you can find us if you can't get any money," I said.

Chris wasn't sure he could find his way to the next bank. He wasn't sure where our hotel was. I was adamant. We left him standing doubtfully on a corner, towering over the portable *tiendas* and their milling customers and Indian attendants, with a dozen shoeshine boys and beggars plucking at his pants.

I had to spend the rest of the afternoon pacifying Vivien.

"Why did you tell him to come over to our hotel?" she asked at the Mayan museum while we were staring at the expressionless stone head of some god or bureaucrat (did the Mayans perceive some essential identity?).

"He knows where we are and he'll come over anyway if he's inclined to," I explained. "We'll go home when the place is closed and use our outside key."

"What if he's waiting for us?"

"We'll outwait him."

"It's people like him who spoil it for everybody else. No wonder the locals are always trying to rip us off."

We had a late dinner that night in the back of a cafe just around the corner from the hotel. Over a bottle of wine we got into a romantic discussion about how our personalities match up to make us a perfect travel team.

As we left the cafe, we peeked around the corner to see if Chris was hanging around the hotel entrance. He wasn't.

Early the next morning, as we were packing to leave, the consulate phoned for us. It was about Chris. His hotel manager had made good on his threat to call the police. The police had gone through Chris's room and found drugs. He was in jail and scheduled to face a tribunal in a week. He'd given our names as friends who might provide bail.

"We only just met him yesterday," said Vivien into the phone.

"How much is the bail?" I asked when she hung up.

"It's not the bail so much. It's the fact that you have to take responsibility for making sure that Chris turns up at the tribunal. What I'm saying is, I know something about the Guatemalan police and how they collect their wages. If you want to help that maniac out, let me know right now so I can buy a ticket and get out to the airport and onto a flight home. I'll be of more use to you from Canada than I would be from the next prison cell."

Half an hour later we were on a bus. We were going north to buy blankets.

Safari
to Malaria

So it's back to work, the air starting to cool off at night so my glasses fog when I step into the bank machine or the college, the motorhomes gone off the highway that runs through town, the trees on the surrounding hills almost bare, golden cotton-wood leaves dying in the gutter, a cold morning fog smelling of sulphur, wood smoke, and snow.

"This is the best time of the year," says Barry as we head down to Spruce Centre Mall, to the Gourmet Cup and Sears cafeteria, our insulated travel mugs jammed into our jacket pockets.

"What about summer?"

"Always a disappointment."

He's right in a way. You set yourself up for four months (four months!) of production — get that book out, write those articles, plant that garden, or go to New York for two weeks in the jazz bars. Sometimes you do some of those things. Usually you do a lot more drinking, lying around, sleeping, having your teeth drilled, getting the truck fixed than you figured.

Then, before you know it, September. When life is ordered, out of your hands. When the responsibility of freedom is off.

But my case, this September, is different. I've just gotten back from a year on sabbatical leave. Including holiday and professional development time, my leave encompassed a summer, an autumn, a winter, a spring, and another summer.

Eternal freedom, it seemed then.

Now I'm addicted.

Not that I was without official responsibilities while on sabbatical. In that time I wrote, or rather rewrote, or rather tried to rewrite, a novel. Writing a novel was my sabbatical project, for which the college paid me two-thirds of my normal salary. I also travelled. As I'd explained to the committee that approved my application for sabbatical, and to the Arts Council that granted me some travel money, travel would add colour and thematic depth to my writing.

But I didn't know then, and don't know now, what would add that to my writing. More likely the missing spark is something like cancer.

I wasn't travelling because of my novel, really, but because of Vivien. She'd long been wanting to take me off on another "adventure," as she always puts it. Vivien believes that travel builds character, which could, she further contends, be the spark missing from my writing. Even if it isn't, travel means material.

"Navel-gazing gets you nowhere," she affirms.

Vivien herself is living proof. She's not only an ardent traveller but also, due originally to my encouragement, a travel writer. "You should write that up," I casually suggested to her years ago, shortly after we'd met — after I'd heard a few stories about Tibet, China, Peru, Ireland, Greece, Spain, Turkey, and Central America.

And so she did.

Three years ago she completed *Central America by Chickenbus*. I put it on computer for her, edited it, and published it, using my old imprint as a publisher of literary works. Harvey designed the cover. Another friend, Art, emerged from the basement of Wayzgoose Printers, smelling of grease and blanket wash, to do the electronic layout. All Art wanted was an acknowledgement on the title page and a continuous supply of beer while he worked. All Harvey wanted was money.

Imagine my surprise when this book, a mere two hundred pages with a few colour photos bound into the centre and some hand-drawn maps scattered throughout, quickly became the first choice of discriminating backpackers heading for that part of the world.

"This is the one you're looking for," said one reviewer.

"When the tough get going," said the catalogue of a large American distributor.

There are a lot of crazy people out there, I thought.

Since then orders, mostly from hiking supply stores in Canada, Europe, and the U.S., have dribbled steadily into my rural mailbox, and Vivien and I have spent hours packaging and mailing books.

Vivien had another good argument for travelling. Travel, particularly third-world travel, which is Vivien's specialty, is cheaper than living at home. Airline tickets are expensive, but if they can get you to a place where meals are cheap and beer is twenty-five cents per bottle, you seem to *make* money.

"How do you think I can afford to travel all the time?" Vivien had asked me, back when we first began to think about my sabbatical.

"I assumed that you took your railroader husband in a lucrative divorce settlement. Didn't you own two houses? I often see Gord in the mall. He always looks dazed, like he's lost something."

"He did, but it wasn't his house."

I have a nodding acquaintance with, and a sort of sympathy for, old Gord, who sometimes sits with his railway cronies at Pickled Paula's, upstairs in Spruce Centre. Did he not, after all, live for fifteen years with a woman who (I am beginning to notice), while continuing unabatedly on with her own pursuits, is inclined to

involve herself in the pursuits of the men she loves and, ultimately, to outdo those men no matter how great their genius?

Gord fancied himself an outdoorsman, a latter-day Crockett,
until Vivien started going into the bush with him. As she tells it,
the crucial incident occurred one night in the high alpines. Gord
was sleeping, as was his wont, with his back against a rock, his
rifle across his knees, waiting for marauding bears. Vivien started
coming out of the tent to pee and heard the safety on Gord's rifle
snap off.

"He was scared shitless," Vivien said. "After all those hunting
and fishing stories, it took me awhile to get the message. I guess I
thought maybe there was some reason to be scared that I didn't
know about. After that I hiked alone or with Joanne."

Barry has even more sympathy for Gord than I do, figuring
that Vivien would indeed have taken him for as much as she
could get.

"I can *hear* her reasoning. 'Love is love but money is money. A
gal's gotta do what a gal's gotta do.' "

Barry did agree with Vivien's argument about the economic
merits of travel, though his was quite a different perspective.

"If she's going to drag you off anyway, you might as well take
advantage of the situation," he said. "The Arts Council won't
provide any kind of support to academics. Even at two-thirds
salary we make too much to qualify. But they will provide travel
grants if travel is important to your project. You could get your
tickets paid. Also, you can try to pad your expenses as much as
possible, then find cheaper ways of doing things and use the
extra money to cover for your missing salary. Judging by what
Vivien says about prices down there, that could be easy."

"But my novel's got nothing to do with Guatemala."

"Change the novel! Your real objective is to write short stories,
isn't it? The novel's just a front. I hear that George just finished a
detective story that involved a chase around the word. He spent a
month each in Melbourne, Prague, Hong Kong, and New York.

Another writer I know of planned a book of poems about Ming Dynasty ceramics and got to tour China."

"How about if I just tell them that I need to get away from home in order to write about home."

"On the grounds that ironic detachment is crucial in your writing?"

"Good thinking. Can I use it in my application?"

"Remember that there's an added benefit. The people on the leave committee like it if you've got what they call 'external support.' They regard most academic pursuits as weird in the extreme. Writing a novel would be right up there with exhuming corpses in the Peruvian coastal desert or counting marine mammal blow-holes in the Arctic Ocean. So if the long-hairs or eggheads at the Arts or Science Councils are impressed enough to give you some travel money, the committee's more likely to approve your proposal."

As soon as my travel grant and sabbatical were approved, Vivien applied for and received two years of unpaid leave. Her plans were to begin a second edition of *Chickenbus*. We would tour Guatemala through the worst part of winter, then return to Canada where she would write up the results. The following summer she would introduce me to her favourite hiking, in Kluane Park in the Yukon. Kluane is a possible topic for another guidebook.

When I finally returned to work, Vivien would go off to the six other countries of Central America to complete her research. Even now her pile of clothing, equipment, and medicine is accumulating around her backpack in the corner of my kitchen, and she's at her doctor's getting more malaria tablets.

During the first summer of my leave, we moved Vivien's furniture out of her apartment and into storage. Vivien spent that summer on a series of canoe trips with her long-time friend and travel partner, Joanne. This series culminated in a trip down the entire length of the Nahanni River in the Northwest Territories.

Vivien wanted me to come along, but I can't even swim let alone paddle a canoe, and I knew nothing then about the Nahanni.

I was also eager to start on my novel, which was more than just a "front" as Barry put it. I dreamed of getting famous during my sabbatical, returning to the college only to say a snickering farewell to the poor bozos who, due to their lack of drive and talent, had to go on working there.

And I was then still dedicated to projects on the eighty acres of bush and swamp that I call home. My usual activities include painting and renovating my shack, planting and harvesting a garden, cutting hay and firewood, and replanting the forest that I logged years ago. I also drink coffee, make wine, and talk books and politics with my rancher-neighbour Carl. I pit myself, stick-by-stick, knee deep in mud and driven wild by mosquitos, against the beaver (personalized years ago by my kids as "Norman") who annually, from April through June, plugs up my culvert and floods my access road. I drive to town on Saturday afternoon to pick up the weekend *Globe and Mail* and have a cappuccino at Other Art with Harvey.

I spend whole afternoons watching the sky.

I began that first summer of sabbatical by unearthing and rereading the manuscript of the novel I'd written during the semester of unpaid leave that I took after I logged my trees. I hadn't told the leave committee about the existence of this manuscript. It's a rule of thumb among faculty that a sabbatical project should, if possible, be something already started or almost done. This is a hedge against failure, which could be a disaster considering that the college can, if the committee considers that any agreed-upon sabbatical proposal has not been satisfactorily fulfilled, reclaim any salary or part thereof paid out during sabbatical.

I'd have to cash in my RRSPs. I'd have to borrow to send my son to university. Cappuccinos would be out of the question.

Because of my manuscript I could, in the (very likely) event of writer's block, produce a hundred thousand neatly typed words and argue their socially redeeming merits.

In the manuscript, tentatively entitled *Upstream Orpheus,* I attempted to tell the story of how a couple of characters, similar but in no way identical to Barry and me, were hired to help start a new college in a northern mill town that is similar but in no way identical to our town. Barry's character was the hero, the dutiful shepherd who followed the star of poetry wherever it led him, the universe shifting harmoniously to accommodate his passage. My character was his somewhat undependable friend, distracted by personal ambition and women, and inclined to engage in political activity. The main action concerned our struggles with the egomaniacal principal of the college, a veteran of the *Wehrmacht* and an archconservative who had, nonetheless and naturally, a certain amount of common sense and even wisdom mixed into his madness.

I started out that first summer by adding a subplot wherein my character, in the course of a weekend conference on the Canadian novel, falls into bed with a female former colleague from an eastern university and is subsequently found out both by Barry's character and my wife's character — by the latter when she sees the bill for the hotel room and notes the number of occupants marked on it. But this subplot, while it did introduce some badly needed sex and intrigue into the novel, was based (loosely) on my own experiences when my own marriage broke up. Only a fool or a writer would deliberately set out to galvanize old regrets. By August I was blocked and depressed. I put the manuscript aside and turned to writing reviews — good therapy for writers with doubts about their talents.

The novel was still aside when, in October, Vivien returned from her adventures on the Nahanni, her body tanned and her notebooks bulging. I devised a will, had it notarized, and delivered it to my kids. I said goodbye to my friends, including Barry, who had important news for me.

"I hate to tell you this now," he said, as we settled into our favourite lounge, "and it's not that I'm not eager to see you go. Having you hanging around the college in your dirty Bermuda shorts is driving me crazy. But I read an article in yesterday's paper about some retired American guy in Guatemala who got his head cut off. The American government is protesting."

"Don't worry, Vivien's already told me. He'd gone into his banana orchard and stumbled into a drug deal involving the army. They took his head off with a machete and put it on the front steps where his wife would find it."

"How does Vivien know all that?"

"The wife wrote to her. They're friends. Vivien stays with them when she's down there. She was hoping we could stay there this time too, but the wife's closed up the hacienda and gone back to the States."

"Isn't Vivien scared?"

"Are you kidding? She figures things there will be quiet for awhile now. She figures gringos will be extra safe. The guy's death has become 'a window of opportunity.' She's probably trying to get the key to the hacienda from the wife."

So Vivien and I flew as planned to Mexico City. For three days she shepherded me around the great artifacts of Mexican culture, a humbling yet exhilarating experience. Then, dizzy from pollution, we boarded a bus and headed south through the Sierra Madre to Guatemala.

Even this small part of the trip became, to Vivien's great joy, an adventure. In the middle of the night, on a long descent, our bus lost its brakes. Our driver, obviously a good man in an emergency, rammed the back end of the companion-bus in front of us, and that bus eased us down around a couple of hairpin curves into a pulloff in the valley below, then left us. Our driver announced that a bus would come out of Oaxaca the following morning to pick us up and that meanwhile we would have to sleep in the bus, with the lights turned off so that no *banditos* would notice our presence.

"Isn't this exciting?" Vivien said as she snuggled up to me on our seat. "You could get a story out of this."

I was recalling Fred C. Dobbs and his difficulties in this same area.

Tiene un cigarro, hombre?

I asked Vivien if she wanted me to hold my pocket flashlight up to the window to signal the *banditos*. "Material," I explained.

"The driver's snoring will bring them."

For the next four months we carried our backpacks and took what Vivien calls chickenbuses into every nook and cranny of Guatemala, Vivien taking pictures and notes and chattering away in her street Spanish to the market ladies, and me hugging our packs and purchases and trying to avoid the eyes of beggars and kids. I was, at first, a reluctant traveller, always yearning for the CBC and *Globe and Mail*, for some English, for some talk that wasn't a sales pitch or request for money, for some public debate that didn't ultimately, somewhere close, involve gunfire.

At first I kept my novel close, in a durable plastic binder with my name, home address, and passport number written inside, and a brief explanation in English and Spanish that there were large numbers of dollars or *"dolares Americanses"* awaiting anyone who found it and mailed it back to me or took it to the Canadian Consulate. I hauled it out of my backpack in steaming hotel rooms, on the edges of smoky markets, and under palm-leaf shelters on oven-hot beaches. But I didn't get much writing done. It was too hot and I was nervous, and in most places, despite the proliferation of acres of green coffee bushes with their inviting red berries, we couldn't find much drinkable coffee, without which inspiration is impossible. It was an odd feeling to sit in the well-appointed outdoor cafe of a relatively plush hotel, looking across at a terraced mountainside of coffee, with a jar of instant and a jug of lukewarm water on the table.

I was so desperate that at one point I stopped on the side of a road and picked some beans to chew on.

"How do they taste?" asked Vivien.

"Like dirt."

"Better than instant coffee?"

"Good point. I'll fill my pockets. Maybe with a cigarette lighter and some tinfoil I could roast them."

Meanwhile Vivien, unaffected by the coffee problem, was scribbling (theatrically, I thought) endless notes for *Chickenbus*.

In the interests of getting comfortable long enough to, as I put it, "take up my pen," I talked Vivien into spending a week in Guatemala City, pointing out that, due to her prejudice against cities and her love of the rural-dwelling Mayans, she had sped through the city in the first edition of *Chickenbus*. We settled into the Chalet Suizo in Zona 1, a lovely place with lots of hot water, clean sheets, and varnished wood doors with large black hinges, a place frequented by what Vivien refers to as "serious travellers" — environmentally conscious, ethno-eccentric, well-organized, upbeat, Spanish-speaking backpackers. There were the usual casualties and disasters too, to make me feel at home, most conspicuously a young, blonde, Californian who, in Honduras, had decided that her malaria tablets were polluting her body and stopped taking them, and who was consequently on crutches, her ligaments torn by tremors. But she was buoyant, recovering, in daily phone contact with her concerned parents, and the object of the care and concern of the staff and everyone who passed through.

Every morning we hiked the five invigorating miles past the comforting, solid, and well-guarded headquarters of the Bank of Guatemala (where our traveller's cheques were always welcome), to the luxurious Zonas 9 and 10, the Canadian Consulate, the Camino Real hotel, and the Zurich Chocolate Shop. The Zurich in particular would have been an ideal spot for writing, as it had excellent coffee and desserts, but it was, ominously it seemed to me, guarded by a machine-gun carrier and four heavily armed teenage soldiers, all embedded in a sandbag bunker. I kept glancing in that direction to see if the soldiers looked nervous or had suddenly flattened themselves out behind the sandbags.

I kept thinking about Vivien's acquaintance, on his knees beneath the bananas.

We are sorry, señor. We love all the Canadiense. We hate only the dirty sons of gringo dogs who take our bananas and give us nothing. So it is too bad you stumble onto our very small mass grave make-work project for dirty street children.

Correction, my brigadier. This hombre has stumbled into *our grave. Ha, ha!*

Silence! Señor, forgive my insensitive dog of a sergeant. You see how difficult it is with us. But tell me quickly, where would you like to take the bullet. The head, I think, is best, but some prefer the heart for sentimental reasons. It is better in the biography, is it not?

How about both?

Señor, I apologize that our government is very cheap with the cartridges.

In the Zurich, the Camino Real, and the Conquistador Sheraton, I toyed with my novel. But I found it, in comparison to Guatemala, colourless and flat. I was beginning, to Vivien's delight, to look around, inspired by the beautiful, deserted museums and galleries over by the airport. In the foyer of one of those museums, I purchased and started to read a couple of exhaustively researched, English-language books on the Mayans and Aztecs. These people, through their civilizations, exhibited some disturbingly familiar compulsions. For example, seeing any number of stones lying side-by-side on the ground, they were compelled (unlike their brothers and sisters to the north) to pile them. I wanted to know why. Then I began looking over and correcting and adding to Vivien's notes. By the time a roaring, belching, and bucking chickenbus, trailing a wake of marimba music, took us out of the relative security of Zonas 9 and 10 and off to some difficult travel (in search of blankets) to Momestenango in the north, I had finally turned into a "serious" traveller. Unlikely as it seems now, I really was, without even remotely thinking of getting a story out of it let alone some colourful imagery for my novel, eager to finger blankets.

So it was between Guatemala and this summer's trip to Kluane that I wrote most of what I did write on the novel. I started as soon as we returned from Guatemala late in February, settling quickly into my "accustomed rounds," as we novelists like to say. These rounds included my homestead, my younger daughter Jennifer's basement suite (where I kept my computer), Sears cafeteria, and Other Art. I experienced a mild bout of creative energy then, fired (probably) by my reacquaintance with coffee and spurred on too by my lack of significant achievement in Guatemala, by the sound of the clock ticking, and by a vision of the leave committee, their faces flushed with the anticipation of reading my deep and colourful novel.

Vivien was not so happy to be back. She missed her apartment. She couldn't concentrate on *Chickenbus*.

"This is your space," she said.

"You used to love it here."

"As a guest."

Finally, inspired by a friend's account of hiking in the Himalayas, she decided to spend the spring and early summer travelling in Northern India and hiking the Annapurna Trail in Nepal.

Joanne was eager to go along.

"I think you should stick with our plan," I said.

"I've ski'd a thousand circles around your field. I've read *Paradise Lost* and *The Prelude* in your *Norton Anthology*. I've showered in the college gym with the girl's basketball and volleyball teams. I've sat in Jennifer's basement suite trying to figure out your stupid computer. I just can't get things done."

"But you're a traveller. You love to be unsettled!"

"When I'm travelling I'm travelling. When I'm settled I'm settled. I need my china cabinet. I need my petit point. Besides, maybe I'll get another book out of Nepal."

"When are you going to quit collecting material and start writing?"

"When are you going to stop writing and start collecting material?"

Over a couple of beers with an old school friend and once-a-month drinking partner of mine, she promised to write a series of articles on her trip to Nepal for the Saturday supplement of the local paper, which he edited. She would mail them to me, with photos, and I would edit them and pass them on to my friend.

My idea had been that Vivien would spend the spring writing up the complete Guatemala section (150 pages at least, judging by her notes) of *Chickenbus II*. That would give me time, before we went to the Yukon and before I went back to work, to properly edit her manuscript. I knew from my experience with *Chickenbus I* how long this would take. Aside from enthusiasm, relevance, and factual accuracy, Vivien's style is characterized by the, if not endless, at least exceedingly prolonged repetition of a dozen or so basic grammatical errors, the excision of each occurrence of which she fights like a wounded cat.

"You always misplace *only*," I would tell her.

"Show me where."

"'You can *only* get into Salvador if you have a letter from your consulate.'"

"That's true."

"But what it really means is that you can only *get in*. You can't *leave* if you have a letter. That could mean that you would have to ditch the letter in order to leave. But what if the soldiers decided that, since you got in, you must therefore have a letter somewhere, even though they'd stripped you and probed all your orifices and couldn't find it? They might decide to keep you around until you shit or tossed the letter up. You'd be trapped in Salvador. The proper way to phrase it is, 'You can get into Salvador *only* if you have a letter.' "

"Go over that again and leave out my orifices."

"If I write, 'You can *only* drive if you have a driver's licence,' that means that you can't, say, *eat* if you have a driver's licence.

You can *only drive*. Do you want everyone with a driver's licence to starve? The proper phrasing is 'You can drive only if you have a driver's licence.' "

"So 'I only have eyes for you' means no flowers, no chocolates, no kisses, just a lot of staring?"

"So it seems. The 'only' could refer *back* to the 'I,' but that's an unusual archaism and it casts doubt on the objectivity of the 'I' and the beauty of the beloved. Most obviously, the 'only' attaches to the 'have,' which makes an obscure meaning. It should be, 'I have eyes for only you.' But that line was written to accompany a certain tune, which is a different thing."

"No it *isn't*, smartypants. The way I wrote it is the way people are used to *hearing* it. Everyone would understand what I meant. Your alternate meanings are ridiculous and your correction makes me sound like a pompous English instructor who spends all day picking his nose when he's supposed to be writing."

Of course she's right about "only." I can't, as I usually do when marking student papers, insist as a matter of good pedagogy and a student's relative security in any future job, on a conservative application of grammatical conventions. I have to consider "the dialect of the tribe," as T. S. Eliot, that belligerent (God bless him) prig, put it. Vivien is, after all, concerned primarily with conveying perishable information as efficiently as possible to perishable (especially if they try to go where *she* goes) people.

Finally, it is undeniably the case that hundreds of writers concerned with conveying what they hope is imperishable information to posterity, including certain impeccable stylists like Eliot himself, have long ago (1940, "East Coker") given up on "only":

> *Because one has only learnt to get the better of words*
> *For the thing one no longer has to say.*

Surely this should read,

Because one has learnt to get the better of words
Only for the thing one no longer has to say.

Was Eliot here aiming at some more obscure meaning — like, for example, "because one has only *just* learnt"? Was he demonstrating, by reverse logic, that he obviously had not in this case gotten the better of words and was *therefore* trying to say something new and important? Was he, as he said in "The Music of Poetry," attempting to "catch up with the changes in colloquial speech, which are fundamentally changes in thought and sensibility"? For example, was he here concerned maybe that his lines, utilizing the impersonal pronoun "one," sounded pompous enough to need a more colloquial placement of "only"? In which case, wouldn't he have simply (except for the fact, again, that he *was* such a prig) used "you" instead of "one"? Or was he, as he himself put it, "exploring the musical possibilities of an established convention of the relation of the idiom of verse to that of speech"? In other words, you can't in any sort of verse or fiction actually imitate speech (you'd end up writing like Davy Crockett or like Robbie Burns and Yeats in their patriotic modes) but only the ways in which people are accustomed to finding speech imitated in verse or fiction.

But does booting "only" out of its rightful place really do this? Is there much of a literary precedent for it? Doesn't it make the line a shade too Crockettesque? Isn't the more standardized version just (I blush at the implication) as musical?

It was distinctly possible, in short, that my attempts to prevent "only" from moving irrevocably away from the idea it wants to modify were driven, as Vivien implied, at least partly by vanity, in which case my supposedly incisive phrasing could sound, in the ears of posterity, at worst stupid and at best quaint, like the conditional tense, last year's ads, the impersonal pronoun "one," or the average person's average grandfather's diary.

A scary thought.

Anyway, none of my pragmatic arguments worked on Vivien, even though she did manage to master the computer and start on *Chickenbus*. By April, she and Joanne had absorbed all the guidebooks and the latest articles on altitude sickness and gotten all of their shots. I delivered them to the airport.

"Work on the novel," said Vivien as we kissed goodbye. "I love you."

2

I notice suddenly that Barry's no longer walking along beside me. Looking back, I see that he's wandered off into the Nissan lot, rows of pastel-coloured cars and trucks, plastic pennants fluttering overhead. He's examining the window sticker on an orange pickup. I stand and wait, refusing to join him and thus encourage his consumerism which, in my opinion, has gotten out of control over the years. I examine instead the "Arby's Beef on a Bun" sign across the street, with its cryptic JR TURK CLUB promotion suggesting Moslem conspiracy and the resurrection of ancient empires. Adjacent to Arby's is the Health Services Centre containing the Place of Vision, which Barry has renamed the Site for Sore Eyes, and Northern Prosthetics, where Barry wants to work so he can walk up to customers and ask them if they need a hand.

Vivien's trip to Nepal pushed her towards fiction. The articles she'd promised to my journalist friend started to arrive almost immediately on her landing at the airport in New Delhi. The first article described how Vivien and Joanne had been driven into a dark alley off Connaught Circle and attacked by the rickshaw driver and an accomplice who was waiting in the alley. They'd fought the thieves, screaming loudly enough to attract the attention of the armed guard at the nearby YMCA, who raced down the alley and drove the thieves off. I had to clarify the chronology somewhat, as well as correct the grammar and spelling, but I recognized the story as a great one as soon as I read it. This made editing easy.

In fact, editing Vivien's stories was no distraction. They kept me from brooding on her absence. This was something, situated as I was out on the homestead, that I had plenty of time to do. The articles were scribbled on both sides of a lined tissue paper and full of the same stylistic gaffes we usually fought over. I found myself rubbing my cheek against the pages, seeing her so clearly, in a dark hotel room perhaps, or at the outdoor tables of a cafe patio, or on the edges of a smoky market, her legs crossed, writing.

The articles also, I noticed, lacked certain pieces of vital background information, the sure sign of a writer in a hurry and an invitation (to any writer with no great reason to hurry) to improvise.

Joanne's character, for example, needed developing. Vivien tended at times to revert to the singular, forgetting that Joanne was even there. Creating Joanne was easy to do as I hardly knew her. Her job as a medical lab technologist, along with her obvious loyalty to Vivien, suggested that she would be the stalwart, pragmatic, mildly cynical foil to Vivien's impulsive, militant, idealistic heroism.

Also, certain details about setting were obviously missing. In the article on Delhi's Red Fort, Vivien mentioned that the Fort had a moat around it that had originally been stocked with alligators. This sort of detail fascinates me. Why were these alligators placed in the moat? What were their names? Are the alligators still there? If not, what happened to them? Vivien answered none of these obvious questions. Nor did any books and magazines that I consulted for information on the Fort or on the *modus operandi* of the Moguls who had built it. Maybe the Moguls ate alligators as a delicacy. Maybe they worshipped them. In the end I was forced to deduce, and inform local readers, that the alligators were there on the whim of a Mogul emperor with exotic ideas about landscaping. However, the alligators had turned out to be useful for torturing and executing criminals, who were sacrificed through a top-floor balcony over the moat. The deaths of these offenders were witnessed by thousands of enthusiastic spectators who formed groups in support of various alligators. Bookies made a fortune and sometimes these groups actually fought pitched battles, in the course of which even more bodies were consigned to the alligators. Ultimately, during the general decline in prosperity following the collapse of the Mogul Empire, the locals chopped up the alligators, poached them in moat water, and ate them.

In addition to the novel and Vivien's articles, I also had to work on a monograph about the novels and poetry of my friend and mentor George that I'd written for an eastern publisher eight years earlier. This monograph hadn't come out due to the publisher's financial difficulties. Every Christmas I got a card from George, each one containing a variation of the same message, *viz.*, "Dear John, I just met this debutante who says she'll fuck me if I can prove I'm really famous, so I mentioned your book about me and she says when I show it to her … Happy New Year. George." "Dear John, there's this stripper at the Waldorf … " Anyway, my publisher, having solved his financial problems (and having received, perhaps, similar cards from George?), asked me to bring the manuscript up to date, so I had to read and write about George's three new novels, three new books of essays, and seven new books of poetry.

It was some comfort then, and is even now, to think that my monograph about George, should it appear fairly soon (which looks doubtful now due to recent cutbacks in government funding to the Arts Council), might, in addition to improving George's love life, help save my job should my novel not be well received by the committee.

Also, George's bizarre experiments in fiction, inspired though some of them so obviously were by the simple hope of wringing money out of the grant system, gave me further ideas for my plot. I decided to add a third point of view to the novel, that of a previously minor character, Harvey. This character would stand outside of, and comment on, the struggle between the *Wehrmacht* principal and me and Barry. Harvey would be, as he is, Barry's first, most loyal, and yet most cynical disciple.

Vivien returned from Nepal in June, tanned black, with her notebooks stuffed full of information for a possible guidebook and with a wad of stories for the newspaper. She was now, due to this newspaper work, more interested in stories than guidebooks. She'd enjoyed writing the stories and was surprised by the enthusiastic response of local readers, a response conveyed to her by my newspaper friend.

"There's a lot of weirdoes out there," he said by way of explaining Vivien's growing reputation.

Vivien liked most of what I'd done to the stories, once she got over the shock of seeing the literal truth altered. Joanne wasn't so sure. She had to confront her colleagues at work, who now felt they *really* knew her.

"I'm not used to having someone else hang out my laundry," she informed me.

Vivien ignored her, asking me what it was like to write fiction.

"Agony," I told her. "I wouldn't advise my worst enemy to get into it."

"Show me how to do dialogue."

So we worked together on the wad of stories about Nepal, delivered them to my journalist friend, loaded my truck, and left for Kluane.

There I lost myself in rock, willow, water, and air, thinking mostly of my cup, bowl, and sleeping bag, and sometimes of old Gord and the bears, watching Vivien's bare but (due to the bears who, according to Vivien, go into a feeding frenzy at the smell of sex) inaccessible legs ahead of me, wondering what I'd done when I got her to lift the mirror of standard English up to her previously self-justifying passions, and yearning for the *Globe and Mail*.

But I did manage, as I had in Guatemala, some days of rest. After two weeks of hiking, Vivien and I settled into a picturesque A-frame cabin on the shores of Kluane Lake. While Vivien drove up and down the Alaska Highway collecting notes on available accommodation and food, I toyed with dialogue. Harvey's character, I discovered, had a more interesting voice than mine or even Barry's, a voice that I could now carry beyond his discussions with me and Barry into his fights with his parents (heavy drinkers), and his conversations with his fellow student Rudy, an up-country yokel who'd been kicked out of his Forest Service job in a firetower for getting so involved in dope and Wittgenstein that he had failed to report a blaze until it just about took out the tower itself with Rudy in it. Rudy decided that he needed an education and came to the college, where he made friends with Harvey and took to courting Harvey's sister Angela.

I found I was better at getting ideas for the novel than I was at writing those ideas up. Mostly I stared out the window, watching blizzards of rock dust from the Kaskawulsh Glacier roll out Slims River and across the ice-blue water of Kluane Lake. I wandered up and down the lake's shoreline and explored the wreckage of Silver City, a turn-of-the-century mining town.

A few weeks later, Vivien left me again, for a week, while she canoed with Joanne on the Yukon River. I was to work on my novel and uncover any interesting facts concerning the flora and fauna and the natural, human, and geological history of Kluane. This would be my contribution to the hiking guide. I settled in at the Yukon Archives in downtown Whitehorse, just down the street from a first-rate natural-foods cafe and an excellent bookstore.

But here, as in Guatemala, I got interested in the material in front of me and ignored the novel, which seemed anemic in comparison to the colourful history of the Yukon. One of Pierre

Berton's northern histories took me away from the Yukon even, and over to the Nahanni River in the western part of the Northwest Territories. I recognized the setting because of Vivien's canoe trip the previous summer, but now I became fascinated with the story of the place — a much more colourful story, it seemed to me, than anything the Yukon had to offer. I found a complete account in R. M. Patterson's *Dangerous River*, a book that I discovered in the bookstore and devoured in one afternoon over many coffees in the natural-foods cafe. It was the story of a lost gold mine and the men who went looking for it, most of whom ended up as headless bodies on the banks of the Nahanni or Flat Rivers.

A glance at a map on the wall of the archives showed a road beginning near Watson Lake in the southeast corner of the Yukon and ending at the town of Tungsten in the western Northwest Territories, close to the Nahanni. The road and Tungsten were marked, with a felt pen, "abandoned." The archivist confirmed that they had been abandoned fairly recently and he produced some mining-company reports that gave me an account of Tungsten in its heyday and of the circumstances that led to its closing. Terrain maps showed an exploration road running north of Tungsten to the Flat Lakes and beyond. Into the north end of those lakes ran Zenchuk Creek, flowing down a valley that offered, it seemed to me, a clear route up into the headwaters of the Rabbitkettle and down the Rabbitkettle into the Nahanni.

I was researching Zenchuk, as well as his trapper/prospector colleagues, in Dick Turner's *Nahanni* when Vivien returned and we were on our way back into the park and up to our last glacier, the Donjek. I described my Nahanni research to her as we picked our way up a creek into the mountains, but she was not interested.

"When we get home, I'm going to write the archives in Yellowknife," I said.

"You said you were going to put in a few hours on your novel."

"Later."

"There is no later. It's August."

"Later."

On our return from Kluane, our notebooks stuffed with information, we once again settled into my cabin. I began my preparations for September, and Vivien scoured the leafier suburbs of town for a suitable "love nest." This was a mutually frightening proposition, but one we'd been tossing around for some years. We'd finally agreed, in a passionate (but, due to the bears, sexless) moment in a tent overlooking the sparkling expanse of the Donjek Glacier, that after a decade or so of "dating," it was time for us to live together. While I preferred to stick with the cabin and its surrounding acres, all of which is paid for and offers ample opportunity for recreation in simply getting in and out, Vivien convinced me that we needed, as an investment for our old age and in order to efficiently pursue our burgeoning commitment to writing as well as our college careers, some creature comforts like electricity, running water, and central heating.

Of course my commitment to writing is hardly burgeoning, and my college career has long ago set into a bearable routine with which I am increasingly reluctant to tamper. Also, I love the cabin as, next to Sears and Other Art, an ideal place to both write and mark and escape writing and marking. But I keep quiet about this. I simply want to live with Vivien. I have tried to make it clear that I will live in the house only when she's in it, but I can't tell if she is processing this important information.

The fact is that Vivien is getting famous. We need a permanent office with fax and telephone-answering machines to handle book orders. Three thousand copies of *Chickenbus I* are almost sold out. A TV crew from the national network is negotiating to make a fifteen-minute special on Vivien. People stop her on the streets and in the stores to comment on her articles. Those articles, put on the wire by the local paper, are being picked up by much larger papers all over the country. My journalist friend recently told me that Vivien's writing was vivid and easy to read and that maybe I would get somewhere if I cultivated a style more like hers. He particularly praised the article on the Red Fort, an article that he considered a classic example of travel journalism at its best.

"Imagine," he said, staring thoughtfully down into his beer glass and shaking his head, "those crazy Indians fighting over alligators. She made me want to *be* there, almost."

Even Carl, who reads Vivien's articles carefully, partly because he has sensed and wants me to account for my intrusions, but mostly because he enjoys the articles, gives me similar advice.

"When she writes about people," Carl says, eyeing me piercingly over the rump of a cow or the wheel of a tractor, "she's bloody good."

I don't entirely trust Carl's opinions on Vivien, having long ago decided that his judgment is impaired by the fact that he is, in a gentlemanly, fatherly sort of way, in love with her. She's the only person I know who can safely refer to one of Carl's prized bulls as a "big cow" or walk into his shack and start putting things "back where they should be."

During the four-day hike back from the Donjek, even on the Atlas Pass where one slip of the foot could have rendered the discussion irrelevant, we expanded on our idea, reasoning that the purchase of a house at this last possible point in our careers where such a thing would be deemed credible by the banks could be a good investment or, at the very least — since neither of us is particularly optimistic about the town's future even *with* the new university that is rearing itself up on a hill west of town — a method of forcing me to save some money for retirement.

So while I jumped on the teaching treadmill, rushing around meeting classes and xeroxing assignment sheets, Vivien searched for a house. A few days ago she found one, available in November, and we acquired a mortgage.

The only thing that worries me now is what I'll do with the house when Vivien's away. I can't see myself, without Vivien's support and encouragement, lifting dog poop off the front lawn, renovating the rec room, and waving at the neighbours.

Hi, Len.

Yo, John. Sorry about that damned dog. Where's Vivien now?

Vivien's solution is simple. "You rent the house out," she says, "and I get half."

"After expenses?"

"Which don't include cappuccinos when you're on the way to collect the rent."

Last week we removed my computer from Jen's basement suite and set it up in Joanne's basement. Vivien's busy writing up her notes from *Kluane* and planning the Guatemala section of *Chickenbus*. The TV crew may decide to film her, on a local mountain, next week.

And then, in only two weeks, she'll be gone.

Again.

3

Barry's entirely disappeared now, somewhere in a row of 4x4 supercab pickups, down on his knees maybe, examining tires, mufflers, gas tanks, and door latches. Maybe, for his own good, I should go over and distract him. I could tell him that it would cost an arm and a leg to get ahead in the prosthetics business. But no. Barry's fussy. "Get ahead" goes beyond the proper definition of prosthetics. "Keep abreast" would be better.

It's probably some sort of post-sabbatical depression; the old thrill of September that is presently animating Barry is not with me. I'm still, as it were, standing on a nearby hill feeling the breeze on my cheek and taking in a broader vista that makes the action in my immediate vicinity look, frankly, pitiful. Here I am, back for my twenty-somethingth year of teaching future book-keepers and technicians how to write standard English. Where are the books I was going to write?

And here I am, waiting for my friend who could even be asleep out there, on his back, his head under the V6 engine of one of the new 4x4s, dreaming.

Of what?

On a more pragmatic level, if that word can be used in connection with my literary endeavors, I'm also trying to think of some simple twist that will straighten my novel out, infuse it with wider significance, and/or simply enable me to *end* it in a more satisfactory way than the suicide that I'd arranged for the sensitive poet-daughter of the chairman of the college board — a man who encouraged the *Wehrmacht* principal in his worst excesses, like his attempt to force instructors, many of them militant pot-heads, to enforce his ban on the smoking of marijuana on college premises. Perhaps I can strip Harvey of his sister and set Rudy to courting, instead, the poetess.

If I could find an ending, I could remove the novel from the reserve shelf in the college library where the committee lodged it and where, for the past couple of weeks, it has been, the librarian tells me, "hot property." I could slap the novel in front of a famous publisher or film producer, in one stroke eliminating my obligation to the college and ensuring my early retirement from teaching — a retirement that I desperately need soon, or rather *now*, before the piles of grammar exercises on my desk are replaced by piles of progress reports, which will be replaced by piles of instruction memos followed by more progress reports and so on *ad infinitum*.

Meanwhile, my college mailbox is stuffed with memos, textbook ads, minutes of meetings, and agendas for future meetings, so any real mail (should I ever get any) is hard to find. My "electronic mailbox" is full of excuses from students and announcements from managers. This mailbox — personed or, as they say, *augmented* by the insufferably polite but husky-voiced "Jane" — grown up now from her days in the elementary school textbooks with brother Dick, cat Fluff, and dog Spot, but still recognizably *holier than thou* — has been the object of a serious attempt to improve the quality of life at the college. By deft manipulation of the phone buttons, I hope to "make Jane talk." So far, however, I have elicited from her only a series of suggestive words and short phrases.

No ... more ... please enter ... please ... press ....

Meanwhile, too, my students are at work making work for me, and my insensitive (clearly jealous) colleagues, who normally can't seem to remember even important details about me like whether I'm still with Vivien, have kids, am shop steward, or have been sighted in the past month, are harassing me in the hall with smart comments like "Redford plays me or I sue," or "Your title has all the resonance of a flushing toilet," or *"Dives deeply into the surface* — how's that for a cover blurb?"

Most of them want me to kill off the chairman's daughter.

"How?"

"The evil president of the college kills her."

"But she's a sensitive poet."

"Maybe the president could rape her before he kills her."

My colleagues also want to know (and this, at least, is encouraging) if, at a conference on the Canadian Novel in the mid-seventies, Barry really did get involved in a bar-room brawl. And did he then head for my room instead of his own — his reasoning being that the police (in hot pursuit) might have seen or maybe even read his latest book with the picture of him on the back cover and so know his name and so easily locate and arrest him? And, arriving at my room, did he really then catch me and a former colleague from an eastern university in bed together?

And in those moments when consciousness relaxes its, in my case, iron grip, there are warning lights flashing in my brain, synaptic buzzers going off, strange anxieties, some of which I should have shed fifteen to twenty years ago. Is my fly done up? Do I have a class, now, when I think I don't? Are the dates on my course outlines all wrong?

I'm also stuck — in the first month of semester and with no warning — with a new course. Our colleague in the English department, Marcus Vingaard, formerly and at various times head of our department, president of the union, and manager of Developmental Studies (the wily bastard has probably spent less than half of his teaching career in the front lines), has also for some years been the Socialist candidate in this constituency. A couple of days ago an election was called, and Vingaard went on political leave to campaign. The prognosis for the Socialists is, for a change, good. The Conservative premier was caught in a hotel foyer with 20,000 American dollars in a paper bag. He resigned and is about to be dragged into court for defrauding a real estate agent — a rare *volte-face* that proves that fact is no stranger to fiction. The Conservatives replaced him with a stand-in premier who, being attacked by members of her own party as well as by a revived opposition, called an election to clear the air. Word is that, very soon, Vingaard could be Minister of Higher Education.

My supreme commander, in other words.

I met with him last Friday to receive the dusty, elbow-patched, Harris tweed sportscoat of pedagogical power. I received his course outline with the simple comment that there was still, fortunately, time to modify it. This upset him slightly, but we are old antagonists when it comes to pedagogical theory. He countered with a batch of "progress reports" that he had not, in the exciting days leading up to the election, had time to mark.

A salesman sticks his head out of the Nissan showroom and Barry suddenly appears, moving quickly out of the lot as if he's been stung by an adder. "Sweet Jesus," he says, when he gets over to where I'm waiting, "They're giving 3.8 percent over three years if you buy one of these trucks. That's less than half the prime rate."

I've noticed, in the weeks since I got back from Kluane, that Barry's very conscious now about banks, interest rates, and terms of payment. Before, he never knew or wanted to know such details and was impatient with my and Vivien's extensive speculations thereon. He believed, fatalistically, that he and I (he wasn't, interestingly, so sure about Vivien) were, as he usually put it, "fucked." No matter how careful or smart we were, we would be cheated (legally) out of our cash, securities, possessions, and pensions by forces a lot bigger, smarter, and better connected than us. He imagined his future self as an old man with a rusty bicycle and layers of ragged clothing (including the mandatory felt cap with ear flaps), picking up bottles along the roads around town and being found, finally, one spring, frozen to death in a culvert, a ragged copy of his last poem clutched to his icy breast or, more likely, crammed into his ass to keep the wind off his hemorrhoids. Or, in more speculative moments, he modelled his future self after another bottle scavenger, a man about seventy years old who appears every summer wearing a woman's bikini (including sometimes the top), makeup, false eyelashes, steel-toed boots, and a cycling helmet with headlight and battery pack mounted thereon, freaking out locals and tourists alike until fall when he disappears, continuing south (we imagine), still in his bikini and excessively rouged and tanned, to California and the Baja. Barry's theory about money (expressed when I told him, a couple of years ago, about Vivien's idea of buying a house) was that you might just as well "peel it off," and this he does with enviable if foolhardy elan, particularly when it comes to his kids and (when there is money left over from them) his house and (in the odd time when there is money left over from that, or when his indulgent parents are forced at tax time to dump money on him) New York.

However, he has evidently, like me, modified this philosophy to include the idea that any long-term debts accrued in the purchase of quality objects (like Nissan pickup trucks, maybe) can be rationalized as "investments" or "forced savings." Up to last year, such objects included a paid-off house, a five-component stereo, various pieces of antique furniture, some paintings, a piano, a drum set, vibes, a computer, a summer cabin near the ocean on the Sechelt Peninsula, a small boat, a motorcycle, some top-of-the-line ski equipment, and all of the usual condiments that go with summer cottages and houses, including a collection of jazz albums, tapes, and CDs so impressive that local public radio features it (with Barry as commentator) every Wednesday morning (for the commuter crowd), and a library of rare, small press publications that is marked by the new librarian of the new university for purchase whenever Barry makes up his mind or is broke enough to sell.

At the time that Vivien and I left for Guatemala, Barry and Joy were in their usual straits, at the upper limits of a number of unpaid credit card balances and a short line of credit. While we were away, however, they launched into a major renovation of their house, a beautiful, old, two-storey, wood-frame place with dormers and a huge front porch on a double lot occupied by stately birch and willow trees. They redid the windows, siding, drywall, and insulation, keeping (at considerable expense) the place as close as possible in appearance to the original, thus satisfying the heritage people who regard the house as an historical treasure and would like to buy it rather than see it changed, though it is questionable whether they have any money. Barry and Joy also put in a hot tub and new kitchen and bathroom, and surrounded the lot with an eight-foot-high fence, rolling the costs up with their line of credit (at 10 percent) and some scary charge-card (including Sears) accounts (at 24 percent) into a $60,000 mortgage (at 13 percent). Ten years of heavy payments lie ahead.

After which they will still, in Barry's view, be "fucked," but at least they'll know they did their best and didn't let any immature, self-serving, sanctimonious, crypto-communist brooding over individuality, art, and the evils of materialism hold them from the true course of fiscal responsibility. This was the sort of thinking that kept us off the pension plan for twelve years, a circumstance that never fails to depress us whenever we think about it, which is at least once every day.

So now Barry believes that he's "locked in." He watches the "prime rate." When it goes up he's happy and when it goes down he wonders if the bastards at the bank ripped him off. He follows the financial advice on the radio and in the paper, writes off for free brochures and harvests swaths of pamphlets from local banks and trust companies, talks about whether it pays to borrow to purchase a registered retirement savings plan and use the savings on your tax return to pay down your charge accounts, keeps track of real estate prices (which are rising right now due to the new university with its management and a skeleton faculty temporarily housed in a downtown office building), and calculates his equity daily, usually while we are having our afternoon decaf cappuccino in Other Art. He speculates that he will, shortly after being laid off due to "redundancy" due to the new university (which *is* talking about offering creative writing), be disturbed in his new hot tub by an eager buyer, who of course turns out to be the new head of the creative writing department at the new university, a Brit (Barry does the accent by affecting a lisp) who just happened to be driving by the house (in his Riley) with his horsey wife.

We simply fell in love with the place on sight, old boy. Reminds us somewhat of Coleridge's home at Keswick or Yeats' tower at Sligo. And fancy you being a poet too! You must loan us one of your books. It's a bloody incredible coincidence, wouldn't you say Muriel?

I just felt *it as we passed by. Nigel is always amazed at how sensitive I am about these things, aren't you Nigel?*

Indeed I am.

Bitterly cognizant of the fact that the house is really (as Barry intended) much more "reminiscent" of W. C. Williams' house in New Jersey and, worse, that the silly Brit, while purporting to be a poet, didn't recognize Barry despite the picture on the backs of some half-dozen books, one of which was nominated for the country's top poetry prize, Barry's response is simple and (considering that the last house payment is naturally in arrears) delivered with phenomenal elan.

One sixty-nine, nine. No triflers.

Barry also contemplates the fates of people who are either fucked or not quite yet fucked – his parents, for example, both of whom are now, and maybe forever, in and out of the hospital, and Arnold, an old poet-friend who gave up everything for his art and now goes from Arts Council-sponsored reading tours into soup-kitchen and food-bank line-ups and who was recently arrested for wandering into someone's suburban house and (while the people were in the living room watching TV) raiding the fridge and leaving, in exchange for some cheese, bread, and milk, a valuable (he hopes to convince the judge) draft manuscript of a poem with his signature on it.

"Is the old Dodge starting to act up?" I ask Barry, seeking to gauge his intentions regarding the Nissan that he was examining so carefully.

"Doesn't match the house anymore."

We walk in silence for awhile, me wondering whether I should lecture Barry on the merits of his old pickup with its near-indestructible and easily tuned slant-six engine. On the other hand, Barry's flippant response to my question indicates that he expects me to do exactly this and is not looking forward to it.

"They shouldn't have dumped Vingaard's technical writing class on you," says Barry, deftly changing the topic. "They could hire somebody part-time. Now they'll promise an easier load in November to make up, but then they'll say there's too many registered students and you'll be on overtime. They did it to me while you were away, the bastards."

Barry knows that I hate overtime – regard it, in fact, as a betrayal of my holiest dreams. What I want is time. And he, like me, hates teaching other people's courses, especially Vingaard's. Conveying to students the shifting formalities of standard English is a relatively easy and interesting way to make a living, but Vingaard is always pushing the usual simulations to the point of mirror-like perfection where suddenly left becomes right and student and teacher, Alice or Narcissus-like, fall into madness. Possibly a frustrated novelist, Vingaard uses and vigorously promotes the "company model" of teaching. In Vingaard's classes, students are always "consultants," working in a company "owned" by Vingaard and writing reports for various "clients" that Vingaard has dredged out of the Chamber of Commerce or any one of the many service clubs that he belongs to. These people are often drunks and sometimes much more interested in the students than they should be. "That's the real world," Vingaard is fond of saying whenever something unusual happens.

But is it not precisely the function of a school to weed out some of the elements of reality in order to focus the novice mind on the basics of logic, arithmetic, and composition? And does not the conventional method of teaching have the additional advantage of emptying out the malls, residences, office towers, and streets for most of the day so that the real work of the world can go smoothly on? Also, if a student got raped by a client, would Vingaard give that student a grade on how she/he handled that particular (as he puts it) "learning experience?" Would he base further exercises on the resulting litigation? Even if the litigation happened to be directed at him and threatened to deprive him of his pension?

No simulation can really be reality. Vingaard should know this. He is, after all, a sometime student of poetry, which is, as George's friend Red (a lyric poet who, significantly, died of a brain tumour) put it, "the art of writing from the inside looking inside-out." But Vingaard never learns, as I discovered on Friday. In the case of the particular class that I have just inherited from him, a class of students taking electronics or drafting technology, Vingaard has set up a special arrangement with the technical instructors. The instructors assign the students a tangible project which the students complete in the technical course while writing a long report about the completion of this project in Vingaard's class.

Progress in Vingaard's class is, in other words, dependent on progress in someone else's class. I could see the immediate results of this in the reports that I marked over the weekend. I knew immediately why Vingaard had not "happened" to mark them. He knew how depressing it would've been.

Few if any of the students had any progress to report. None of the students had done any writing or planning for writing. All of the students had good reasons for being stalled: "I am presently waiting for my volt-stretcher to arrive from Tokyo and when it does I am confident that I can install it into the maze table and have my project completed by the end of November as stipulated." As an experienced teacher, I can easily translate this into its true meaning: "For reasons built into the assignment you handed me, you incompetent creep, I have a perfect excuse to sit on my butt all semester and do nothing but write a pile of repetitive no-progress reports."

Was I supposed to slog through the rest of the semester with the details of video genlock synthesizers and concrete domes crowding my teeming brain? Or lie awake at night in a cold sweat because some gizmo was lost in the mail or crossing the Pacific Ocean on a slow boat from Tokyo? Let the "real" instructors sweat over things like that. My job is to sweat over how students spell, whether their brains can be trained into sequences of pro-con, time-space, comparison-contrast, induction-deduction, and cause-effect, and whether they have imagination enough to accept gracefully the necessity of, and learn the tricks involved in, fixing the dialect into the shifting formalities of the standard so that the questionable work of the world can be routinely carried on. And that is, as a possible affront to human nature or (as the Babel story indicates) a deviation from the divine order of things, enough to sweat over.

"Vingaard told me to take attendance, give spot quizzes, photocopy all their assignments, and keep a file on them," I complain to Barry as we wait for the pedestrian light so we can cross the highway over to Spruce Centre. "He's convinced that if I don't do that they'll all just screw around."

"Of course they'll screw around," says Barry vehemently. "You won't have a clue what they're talking about in connection with their projects. Also, they can play you off against the instructor responsible for the project. I've been through it."

"Maybe I should hand the course outline over to the Conservatives. They could use it against Vingaard during the election."

"As usual you've got it all wrong. The public would *love* Vingaard's course outline. Vingaard would be a hero. That kind of Quixotic educational experimentation is very popular. People *love* to see teachers and students being tortured."

"True. And if he wins, we win. We get rid of him. And he's probably better at politics than teaching."

"He's a good enough teacher, despite his ideas. Also, he likes you, for reasons that are beyond me, and he wouldn't do anything against you unless you make things impossible for him, which would be really stupid not to mention unnecessary."

"But he could be dangerous. He gets all these *ideas*, which he converts into opinions and then into causes and then into pedagogical experiments that blow up in *our* faces as well as his. If he wins and becomes Minister of Higher Education, he could really screw us around."

"He'll have other much more serious things to worry about, like the new university which, if they give him the Education portfolio, is going to be his Waterloo, though of course if it comes to that he'll make sure it's someone else's Waterloo. Like ours. Anyway, the system's too opaque. I've never heard of a directive making it from up there to down here in one piece. We should support him. Especially since he could save our butts once the university starts up."

"You don't believe that."

"He promised us."

"He did?"

"While you were away in Guatemala pretending to write a novel. He said that, if elected, he'd fight to make sure that all present college programs remained intact. He even made a ponderous joke to the effect that if he didn't protect the university program in particular, he could in the future be without a job himself."

"You believed him?"

"Of course not. While he was talking I felt a cold breeze stab my sphincter. But who else would try to save us?"

"So you're saying that we should keep our mouths shut?"

"Especially you."

4

I did what I had to do with Vingaard's students. I stayed on my side of the mirror. I spent Saturday morning on a detailed marking of the progress reports, ferreting out every misspelled word, every noun-verb disagreement, every nonparallel structure, every format error, every double-space between a comma and the next letter, every (when another splash of red ink seemed in order but hard to justify) misplaced "only." Then I wrote, in exemplary format and style, a memo telling the students that the project and the project report were two quite different things and that the latter could (hard as it may be to believe) coexist with, nay even *pre-exist*, the former, and that I in future wanted to know not only what they had done, were doing, and would be doing, but also *and more importantly* what they'd written, were writing, and would be writing. Furthermore, I expected to proofread those parts of the report that they reported writing as they reported writing them.

This morning, armed with my folder of marked reports and

my memo, I met them for the first time. Nice kids, some of them adults actually, all busy designing and/or building and/or pretending to design and/or build their cement domes, equestrian facilities, accident-proof access scaffolding, solar-heated houses, video genlock boards, and robotic arms. All bemused at if not slightly impatient with the institutional madness that requires them to hold the mirror of standard English up to the realities of drafting floor plans and soldering components. At the same time, they're probably also all (mostly correctly) convinced that most of their practical and all of their theory courses are just some kind of kinky initiation that will soon be over. Then they'll be out in the real world, unselfconsciously designing houses, wiring circuits, reading (only) the newspaper and writing (only) postcards.

I introduced myself to the class as briefly and humorously as possible. I informed them that I would be making certain changes in the course in the next couple of weeks, after I had figured out, or been unable to figure out, what was going on. The students extended some sympathy to me on this point. I then handed the progress reports back, with the memos. They found out their grades. The honeymoon was, as they say, over. They read the commentary on their reports. Frowns. They read the memo. Groans. Sullen faces.

The women, all of them in drafting, started comparing their progress-report results. One of them didn't fare too well in the comparison, had had a problem grasping the concept (basic to the plan of any progress report) of past, present, and future.

"But there is no such thing as 'Present Work'," she hissed. "There's only work that I've done and work that I still have to do!"

Her friends sighed sympathetically but complacently. They hadn't gone into things quite so deeply, proving again that too much thinking is dangerous, even (perhaps especially) in school.

Their minds were now on the big report. They felt that the real problem of time at this point was more along the lines of "How can we write about doing things that we haven't done yet?"

"Do the background stuff," I explained to them when they finally asked. "Sketch out any summaries, abstracts, recommendations. If you're actually building a piece of equipment, produce the instructions for using it or for maintaining it. You can even guess what steps you'll have to take to finish and what the results could be. Start your diagrams. The details can always be adjusted later. Remember that you have to have a 3000-word report written in two months. You can't write that much in the last few weeks of the semester. You have to start now." I thought of adding, "And possibly invent reality as you go," but I thought better of starting a philosophical debate that the students could, if not win, at least prolong indefinitely.

More groans, but less convincing now. Probably they would brood over it for the coming week. "Work in Progress: brood over whether or not it is possible to write up something that you haven't actually done."

Like, for example, murder your uncle for killing your father and marrying your mother.

Like find out that, for years, you've been married to and ardently impregnating your own mother.

Like hand your kingdom over to your kids because they tell you they love you.

The male drafting students, demonstrating that certain aloofness (the result, probably, of the popularity of some rock star or television actor) that characterizes young men this year and is turning out to be a windfall for us teachers, deciding that meaningful class discussion had ended for the time being, turned on their computers and started to hack up the next progress report, cocking their ears to the women just in case any pertinent clues to the nature of time or their new instructor revealed themselves.

The electronics students grabbed their memos and marked reports and left, all except for one, Shane. I'd noticed his name when he picked up his near-perfect progress report.

Shane appeared to be some kind of leader. Probably his job was to deal with me for the other guys, who would maybe deal for him with the lab technician. He was either a good writer or a good cheater, and he didn't look physically capable of working in a lab. Or maybe he preferred hanging around the women in drafting and construction. He was massively fat, a good 250 pounds at least, with thin, blonde hair and a pasty face covered with damp zits. He wore a T-shirt that didn't even come close to covering his belly button. He overflowed his chair. After picking up his marked report, he leaned so heavily back in his chair that I thought it was going to flip out from under him. Then he took his keyboard and placed it on his paunch. Wheezing rhythmically, he started poking away at amazing speed with his stubby fingers, half looking at the distant monitor and half (it seemed) at the ceiling, like he was meditating.

Barry says there are two rules of teaching. The first is to keep your eye on your discipline, without which you will be totally adrift, like Vingaard and the managers, in a sea of expediency and end up going into politics or arranging your home life around the vagaries of your latest neurotic spouse or the bowel movements of a basset hound. The second is to identify the leader in any class and make friends.

I'd hardly understood a word that Shane had written in his progress report. It was mostly electrical hieroglyphics. His project, a video genlock synthesizer, useful (evidently) for playing video images alongside or on top of regular TV programming, was being held up because of resistors. That had a logical sound to it. He had the usual if not simple at least standard concept of past, present, and future. And, thank God, he didn't seem concerned (at least yet) about having to write about something that wasn't happening.

"The present is a state of mind," he said dreamily, evidently to the hissing woman who was sitting beside him. "Future Work will never become Work Done if you don't do something *now*, and there is no *now* if you aren't *doing* something. Sometimes I think women lose their brains when they get their first period."

I blinked. Disregarding the comment about women as the gratuitous posturing of a (rightfully) insecure male, it was one of the best commentaries on "Burnt Norton" that I'd ever heard. Maybe electrical training, like poetry, requires a special ability to see abstractions as tangible things and tangible things as symbols.

The woman glared at him but said nothing. Probably she was used to him. It was possible, even, that she liked him. The glare was not entirely baleful, as we novelists like to say.

"Vingaard drew us a chart, sir," Shane continued, still staring at the ceiling and poking away at the keyboard. "Past Work is what you did from the last reporting period to this one. Present Work is what you're doing from this reporting period to the next one. Future Work is everything left to do."

"See," hissed the woman. "It doesn't make any *sense*."

"If you mean that it doesn't fit reality *as we perceive it*, you're right," said Shane. "In a progress report, 'Present Work' is really always the same thing: I am presently reporting on progress. It would be redundant to specify it. But Vingaard's definition *is* workable."

"Sir, what if I did nothing last week?" another woman asked.

"Nothing?"

"Major drafting test."

"None of us did anything on our projects."

"It was an awesome test."

"Just report that you did nothing."

"I reported that last week. Don't you say in this memo that you're going to fail us or something if we report that again?"

"Right. I want you to start writing your big reports so, after reporting nothing under Past Work, under Present Work tell me that you're presently writing. You could say, for example, that between this Wednesday and next Wednesday you will be writing the backgrounder for your report. And under Future Work you'll be writing, say, your maintenance or operating instructions or starting your diagrams."

General silence. They knew that once I'd gotten them to promise, in writing, to write, they would have to do it and, worse, show it to me, and then possibly rewrite and show it to me again and so on *ad nauseam*. They would fall into my side of the mirror. They would be, irreversibly, in a *real* English course. Even Shane, who had been pounding away on his keyboard through most of the discussion, stopped.

Shit, I thought. I'm pushing them too hard. Now he's going to start, then they'll all pitch in. Students always know when solidarity is called for, and it's hard to argue with twenty people at the same time, especially if some of them are smart. It occurred to me too that Vingaard had set the due date for the preliminary outline of the final report ... when? Close to the end of semester. What was he thinking of? Of what was he thinking? That it would be too late by then to do anything about the actual projects, so he could assign a short (and easily marked) book review at the end as a substitute for the big report and blame the whole disaster on the technical instructors or on fate? Or that, given the political situation, there would likely be an election and this course would be a last joke on some politically unimaginative colleague like, for example, me?

Fortunately, I had already told them that I would revise the course schedule.

But Shane had none of this on his mind at all. "Sir," he said, "is there a place in Africa named Malaria?"

The woman beside him, who was hacking on a progress report that does, I hope (since it's now on my desk), deal adequately with the concept of present time, giggled.

"A place?"

"Vingaard says I get a point on the grammar test if there's such a place. Beam me up. Sentence 65."

I hit the keyboard and brought his screen up on mine. Yes, it is true that some teachers, like most of my younger colleagues, even those with a Ph.D., would lick my hemorrhoid to get this job. Experience at teaching on computers always looks good on a resume. Computer literacy, as Vingaard called it back when he was lobbying for the computers. What next? Aural literacy? Comedic literacy? Manual literacy? The literacy of silence? Vingaard also talked about keeping up with the Japanese. Too bad the Russians fucked up; they seem (because of my ethnocentric reading of Chekhov, Turgenev, and Dostoevsky maybe, or perhaps because of my World War II Vancouver childhood) less threatening than the Japanese. Vingaard's smart. Thanks to him, I'd have a great resume if I ever needed one, except for the unalterable, unavoidable little fact that I'm fifty years old and therefore almost certainly (in some minor way, I hope) gone in the head.

Sentence 65, in a file entitled "Basic Grammar Exercises: Modifiers," was highlighted. The sentence read "You may be exposed on the safari to Malaria." Clearly the upper-case "M" in "Malaria" had not originally been there, and the correction that Vingaard had in mind was "On the safari, you may be exposed to malaria" or even "You may be exposed, on the safari, to malaria." Shane had simply converted "malaria" to a place name. I chuckled to myself. That was a good one, loosely reminiscent of Groucho's "When I was on safari I shot an elephant in my pyjamas." Of course, safaris don't *go* places, do they? Aren't they more *in* places? Maybe not. Acknowledgement must be paid to changes rung in the dialect, so long as such changes aren't too extreme. It's a nuisance, like "only," but as Eliot knew, a language that falls into the hands of bureaucrats and doesn't allow change, dies, and I'm too old to learn Japanese or Russian. Besides, I'm supposed to be a novelist, really, and not a bureaucrat at all. I'm a novelist, supposedly, filtering the energy of the dialect through the formality of the standard and thus (like Shakespeare and Eliot) invigorating the standard and taming the dialect and impressing everyone with a genius that could not possibly be my own. Obviously Vingaard thought you could "safari to," and that was good enough for the purposes of technical writing, though if he'd wanted to deprive Shane of his grade, the matter of proper idiom might've been a more legitimate rationale than questioning the actual existence of a place. This surely is the concern of geographers rather than grammarians, who do often introduce fantasy into their tests and examples as a means of either venting their frustrated literary aspirations or avoiding the interminable boredom of devising and marking grammar exercises.

Vingaard might know better than I whether you could "safari to." Not that Socialists are generally known for having any sense for language. Their theme song "Solidarity Forever" utilizes a plagiarized tune and words so stupid that they make you blush even if you vaguely believe them, though it is possible that the song is actually a *parody* of "The Battle Hymn of the Republic," deliberately designed to drive American rednecks crazy, in which case I've been missing the point for years. But Vingaard, though he seems to have not the slightest ambition as author or critic and is, unless it suits some political purpose, disgustingly noncommittal about the entire discipline of English, can turn out vivid and (when he's angry, which is often) dangerously sarcastic prose in defense of his ideas, and so is a writer to be reckoned with.

And of course you could be "exposed" while on safari. As a coward, for example, as in "Macomber."

Good old Hemingway. I wonder who's teaching him now?

I scrolled up and down, wanting to look busy and not having any immediate answer for Shane about the possible location of Malaria. The other sentences looked alright. But wait a minute. Number 25 read, "Mr. Smith! A man of great integrity has never been promoted." It had obviously originally been "Mr. Smith a man of great integrity has never been promoted," and was meant to be corrected as "Mr. Smith, a man of great integrity, has never been promoted," or "A man of great integrity, Mr. Smith has never been promoted."

It occurred to me that doing grammar exercises backwards could be fun. I started to wonder if it would be valuable to ask students to *introduce* specified grammatical errors into correct sentences.

Probably not. That would be too far on the opposite side of the pedagogical spectrum.

"What did you get on this?" I asked Shane.

"Ninety-nine percent."

So Vingaard had had no problem with Shane depriving Smith of his integrity and attributing it to some unknown, unpromoted person and then, as if to add insult to injury, implying (by bringing it so forcefully to Smith's intention) that Smith might in some way be responsible for the unknown person's pitiful condition. Or maybe Smith is a union shop steward, like me, responsible for correcting such injustices. Good old Smith!

But that was sentence 25, and by sentence 65, Vingaard had — in a funk, perhaps, after marking some seventy-five grammar tests in the first three weeks of the course instead of going to meetings, socials, and christenings like a candidate on the cusp of the greatest battle of his political career should — twigged to Shane and wanted the doubtless dusty, sleepy, and ramshackle town of Malaria pinpointed on the map (southern Sahara, I'd guess) before he "gave" Shane a grade.

I sympathized. Sometimes even a veteran like me inadvertently pushes the simulation too far, and when you do that you don't want smart people like Shane tittering behind your back. But it was a clear case of oversensitivity; this was, after all, merely a very conventional grammar test. Shane deserved his 100 percent. He wasn't giggling at Vingaard but coming right up to him and showing that he perceived the anomalies but was willing to go along and answer long lists of grammar problems that were beneath him and irrelevant to his career goals and to the simulation at hand, but that at the same time might be useful to the dummies who made up the rest of the class. His answers were an acknowledgement of kinship, a signal from one civilized person to a(hopefully)nother that the mind didn't just exist to provide rationales for whatever the passions wanted, from time to time, to do, but had a passionate life of its own. And Vingaard had rejected Shane's advances and had to be punished or, rather, forced into enlightenment.

On a particular point like this I couldn't break ranks. Shane would understand this and also understand that I understood that a 100-percent grade on a stupid grammar test was not the point.

"There's an atlas out in the foyer of the library," I said.

"I looked there," said Shane. "I need a bigger atlas, one that concentrates on Africa."

"The place wouldn't have to be in Africa," I said. "You could conceivably have safaris in — to — other parts of the world."

"That's *right*! Surfin' safaris. It could be a beach."

"Shopping safaris," said the woman beside him, smirking. "It could be a shopping centre or even a store."

Safari to mall-area? What Barry and I were about to embark on?

A metaphor is a fair comparison, but a pun, though fun, is evasion.

While I was pondering the implications of this, the buzzer sounded. It was 8:45. The students logged off the network and rushed, Shane lumbering along behind, to their next class, and I went around slowly, my head aching and my shirt wadded into my armpits, collecting the start-up disks.

5

"Bank machine first," says Barry as we enter the Spruce Centre parking lot. So we bypass the side door to Sears (locked anyway until 9:30) and cut across to the mall entrance where the bank machines are lined and lit up.

Last year Barry was the one in trouble and I was calming him down. His troubles are, however, less tangible than mine in that they can at any one time be a matter more of depression than circumstances. Barry, like (I assume) most lyric poets, suffers from recurring bouts of acute depression. By the time Vivien and I left for Guatemala, my clinical interest in him as a protagonist in my stories was giving way to concern for him as a friend. He looked awful. He raved about how he'd worked for twenty-five years and had nothing. When I pointed out that he'd simply spent all of his money instead of saving and investing it, he turned silent, then talked about his migraines and how he had insomnia all the time.

He'd told me how, one night or early morning, he decided that his insomnia was caused by the stink from the pulp mills. He'd phoned up the mill just across the river from the town and asked the guy who answered if there was something wrong with the mill.

"Why?" the guy asked, evidently alarmed, obviously assuming that Barry had seen a fire on the grounds or some escaping chlorine gas.

"It stinks."

"Oh that," said the guy, relieved. "That means it's working right. The stuff you can smell is harmless. It's the stuff you can't smell that'll kill you."

Barry's on a new regimen now, appropriate to a mortgagee and hot tubber: decaf only, beer on Friday and Saturday nights only, swimming Tuesday and Thursday nights. He looks thinner, tanned. He always has argued that debt has a calming effect.

But then so does satiety.

Barry could be addicted to spending. After all, shortly before I left for Guatemala I had, I thought, convinced him to lay off the house. I explained to him that, according to reports I'd collected over the years from the drafting and construction tech students, you seldom recover your investment from a major renovation. It's better to buy up to a newer house. Also, the siding, which Barry was particularly worried about because he had to paint it each year because the paint bubbled and flaked off, was cedar.

"According to the forestry students, it would be solid as stone underneath," I explained. "Even if it has some water in the surface, no water could get through into the wall. Cedar doesn't rot and the lumber they used back then was the best."

Anyway, things must be working out, financially, so far. When I was last at Spruce Centre with Barry, in April, he'd flipped out. Joy had gotten to the bank machine first and left only $27.36 in the account, and it was still a week to payday. Now he doesn't even bother checking his balance, just punches in a request for $100, puts his card back in his wallet, calmly pockets the money, and gives the balance slip a cursory glance before tossing it in the garbage.

"Feed's on me," he says. "You paid last time."

Just inside the mall's main entrance, we pass up the Gourmet Kaiser shop, also a regular stop. We prefer the kaisers to Sears breakfast, but the shop has recently been bought out by some Chinese people, and though all the same German ladies are still working out front, the kaisers are a bit thinner now. The German ladies are definitely bitchier. The last two times we went there, there was no gruyere. One of those times the crusty buns had been replaced by something that had obviously been kept in a plastic bag. The German ladies were acutely embarrassed, and a number of customers refused their orders, but is it politically correct to expect a Chinese family to be fanatically committed to the perfect Kaiser? Is it politically correct for a Chinese family to *own* a delicatessen? Anyway, the Gourmet Kaiser has no tables, so if you buy a kaiser you have to eat it in the mall, sitting on one of the benches. Out in the mall there are lots of distractions. If you want to mark or plot, you go to Sears.

Today we're meeting Stan who, according to Barry, wants us to commit ourselves to writing regular columns for the union newsletter.

I miss the newsletter, which, before I went on leave, I used to edit. I miss my old office too, which Stan inherited along with the newsletter, and my decade-long dialogue with Kurt, my office-mate. I wonder if Stan has learned to appreciate Kurt. Kurt is alright once you get used to him, which takes, due to his extreme reticence, longer than one semester or even two. Also, his convictions, too narrow to have any connection to reality, have a logical consistency that makes them attractive. This consistency was arrived at in the course of twenty years of lecturing about his convictions on the pedagogical grounds that this inspires students to develop their own convictions and write them up in what he calls "themes." Barry adds the adjective "wet" to this designation. These themes convince readers due to the systematic application of logical formats like thesis, antithesis, synthesis. The fact that the younger students regularly protest Kurt's approach to teaching, accusing him of using the podium as a soap-box or pulpit, merely convinces Kurt that he is onto something, and he continually devises increasingly controversial theses. He also points out that his older students, even if they are few and far between, are often enthusiastic about his approach and love engaging in political debates in class. The student protests that result from Kurt's first lecture (in his composition classes) on the merits of fascism as opposed to democracy or (in his literature classes) on "Leda and the Swan" as literary pornography are ritual events at the college, dreaded by management certainly, but perhaps even more by faculty who have to face a sudden flood of offended students trying to get out of Kurt's class and into any other. It seems that, in particular, Kurt's comparison of the Yeats poem to assorted famous paintings of the Leda story — among them a painting, a copy of which Kurt actually brings to class, that once hung over Hitler's bed at Berchtesgaden — causes particular offense.

"They need to learn that our most sublime art may affect us powerfully through its appeal to our basest instincts," says Kurt.

But it's the newsletter that really hurts, mainly because Stan is doing a much better job on it than I ever did. While I was on sabbatical, Barry sent me some copies of the newsletter care of the Consulate in Guatemala City, and I carried them around with me for a few days until it occurred to me that with their Status of Women Committee Reports and appeals for the Nicaragua Relief Fund, they could be taken for communist literature, the possession of which is, according to Vivien, illegal in most Latin American countries.

You are no de writer, you are de espider, and we shoota de espiders ....

So I shredded the newsletters into washroom wastepaper receptacles and covered them with used toilet paper (which generally cannot be flushed in Central America due to extremely low water pressure in most toilets). I knew as soon as I read them that I wouldn't be agitating on my return to get my editor's job back. I'd held that job for almost two decades, taking the magazine beyond the usual notices of meetings, lists of officials, accounts of negotiations or arbitrations, and announcements of socials. Barry wrote poetry and reviews for me, Don wrote reviews, and Kurt wrote philosophical articles on why the monarchy was necessary, why all university students should study a foreign language (ideally German, which has maintained its purity), why the concept of human rights erodes parliamentary democracy, and why French existentialism (where the ultimate act of freedom is to kill yourself) is inferior to German (where you kill someone else).

I myself specialized in satire.

But all of it was armchair journalism. Stan actually goes out and makes news. He creates scenes at meetings and then writes about what happened. He crashes into people's offices and homes and gets interviews. He polls faculty and students on various topics.

He's also a good writer. That is, his prose is good.

Barry stops in front of Treeline Outdoor Wear, next to the Gourmet Kaiser, and starts pawing through a table of stuff that has just been rolled out by a salesclerk. He lifts up some steel-reinforced coveralls, 50 percent off.

"Got a pair of these?" he asks me.

"No."

"They're hard to find. You should wear them when you use your chainsaw. You don't often see them on sale."

"I won't be doing much of that anymore."

"Don't be gloomy. You told me you could rent the house out and return to the bush whenever Vivien's away, which is half the time. Actually, now that I think of it, it seems to be more and more as your relationship develops."

"How did Stan make out last year?" I ask. "With his scripts?"

"I wish I could judge," Barry replies. "They generally sound stupid to me, but TV generally *is* stupid. I think he knows what he's doing. I'm considering giving him the second semester of creative writing; he'd be exactly what the students need at that stage. It's a whole new world and, frankly, I'm not interested in it. I'm not even interested in creative writing anymore. In fact, I think I've stopped writing altogether."

"I'll inform the Canlit establishment. What kinds of scripts does he write?"

"Most of them are violent. Usually there's this Korean kid, or guy, very much like Stan himself, who was raised in a small Interior town full of loggers and Indians. He's the only oriental in town so he has to fight his way into school every day. He gets tough, self-disciplined, etc. Learns karate, tae kwon-do, judo, you know."

"Yu-Noh?"

"Also, the Korean kid has family problems. Usually his father is absent, maybe dead, and sometimes his mother is still back in Korea or dead. Anyway, he meets an old man, or woman, an authority figure, a substitute parent, usually native, who teaches him how to carve canoes and paddle out to scratch killer whales behind the ears. But the old Indian man is being persecuted by the local white rednecks, usually on motorcycles, skidoos, or power boats. The kid, of course, outsmarts and/or beats up the evil leader of the motorcycle gang. He saves the canoe, the old Indian guy, and/or the whales. Usually there's a symbolic brotherhood scene at the end. The Korean kid learns his place in the order of things."

"That Koreans are simply Indians who couldn't see crossing two hundred miles of eminently floodable land-bridge? Or they did cross and then discovered they looked stupid in paint and feathers or hated buffalo meat, so they returned home to Seoul?"

Barry leaves the coveralls and we swing past Moodie Chocolates, passing along the edge of the mall's foyer, a large, open area under a pyramid-shaped sun roof. Its centrepiece is a pond that contains a twenty-foot-long model of one of the old paddlewheelers that used to ply the river here in the few months when dog teams were impractical. The paddlewheeler's paddlewheel rotates constantly, making a pleasant splashing sound.

Sitting on one of the nearby benches (like giant children's blocks, the low ones for seats, the middle ones for tables, and the higher ones with holes in the top for garbage) is one of the mall's major distractions, another reason why we generally eat at Sears. It's Alphonse from the Sunset Lodge nursing home down the street.

"He's still alive," I mutter to myself. He looks a bit frailer, a bit more huddled into himself, but his eyes are the same: alive.

Alphonse has been in Spruce Centre as long as I have — since the place was built. He disappears once in awhile for long periods of time and then reappears, resurrected by modern medicine. He's just mobile enough to make it to the mall every day, though in winter he's not so dependable, and he must like the paddle-wheeler because it's always been his favourite spot. Or maybe it's not the paddlewheeler so much as the commanding view of the main entrance. He's wiry, probably only a hundred pounds, about five-foot-six, wears a blue pinstripe suit, a blue toque, a blue overcoat, work gloves, and running shoes, and talks only about sex or his son, who took all of Alphonse's money ("thousands!") and spent it and dumped Alphonse in the Sunset.

We tend to sympathize with the son. Alphonse is a pervert. Worse, he doesn't talk with us but at us, and he won't leave us alone. Maybe it's our Harris tweed sportscoats with the elbow patches, our glasses, our mustaches, and our grey hair, all warranties that an approach will be greeted with clinical detachment rather than a punch in the nose. Or maybe it's me personally, the signal that I seem to send out to drunks, weirdos, and bums (even in Latin America, much to Vivien's amusement) so that they invariably weave their way across crowded streets or rooms and appear at my side to babble their inane stories, like overaffectionate dogs or cats who love to sit on the laps and chew the armpits of the shirts, sweaters, and coats of people who hate them. We've tried moving to other seats, but Alphonse always finds us. We've tried cramming our asses together onto one of the isolated seats, but he pokes his hard, shrivelled ass between our somewhat shrunken but still flabby ones until he's got an inch of space, braces his hands on his knees, and starts talking.

"Get all you can, while you can," he says. "I never did and boy am I sorry now."

Usually he gets around to Vivien, who he's seen with me in the mall the two or three times that I've talked her into coming here. On one of those times he cornered us on a bench in front of the Gourmet Cup and asked Vivien if he could sit on her lap.

"The little ones are the hottest," he told me, while she sat staring with her eyes wide. "You can tell the best fucks; the tops of their legs don't rub together. The fat ones bring themselves off just by walking around. That's why they're always smiling. I bet yours wears you right out. Steroids won't help. They turn you into a faggot. Your dick is an organ, not a muscle."

"Friend of yours?" Vivien asked as we moved away from him. "One of the main reasons you frequent this wasteland?"

Barry has suggested, in front of Alphonse, that we stuff Alphonse into one of the garbage containers or corner him in the washroom and put the boots to him, but he does that only to find out if Alphonse can hear anything besides the sound of his own voice.

He can't.

"I thought when I got old I wouldn't need it anymore," says Alphonse near the beginning of one of his favourite monologues. "But I'm whacking off two, three times a day. My doctor says it's normal but he's too young to know anything. I could pork some of the ladies in the Lodge. Half of them wouldn't know I was doing it or remember after. But liver spots don't turn me on and the orderlies are always watching. I could buy something young. This mall is crawling with whores. Let me know if you want one and I'll point some out. What do I care about AIDS? But the little bastard, who hasn't visited me for weeks, got all my money, and on my pension it would take me ten years to save up for it. I don't have that much time. At least, I sure hope I don't."

This particular monologue started me brooding over a modern romance, possibly for *Playboy*, entitled *Spruce Centre Moll*. Alphonse could be a kind of perverted yet avuncular counsellor to Moll. Together they trick Alphonse's son, get the money back, and ride off to the Baja with a bronzed, bikini-clad cyclist who writes poetry. In the course of all this, there would be lots of graphic descriptions of blow jobs on the garden tractors in Sears or in the motorhomes being raffled off by Rotary and Kinsmen.

In reality, Alphonse wouldn't be up to any of that. He's sick in the literal meaning of the word, also. The one thing that halts his speculations about sex or his son is his cough. He stands up, his body racked with spasms, leans dizzily over the garbage container, and spews into it, which lowers infinitely our appreciation of the kaisers and coffee. Then he sits down again and goes on talking.

Barry worries that someday we'll have to do cardiopulmonary resuscitation on Alphonse.

"Don't worry," I tell him. "Our tickets are expired. He could sue us if we don't let him die."

Alphonse sees us and struggles from his seat in order to follow. I doubt he'll be able to catch up before Sears opens.

Barry doesn't see Alphonse. He's too busy summarizing Stan's scripts.

"Or," Barry continues as we pass a line of soap, perfume, flower, and women's clothing stores, "Stan's hero is a Korean detective in L.A., an expert on martial arts, self-disciplined and tough because he was raised in a town full of loggers and Indians and didn't have a father or a mother. He's a troubleshooter, gets called in to solve the tough ones. But he's lonely, doesn't know his place in the order of things. He gets handed this case involving some pervert in the Korean district who takes blowtorches to prostitutes. He looks at the latest victim. Something about her, or about the burns on her body, disturbs him. He does computer searches but can't quite put it together."

Barry stops to check the interest rates posted inside the locked doors of the bank, then he continues.

"There's another murder. The burn marks match those on the previous victim. So it's not random. Then the detective vaguely remembers, from his childhood in Korea, before his family got broken up by war, or revolution, a religious fire ceremony that he attended with his father, a high-up in the Korean government. In fact, there's a small, delicately shaped burn on his arm that exactly matches a small burn on the arms of both of the dead prostitutes. He goes to Korea. He finds a priest who explains the ceremony."

"There's a Korean fire ceremony where they burn people?"

"They burn them ritualistically, like tattooing. The burns on the dead prostitutes are identical to the ritualistic burns except that, after he burns the prostitutes, the killer shoves the blowtorch into their mouths and boils their brains until they explode out their ears, noses, and eye-sockets. Anyway, the priest is surprisingly friendly and even wants to accompany the hero to L.A. to help find the killer. The hero agrees to take him along, so long as he stays out of harm's way. Back in L.A., the hero disguises himself as a prostitute and hangs around the Korean district until the killer shows himself, brandishing a blowtorch. The killer is also an expert in martial arts, gets the hero down, handcuffs him, and starts to burn him. However, he stops in shock when he sees the ritual burn on the hero's arm. Then the priest intervenes. He identifies the killer as the former Director of Security in the former Korean dictatorship, a renegade priest, a man convicted *in absentia* for crimes against humanity when the new regime took over. The killer identifies the priest as the ex-president's best friend, who advocated liberal policies and had to be shelved soon after the revolution. The kid realizes, from what the killer says, that the priest is actually his own father. Then there's a back-alley blowtorch duel that the father wins."

"I don't think blowtorches have *that* much range."

"Don't ask me. Never owned a blowtorch, though I should get one for soldering those old copper pipes in my house. Maybe we should go into hardware and check them out. The father then explains that he had to abandon his family and go into the priesthood after he was kicked out of government. He stayed in hiding because the new regime was shaky and guys like the former Director of Security were still at large. He had actually recognized his kid earlier via the ritual burn. He tells his son how proud he is of him and points out that the killer has completed his ritualistic burning. The hero now understands his place in the scheme of things."

I could see that Stan was trying to process the usual shovel-load of reality that had been thrown at him. After his hiring interview, Stan told us that he was raised in a small town just south of here. Still later, when we took him for dinner, he mentioned that his family were refugees, kicked out of Korea for political reasons.

However, the results of Stan's hangups, at least as Barry describes them, are too speculative, too embarrassingly close to real fantasy. What, for example, does "crimes against humanity" mean? Murder? Rape? Buggery? Can there be such crimes, considering humanity from the perspective of, say, a killer whale, alley cat, or God? Do killer whales have ears? Could a hero who knows karate have nice enough legs to attract a killer into an alley? Is Barry adding things to Stan's scripts just as I added things to Vivien's articles?

At the Gourmet Cup, as we wait for our coffees, I watch Alphonse. He limps painfully toward us past VideoMart, hunched forward, his gloved hands in the pockets of his trenchcoat and his arms held tightly to his body as if he were freezing. He looks determined, an Ancient Mariner with a message of perverted love. Luckily, there's only one other customer in front of us at the Gourmet Cup, so Alphonse will never catch up. Barry adds cream while I examine the lineup waiting for the lottery booth to open. I've noticed over the years that most of the people in the lottery line are the same people who buy their clothes at Mighty Mart and eat Pickled Paula's pizza dogs rather than gourmet kaisers or even Sears breakfast. I've noticed too that Alphonse never bothers them.

As we turn the corner by the Briar Patch (tobacco and magazines) and head down the quarter-mile stretch of shoe, clothing, and jewellery stores to Sears' mall entrance, I can see, out of the corner of my eye, Alphonse hesitate. Maybe he'll decide it isn't worth it. Our travel mugs, since they have lids, are perfect for this operation. And then, a lucky break. The tall, good-looking woman who runs the men's area in Sears and who always wears short skirts is opening up today. The ardent shoppers slip in as soon as she has one of the panels slid out of the way. They fan out through jewellery and ladies wear. But we gaze patiently and from a polite distance at her ankles and the muscles in her calves until the entrance to Sears is wide open and the woman disappears into the "Arnold Palmer" section of men's wear. As we go through the entrance, Alphonse appears around the corner by the Briar Patch. We pass through men's towards furnishings. Behind furnishings are the stairs and the service elevator to the basement, where the cafe and bill payment offices are.

Barry stops at the edge of men's wear to look at some leather jackets on sale. The leather jackets do actually interest me, but this is only nostalgia. We gave up riding our motorcycles years ago. Too hard on the body, my hemorrhoid activating routinely after only a few miles, and Barry's back starting to ache. Also, Joy and Vivien wouldn't cooperate, refused to grace our adolescent dreams by donning tight jeans and the leather jackets that we bought for them and taking a few runs out to Willie Nelson concerts in corn fields in Idaho. Joy hated to get bugs in her hair and Vivien couldn't stand the inactivity. So I gave my motorcycle to my son and Barry mothballed his in the woodshed when his "black box" went. After checking at the dealership about this crucial part, which is about the size of your thumb, Barry concluded that it grows only on the upper slopes of Mount Fuji and can be picked, like Canadian wild rice, only by the aborigines, of which there are only two left in Japan, both male, over a hundred years old and glowing with radiation. You have to pay a high price for these parts.

I can see Alphonse now, standing none too solidly at the mall entrance to Sears, trying to spot us. I warn Barry and we duck our heads and disappear into the rug section, where we can walk upright, protected from view by the floor-to-ceiling displays. The salesman in the rug section, an East Indian guy (no coincidence, Barry argues, any more than the handsome woman with short skirts in men's wear, but the result of sophisticated management and marketing strategy) waves familiarly at us.

"Do you know that guy?" I ask Barry. "He's never waved at me before."

"We bought a rug here while you were away. It was a perfect match for the new living room. He brought it over and laid it himself, so I had a few beer with him. He's from the Punjab. It was a funny scenario, you know. He was right there on our front porch with the rug when we got back home from buying it. *No truck*. And he *walked* off after having a couple of beer."

"Your point?"

"Obviously he flew the rug over."

"Why didn't I think of that?"

"Joy and I were having a few beer a couple of nights ago. We were talking about the rug. I could've sworn I felt it move. Joy wasn't so sure. She went to the can, so I laid my head back, closed my eyes, and repeated some funny sounds I heard the guy make while he was laying the rug. I opened my eyes and I was staring right at the ceiling from only six inches away."

"What happened next?"

"Joy was shaking me awake."

Just past the rug merchant's desk is the side entrance and the service elevator and stairs. Here, we're safe. Alphonse never comes down into the basement, maybe doesn't even know it's there, maybe can't manage the stairs or service elevator, maybe owes Sears money. If he ever does find us, it would be the end of our long-term marriage to the cafeteria.

6

While Barry and I eat our, respectively, scrambled and poached eggs, Barry tells me about our new college president who arrived while I was away.

"I've seen him around," I tell Barry. "Tall, dignified, bald on top with a fuzz of white hair on the sides and back. Vivien's already met him over some Early Childhood Education business. She says he's sexy."

"Yeah?"

"She says if she didn't have me, maybe she'd go for him. She says bald men are supposed to be great lovers. The passion burns all the hair off the tops of their heads."

"She's pinned him alright, but she's already too late to get him. It seems that after he got here, he fell for one of the executive secretaries. His wife found out and went nuts. She hangs out with a member of the college board, a real estate agent who hangs out with Joy. The three of them sit in the hot tub once in awhile and drink wine; I have to stay clear because all men are scum. Joy says that the wife is after the house, a big place along the river with a pool and tennis court. The real estate agent is providing moral and legal support and also trying to figure out ways to get her fellow board members to vote against the principal so he'll resign. The board probably wanted to fire him, originally, but they'd just hired him so it would've looked bad."

"Why does the wife want him fired? How'll he pay the mortgage and support if he's out of a job?"

"Right now she wants revenge."

"Is he still with the secretary?"

"I think so. He moved her south. She's out of sight and he's down there at meetings half the time anyway."

"So he's screwed himself up politically and we can't count on him for much."

"Maybe now we can. He's got class, though once in awhile he still gets that look on his face like a man who wakes up in a Guatemalan hotel room and discovers that his passport is missing. He's starting to take control. I think the board is generally impressed with him. Some of the members even like him."

Barry takes our mugs over to the urn and fills them up. He stops on the way back to talk to the store manager, who is having coffee with his departmental managers, all bright-looking young men in suits. The manager has a suit on too, but it is slightly rumpled and considerably more expensive. He makes a point of interrupting any talk with his subordinates to talk with the patrons in the cafe. As I watch, he and his group break out laughing. Probably Barry has asked the manager for a job in the lawn-mower shop. Barry has always wanted to work there so he can wear a dirty jumpsuit and, as he usually (with his eyes raised to the ceiling) puts it, "talk to the people," *viz.*:

Rod's bent.
Good thing it's still on warranty.
Must've been some rock you hit.
Didn't hit no rock.
Hell of a dent in the blade.
Well ....
Voids the warranty.
Well fuck you then.
Fuck YOU.

Such talk, Barry believes, is a primitive kind of poetry.

Barry comes back with the coffees.

"The manager says he always listens to my jazz spot on the radio. Finally figured out who I was by my voice. He says he plays trumpet so I told him where we'll be on Friday night. He can come down and listen; if he thinks he's good enough, he can come to a rehearsal."

Just then Stan walks in. The manager and his young men all turn to look. Stan's wearing a long, purple trenchcoat that reaches right down to the tops of his heavy and highly polished army boots. He carries a thin file folder. He stands and stares through his Coke-bottle glasses at the menu board and then goes back around the display counter and looks through the door into the kitchen. He comes back out front, takes a tray, puts his file folder on it, and starts to make his way down the counter, taking plastic-wrapped items off the shelves, holding them up directly in front of his face, and putting them back again.

"I should warn him," I say. "Some of that stuff's been there since they built the place."

"Don't worry about him," says Barry. "He's a *very* experienced consumer."

Barry's right. When Stan arrives at the table there's nothing on his tray but a carton of milk and two cartons of apple juice.

"I can't believe that you guys actually eat here," he says.

"I've got to admit that it feels strange to be back," Barry answers.

"You didn't eat here while I was up north?"

"Are you kidding? Aren't you going to eat something, Stan?"

"I ordered French toast."

"French toast isn't on the menu board."

"I never order things off a menu board unless the cooks are teenagers with terminal acne. The ladies out back look maternal enough, like they've spent years at home making French toast for their husbands and kids and even eaten it themselves."

"What did they charge you for it?"

"Four bucks."

"Same as the eggs."

Stan opens his folder and hands each of us a sheet of paper. "I want you to read this," he says.

"Another script proposal?" says Barry. "What happened to the last one about the escaped psycho who kills his prison psychiatrist, assumes his identity, and cures a new patient who falls in love with him, fucks him, and turns out to be his own long-lost sister?"

"It's with my agent."

The sheet says "Wolverine" on top. It starts with a summary:

1. Wolverine ACCEPTS his wife's death.

2. Wolverine KILLS Jack's son.

3. Jack TRACKS Wolverine.

4. Wolverine SURRENDERS to Jack.

5. Wolverine KILLS Jack.

"He does this once a week," Barry explains, as he starts to read. "Don't worry. It doesn't take long to go through these and usually his agent has the brains to reject them so they don't actually get written up."

"I don't know anything about scripts," I say, putting the sheet of paper down on the table.

"I know," says Stan, opening his first juice carton.

I look over at Barry. He's already got his pen out and is writing comments on the script. He seems to be taking this seriously.

I take a deep pull on my coffee, sigh noticeably, pick up the sheet, and read that, in Act I, Colonel Jack Gore's covert hunting party HUNTS aloof mountain man Frank Wolverine and ABANDONS him for dead.

I put the sheet back down on the table. I'm bored already. The characters have names that identify them as mere caricatures. This is an old-fashioned technique, long abandoned by contemporary realists.

Stan looks at me. "Nobody has 'Wolverine' for a last name," I tell him. "It's got to be a nickname. Put it in quotes."

Stan is opening his second juice carton. "He's *Indian*," says Stan. "Read the *whole thing*."

"Jack *Gore*?"

"Alright," says Stan, taking a pad of paper and a pen out of his pocket and making a note.

So, feeling guilty about misrepresenting Wolverine, one of Stan's ancestors who crossed the Bering land bridge to North America and acquired a taste for feathers and buffalo meat, I read how Wolve's native wife, Sarah, DEFENDS her eleven-year-old daughter Kate from Jack's sadistic son, Manfred, and BLOWS UP the cabin. Wolverine solemnly BURIES his wife's few remains and PADDLES his comatose daughter to the nearest doctor. <u>Wolverine accepts his wife's death.</u>

I put the script down again. "What IS the significance of the upper case verbs and the underlining? I'm already starting to THINK like that and I can tell that it's going to <u>drive me nuts.</u>"

"Will you shut up and read," says Barry. "You're distracting me, which in the case of this particular story is very easy to do. Stan, are you sure the infrared tattoo and the electronic tracking device are good ideas? There's too much stuff on the poor guy's *head* and I hate movies that replace psychology with equipment. Maybe Wolverine is attracted to violence. Maybe he wants to die. Maybe he misses his cabin more than his wife, whose death he accepts too quickly. Let him have a personality."

Stan opens his milk carton. Then he makes another entry in his notepad.

"How about if I cancel the tattoo and keep the tracking device?"

It strikes me as ironic that I escaped Alphonse just to be trapped by Wolverine. Is Stan cracking up? Too many script-writing seminars? Will it be safe to let him carry on with the newsletter?

In Act II, a smiling Colonel Jack Gore AUCTIONS OFF the right to hunt Wolverine, their club's yearly human quarry. Each hunter BUYS 24 hours of hunting time. Wolverine ESCAPES the first hunter and DISCOVERS an infrared tattoo on his forehead. In Act III, Wolverine THWARTS three more hunters. He WONDERS how they are finding him so easily. He DISCOVERS an electronic tracking device surgically implanted in his head. He REALIZES they left him for dead on purpose. Who would do it? Why? Manfred gets his turn to hunt. Jack WARNS Manfred to be careful; Wolverine is Special Forces. Wolverine DREAMS he is talking to Sarah. He AWAKES and SCREAMS out her name. Manfred FINDS Wolverine. <u>Wolverine kills Manfred dead.</u>

I put the script down again. It's the old "dangerous quarry" scenario, the hunt for a human being who turns into the hunter. Also, Stan doesn't bother hiding the strings that hold together his plot. Take the "surgically implanted tracking device." Wouldn't it take a doctor to do a surgical implant, especially one that is completely hidden and doesn't itch? Who was this doctor? Mengele — one of Jack Gore's mentors? Was it the same doctor who took Kate into her/his care? Did Wolverine discover the device because he was scratching his head, trying (like me) to figure out what was going on? Did he *then* go to the doctor to have it removed?

Holy shit, Wolve, that's a hell of a lump on your head.

I know, doc. Do you think it's cancer?

Lookee here! There's a bitty antenna sticking out of it! Hold on, tough guy. I know you hate anaesthetics. I'll just yank it out with my forceps. Yaaaah!

In Act IV, Jack FULMINATES over the body of his son and PREPARES to hunt Wolverine. Kate AWAKENS from her coma in a hidden location. Jack TRACKS Wolverine, recalling that Wolverine HUMILIATED him in Nicaragua when he refused to TORTURE some peasants. Wolverine was discharged but the whole affair DESTROYED Jack's career advancement potential. Wolverine finds and destroys Jack's trophy room of endangered species. Jack PRODUCES Sarah as hostage. Wolverine SURRENDERS to Jack.

Did the doctor go with Kate into hiding to look after her to make sure she came out of her coma? And if Sarah is still alive, what "remains" did Wolve solemnly bury? Her moccasins? Shouldn't Wolverine know ptarmigan or moose bones from human bones? And why would Wolverine destroy the trophy room, thus giving Jack a perfect excuse to shoot (as he would no doubt take great pleasure in doing) another collection of endangered species?

In Act V, Jack tries to get Wolverine to TORTURE Sarah.

Wolverine LOOKS into his heart and ATTACKS Jack and KILLS HIM DEAD. <u>Wolverine, Sarah, and Kate embrace in a new wilderness cabin far from civilization.</u>

Did they remember to pay the doctor?

I put the script down. Stan looks at me.

"Why are you doing this, Stan?" I ask.

The PA system announces "French toast." Stan goes over and gets it, returns, and starts to pick through it. Amazingly, it looks good. There's bacon and it's cooked but not hard. The toast is cooked through. Most amazing of all, he has a bottle of real maple syrup.

"We don't get bacon with ours," says Barry glumly.

"We get hash browns," I point out.

"Take a piece," says Stan.

"Joy says I shouldn't," says Barry, taking a piece and popping it into his mouth.

"I can't believe you got real syrup with that French toast," I say to Stan. "It's expensive."

"I don't think they normally have syrup here," says Stan. "I think one of the ladies had to go find some."

"Obviously she was in a hurry, so maybe she bought the wrong stuff by accident. Or maybe she saw you peeking into the kitchen at her and fell in love. Maybe she recognizes in you the characteristics of a long-lost son who was kidnapped years ago from an L.A. shopping centre and transported to a lumber town full of loggers and Indians."

"That settles it," says Barry, taking another piece of bacon. "From now on, I get the French toast."

As Stan eats, he explains to me that he has to sell a script because he's broke. It's the predictable litany of credit cards and mortgages. At least Stan is candid about it. Perhaps he's influenced Barry in the year I've been gone.

"I know what you're going to say," Stan finishes. "You told me last year when I came here that if I wanted to write I'd have to bank money and buy time off teaching. I just can't do it."

"I tried to slow him down," says Barry, sensing my reaction.

"*You* thought the townhouse was a great idea!" protests Stan. "*You* picked out the stereo!"

"Let's get out of here," says Barry. "I have a class."

7

Outside, the sun is warmer. The morning fog has burned off, but the air now stinks of auto exhaust and the smell of wood smoke is stronger. In fact, it's acrid. I look up and see that it's coming from a necklace of slash piles around the university construction site on the hill.

As we walk, Barry tells Stan about the spitball-throwing physical education majors in the back row of his composition class. Then Stan tells Barry about the social services students in *his* composition class who seem to think, or may have been told by their teachers, that the English and math requirements aren't important. Apparently all you really need to be a social worker is the experience of being abused by parents, teachers, police officers, or even, for lack of someone else, yourself.

"You've got to have something to say in group therapy sessions or you fail the program," Stan explains. "I tell them to make it up and get them to do it right there in my class. Some of them are good at it too. Probably this is going to get me into trouble with their instructors, but I don't see how a student's personal problems are relevant to his/her career in social work. Do you have to spend years in jail to be a criminal lawyer? Do you have to have cancer to be a good doctor?"

Or a good novelist?

Looking at the fires as we walk, I think about how the Romans might've felt at the end, the city surrounded by barbarian armies. Probably they were relieved. All that marble to scrub. All those laws to obey and taxes to pay. All the lying politicians and psychotic neighbours.

All the boredom.

Except that in this scenario we're supposed to be the barbarians and the university people are the Romans.

Anyway, the image is too romantic. It reminds me of another image, from a poem I studied in German literature during my freshman year, an image from Goethe maybe, or Heine, where the mists on the Rhine are described as the campfires of the Norse gods convening to hatch the German future.

I hope this sort of thing got bombed out of the Germans during the war.

We enter the college and Barry rushes downstairs to get to his class. Stan asks me if I've got anything in mind for the newsletter, which has to be ready to print in a week. "Something on the university," he says. "People were telling me last year while you were away that they missed your satires."

"I'm bored with the university."

"I am too," says Stan as he runs off. "But people never tire of a good joke. Whatever you do, I need it on Monday."

I go to the mail room. There's nothing in my box from Hollywood or any famous writer or publisher, so I put the pile back in to ripen. I head for my office which, since I returned from leave, is in one of the old portable buildings on the outskirts of campus. The building used to hold our library and now has overflow faculty offices, a smokers' lounge, the Indian Assistance Program office, the Woman's Advisory Office, and the bookstore. It's been condemned a half-dozen times by the fire marshall and fixed up by the college, but it's still run down and smells like there's a decomposing body under the floor.

The entrance is dominated by the name "MOO," huge letters carved into the door with a screwdriver or knife. I know that

Moo is a name because in the toilet cubicle of the washroom across from my office there's a rhyme:

> *Moo came here*
> *to take a shat*
> *because he knows*
> *this is where it's at*

Moo's name is scratched indelibly on walls and blackboards all through the building. Because I naturally sympathize with anyone seeking to draw attention to himself by literary means, I've been trying, since I moved into the building, to devise a more standardized version of the poem that would express the same idea with the same feeling but without the forced rhyme and the phrase "where it's at," which doubtlessly will have only a temporary resonance:

> *Moo came here*
> *to take a shit*
> *because he knew*
> *that this is it*

I could even reverse the first line and get a rhyme out of "Moo" and "knew." But the "this is it" is even vaguer than Moo's last line and at the same time has a colloquial significance not intended by Moo.

Why do I concern myself with Moo? Surely there are more important literary matters to set straight. Like my novel. Or even, speaking of poetry, my decade-long attempt to revise "Thirty days hath September," an infinitely useful verse and one that even Moo might know, at least as far as the first three lines, after which it skips a rhyme and then becomes too cryptic to memorably explain leap year. So far my version is as follows:

> *Thirty days hath September*
> *April, June, and November*

All the rest have thirty-one
Except that dark and dirty one
February with twenty-eight
Every year for three years straight
Then on the fourth with twenty-nine
To keep the days and years in line.

But the description of February in my version is hemispherocentric and the entire poem is one of those long, breathless, hydrocephalic sentences that I specialize in.

Perhaps Moo reminds me of my own long-abandoned career as a poet, specifically my unfinished masterpiece *A Paean in the Ass*, a slim collection of poems on the subject of, to put it bluntly, farts. I still believe I was onto something in this book and am encouraged to think so even now by Barry, who has had on his office wall for some fifteen years my poem about "fire from heaven," or the spontaneous combustion of human beings. He regards the poem as "a trifle Yeatsian" but the concept behind the poem as fascinating, even irresistible, and he sometimes quotes, at salient moments, from the poem's conclusion, where I say of the burnt and exploded bodies of victims that, in comparison to books, symphonies, and other remains of the glorious dead,

There's more philosophy in these spent casings
The ghosts that haunt them like the smell of cordite

But did I intend to suggest, as Barry thinks, that life is shit? Did I fail again — in this case not making it clear that shit merely symbolizes the organic mass out of which that will o' the wisp, the mind, arises, like a swamp-fed gas, and into which it must constantly delve, at incredible risk, as an act of renewal?

That's why I abandoned poetry — the infinite possibilities for interpretation. I sympathize with my students who, in their reports, cut the Gordian knot with deft strokes like, "This poet was obviously on drugs at the time he wrote this poem." Or,

"This poet clearly exhibits multiple personalities." On grounds like these, it is easy to interpret a poem's style, theme, and imagery.

As I round a corner into the hallway that leads to my office, I see Vivien down at the end of the hall, sitting on a plastic chair by my office door. My heart skips. In the dull distance she looks small, bright, and perfect, as from the wrong end of a telescope. Maybe she's brought good news. The Guatemala section of *Chickenbus* is finished. Or a Hollywood producer, visiting his ailing father at the Sunset Lodge, decided to fill an empty hour in the college library, where he found and read my (albeit unfinished) novel and now wants to buy it for a script. Or maybe Vivien has decided, for love of me, not to go back to Central America but to hang out in our love nest through her second year off, baking, running around in negligees, and maybe even marking my papers for me.

Vivien hears me coming and looks up, smiling.

"God it stinks in here! I almost left for Sears to see if I could intercept you."

We kiss.

"What did the doctor say?"

"I've taken too much meflaquin over the past few years, so he didn't want to give me more. but the chloroquin isn't effect against malaria in some areas."

"So?"

" 'Lay it on'," I told him. " 'We'll worry about the side effects later.' "

"Wait a minute. If . . . ."

"We got the stuff from the Yellowknife archives. I couldn't resist opening it. It's all they have on Zenchuk, though in 2010 they'll be able to release transcripts of tapes of interviews with him."

I open my office. Vivien precedes me in and opens a folder of papers on my desk.

"This is an interview with Gus Kraus," she says. "Most of the original trappers and prospectors were interviewed in the fifties, but Kraus was the only one who allowed immediate access. The others stipulated dates far in the future — in Zenchuk's case, 2010. What did they have to hide, eh? Kraus tells about spring break-up in 1934, when he and Zenchuk met at Albert Faille's Irving Creek cabin on the Flat River for the trip out to Fort Simpson. Zenchuk had come up from his cabin at the mouth of the Cariboo River. The story has some interesting details about how they operated. But in the course of it, Kraus talks about how Zenchuk, in the summer of 1947, stood up a fellow named Shebbach who walked all the way from Watson Lake to the Flat River to meet him."

"That's the story Patterson tells!"

"Exactly, but without mentioning names. Probably he feared a lawsuit. Shebbach starved to death waiting for Zenchuk and became another of Nahanni's headless corpses."

"I can just imagine it," I say. "Shebbach probably read Pierre Berton's newspaper articles. They were published all over North America and contributed to a huge public interest in Nahanni. Zenchuk and Shebbach probably met accidentally, in a bar, say. It's winter, going on spring. Shebbach's got a newspaper and is talking excitedly about gold on the Flat River. Zenchuk, well into middle age but still vigorous, says "I have a cabin up there" and "I searched for the lost McLeod gold." There's more such talk, more drinks, and a deadly misunderstanding on Shebbach's part, probably to the effect that Zenchuk was still trapping and prospecting on the Flat and Cariboo Rivers. Shebbach then, as Patterson tells it, turns up in May in Watson Lake. He travels light, a pack and a .22 rifle. By August, he's deep in the Selwyn Mountains and has found the headwaters of the Cariboo River. He follows the river down to the Flat. No Zenchuk. And the cabin's clearly been abandoned for a long time. His only hope is that some trapper will appear to work Zenchuk's old line. But no one shows."

Vivien flips the pages of archival material, finds the spot and points at it. "Kraus was one of the men who went looking for Shebbach. Kraus says they gathered all the scattered parts of Shebbach's body and put them in a bag. There was a diary too, that the police probably returned to his family. We could check the Edmonton phonebook for Shebbachs. And for Zenchuks."

There's a pause, me staring dully at the piles of student papers on my desk and floor.

"Okay," says Vivien. "I'll phone. But we're going right up there when I get back from Central America."

"What about my novel?"

"To hell with your novel. You've got me going on this and you're not backing out now."

"Okay. We're going. Now get out of here so I can mark. And for God's sake don't leave those papers on my desk."

Vivien gathers the archival papers, hugs me, and runs.

"Don't pick me up at Joanne's," she says over her shoulder. "I'll meet you here. We have to start making plans."

I sit down at the desk, find a red pen, and grab a style test off one of the marking piles. With marking, it's best for me if I don't hesitate. Even a split second can be crucial.

The student hasn't adequately corrected sentence number one, "I tried my best but the chainsaw is busted." "Is" has been changed to "was" in the name of tense sequence, but "busted" is still there. I cross out "busted," write in "broken," and put a .5 in the margin beside the sentence.

Shane would've had the chainsaw caught by narcs in a drug deal, or grow big breasts. "The chainsaw is busted by local police for possession of marijuana." Take *that*, Vingaard.

"O la la," thought the peavey. "The chainsaw is busted."

Can a woman be "busted" in this sense? I reach for the dictionary and locate the word. No, she can't be. Then, remembering Shane and his safari, I turn with a mixture of relief and self-loathing to "malaria." It's Italian, *mala aria*. Bad air. I was hoping it would be Latin so that the spelling would possibly be the same in a number of modern languages. I check the Latin dictionary, but no such word. This means that, if there's a place name, it would have to be an English one chosen for proximity to malaria-breeding swamps and not for the quality of the local air. But this is not likely. Anyway, most of those names have, in post-colonial times, been changed back by understandably irate locals, and most of us English speakers are once again, in the literal sense, a long way from the jungle. And who would name a place (or a beach or store) after a disease?

I return to my marking, determined to shake this feeling that I'm still free.

It looks like the chances of Malaria being the destination of any sort of safari are slim.

Which is too bad. It would be a great title for an adventure story.

God
Is Debt

No more quiet mornings reading and marking over an "eggs-istential" and a gourmet coffee with a tasteful mix of rock, jazz, or classical in the background. No more afternoon literary talk over lattes with Vivien, Barry, or Harvey.

I can't speak for the "events" that took place at Other Art. I prefer art to come at me through a solid wall of technology.

"Watching a jazz combo tossing bars of music around reminds me of a family of orangutans picking and eating one another's head lice," I said once to Harvey when he was trying to sell me a ticket to a jazz evening.

"Artists, performing live, convey charisma," said Harvey. "That's what attracts audiences."

"Charisma is just perfect technique."

"Which is the perfect response to the unexpected."

"Which is the elimination of the unexpected."

Harvey. We talked and argued endlessly about politics and art. I miss him as much as I miss Other Art, though I predicted long ago that Other Art would fail because of his misanthropy.

Lilla fixed that.

What actually killed the business was what originally created it: Harvey's attitude to money. Lilla seems to have shared this attitude, but since she is the more reticent of the two, I can't be sure. It might have been harder for her to share it, since it was the few thousand dollars of equity she had in her own house that sparked the explosion of loans, silent partnerships, and investments that sustained Other Art.

A local accountant did the books for nothing.

A local lawyer handled the incorporation of Other Art and did contracts, all for nothing.

A stormy, ever-changing, vocal, and very public volunteer committee of local businesspersons gave advice and drew up business plans.

All of these people had loaned Other Art money or guaranteed loans or invested in the business; they were in love with Other Art and they were trying to hang on to their investments.

Harvey had them exactly where he wanted them.

I doubt he took much of their advice. If he had, Other Art probably would have lived. But not the life Harvey imagined.

Harvey has his own idea about financing, which is that only cash flow is important. Cash flow indicates what's *happening* — how many cappuccinos etc., paintings etc., and tickets to plays, readings, and musical shows etc. are being sold. It is only what's *happening* that's important. Debt, inasmuch as it might indicate how much money is going into generating cash flow, is meaningful. Otherwise it's boring.

"You mean you're just going to ignore your debt?" I asked when I first heard about Harvey's concept of financing. I was nervous because Harvey had previously hit me up for a couple of small loans, and I still believed I might get my money back. The loans, he said, were for paying wages to staff. Harvey knew I would not be eager to put money into shows or equipment. On the other hand, I was likely to be sympathetic to the witty waitress who had just given me an eggs-istential.

"I didn't say I was going to ignore it. I'm just going to let it pile up and I'm not going to pay it."

"How will you get away with that?"

"By not believing that I really am in debt. As I see it, debt is merely the capitalistic version of original sin. Original sin was invented by theologians in order to get everyone into church confessing and contributing. No one could escape penance, not even the virtuous, because no one could atone for the absolute depravity of Adam and Eve's crime in the Garden of Eden. Similarly, debt has been lifted by the priests of capitalism from a common crime to a universal fate. Every Canadian baby is born $20,000 in debt (at 7.5 percent). Brazilian babies, who are poorer than Canadian babies, are ten times deeper in debt (at 12.5 percent). Ninety percent of all the people in the world are in debt from their date of birth on, and are going in deeper at an exponential rate. I'm using round numbers here . . . ."

"Very round."

"But the fact that all those numbers are mostly zeros is symbolic. We're talking about nothing. The world's overall present debt probably exceeds all the value of all the minerals in the earth, extracted and processed into Japanese cars. Soon the debt will exceed the appraised value of the solar system and then of the universe itself. Clearly we're into religion, not economics."

"It does sound suspiciously extreme," I admitted, reluctantly, bidding a silent farewell to my two hundred dollars. The zeros in two hundred seemed significant to me, but of course they were insignificant drops in the pond (or maybe lake) of debt that was Other Art, which itself was insignificant in the vast ocean of world-wide debt that Harvey was describing. Anyway, I knew that Harvey knew that I could survive the loss of only two zeros.

"It's what happens whenever a fixed system, in this case arithmetic which is the heart of science which is at present the heart of civilization, is applied to reality. Common sense is out the window."

"So you're telling me that the Other Art debt is out of control."

"Evidently it's growing fast, but thanks to that growth we're here, warm, with fresh coffee. Last night a full house listened to Celtic Harp. Next weekend, Stephen Fearing will be here. Right now I'm waiting for a load of paintings by a rancher who lives around Williams Lake. I discovered her when I went down for a local show. She's the Matisse of the shorthorn."

"But debt *is* real if people are coming at you all the time trying to collect."

"Too true. The World Bank regularly convinces local charismatic fascists that the debt must be collected. Millions die. Then some local charismatic communist raises rebellion amongst those offended by what the fascist is doing. Millions more die. The communist takes over and refuses to pay the debt. The international financial community boycotts the commie and economic chaos results. Even more millions die. The fascist gets back in, and around we go."

"That's a fair description of modern politics, but I was thinking of you in particular. Your creditors must apply a lot of pressure."

"None at all."

The trick, Harvey explained, is to eagerly embrace debt just as the existentialist embraces sin. Once you go into that black hole and emerge on the other side, you are free to do what you want. Your creditors recognize your fearlessness and act accordingly. They know that, if the whim takes you, you will simply shrug and walk away from debt. And then they alone will be responsible to that debt.

"I've had investors, bank managers, and loan officers down on their knees begging me to hang in there," Harvey said. "If I promise to adhere to their plans to avoid bankruptcy by counting beans, they give me even more money, which I promptly put into another stage show. My creditors have become my colleagues, customers, and even friends."

At some point in our discussions, I saw deeper into the meaning of the Other Art icon. It occurred to me that the icon was a subtle reflection of the town's icon, "Mr. Clearcut," a giant made out of logs and cross-sections of logs, a tinker-toy man. Mr. Clearcut stands at the tourist information centre at the crossing of the two major highways that run through town. He stands with his legs planted far apart, he brandishes an axe, and he wears a hard hat. He represents the strength and militancy of the forest industry in this area, the industry that dominates the town's economy. Miniature Mr. Clearcuts are available in the hotels and kiosks around town.

The locals are attached to Mr. Clearcut — an attachment that is edged with defensiveness. Mr. Clearcut is, after all, clearly a primitive. The contemporary term for him might be "hokey." American tourists have been known to use the term "yokum." Consequently, when local rowdies sneak out to spike a two-by-four penis between his legs, or dress him in a tutu or silk panties, the newspapers and radio stations are full of outrage that can go on for weeks. The Junior Chamber of Commerce posts a sentry.

Harvey's courage and conviction have always made me defensive. I am too weak to follow in his footsteps. Having long ago been tempted into mortgages, pensions, and RRSPs, I sacrificed (only partly, I hope) my modest talent for writing stories and took up marking an endless stack of papers and teaching an infinite supply of hormone-hyped, TV-addicted teenagers to write sentences in standard English and to read literature for its socially redeeming merits.

In exchange for thirty-five or maybe forty years of such work, society keeps me alive and promises, when I'm too old to work, some kind of welfare. The official age of retirement is, apparently, being moved from 65 to 70 due to shortfalls in the Canadian government's mandatory pension plan and to the excessive (it now appears) zeal that society has shown in keeping people like me healthy. There is some concern that I could live well into my nineties. The cost of maintaining me will have to be passed on to the next generation, just as the sins of the fathers were once passed on to their sons.

Harvey treats my trust in society with the contempt that it so richly deserves.

"*Then* you'll write your novel," he sneers. "When you're blind and brain dead, *then* you'll turn into a great writer. Are there any examples of *that* ever happening?"

"I can't remember."

I took this as a warning not to loan any more money to Harvey. Instead, I would buy his art. I would pay cash and hope he was smart enough to stash that money in a hollow tree somewhere.

And so I did. I started with Harvey's painted ties until my sons-in-law, son, and self each had a rack of them. I bought a genuine silver Other Art icon, hand-cast by Harvey. Mainly I invested in a series of papier-mache masks. I'm not much attracted to painting or sculpture, but these masks fascinated me. I seemed to see Harvey in them better than I did in his real face. I also figured that Harvey could eventually become famous for his masks, and I in my old age could gradually sell mine off to buy heart medicine.

Barry followed my example. "I had some doubts about Harvey," he said, "but his designs grow on you." Barry went for the wall hangings made of chopped-up conveyor belts from the pulp mills.

Now that I think of it, it was at the point when Other Art reached its widest range of expansion and its highest level of activity that Harvey started informing me of his theory of finance, and that I started buying Harveyanea. I took his information as a warning. Harvey always seemed to recognize that Barry and I need the security of the herd, the statistical guarantee that we would almost certainly be milling in the centre whenever less fortunate individuals were being picked off around the edge.

At times Harvey must have looked hungrily at our sleek flanks, but he fed mainly off others.

By the time Other Art went down, dragging its numerous

"friends," "associates," and "investors" with it, it had gone through two transformations. Three years after its start, it moved downstairs to street level and became less of an art gallery and more of a coffee house. In this form it prospered, adding the younger, more bohemian, downtown street crowd to its clientele of affluent, middle-aged professionals. Long and windowed, this manifestation of Other Art occupied the busiest corner in town. Customers entered and picked up coffees and food at a central counter, choosing from a large menu that included luncheon soup and sandwich specials, pizza, muffins, and fancy desserts. The customers took their food and drink to the tables or (more usually) to the elevated counter along the windows. There they sat viewing, and in full view of, the street. Lilla kept high-quality magazines and papers for browsing, and most customers did browse, but that was only for the sake of appearance.

Few of them, according to Harvey, really knew how to read, but they wished to look like bohemians.

I avoided this manifestation of Other Art unless I was looking for Harvey.

At the far end of Other Art, the gallery continued but in a shrunken form. Sales of hand-crafted jewellery and cups continued at a good pace. Sales of Other Art icons, T-shirts, and backpacks exploded. Designed by Harvey, these became the rage among the college and university crowd and (in summer) the hordes of treeplanters that descended on the town. In the evenings, the usual round of musical and literary events took place, but the space was not right and the sound was terrible.

This troubled Harvey.

Even as the business began raking in money — bringing, as the newspaper put it, "new life to the downtown core" — Harvey was planning a move.

Two years later, the original debts entirely paid off, the daytime staff up to five not including Lilla and Harvey, Other Art moved to its third and final location, a large space in a relatively new building just across from the elm-shaded park that sits in front of city hall.

"Right in their lap," said Harvey.

In this Other Art, food and coffee were served at tables, each of which featured a table-top montage — my favourite being the "Irish Writers" montage. A huge expanse of wall (there were no windows) hosted an everchanging art show. The corner stage was large enough for a four-piece band. Once Harvey got started on his bookings there was a show every Friday and Saturday night, and sometimes one in the middle of the week. The mid-week ones were usually readings. In cooperation with the new university, Harvey launched a literary series.

My part of it was, mainly, consuming an eggs-presso (scrambled egg and toasted bagel) or eggs-istential (two-egg omelette and toasted bagel) most every morning during some convenient gap in my timetable. A half-dozen other customers — also writers, I suspect — made up the group of silent and withdrawn morning regulars. We drifted out as the lunch crowd — secretaries and bureaucrats from city hall, the law courts, and the government buildings — drifted in for the noon-hour buffet.

The big money, however, Harvey told me, was in the shows and accompanying liquor sales. Musicians played to full houses. The newspaper printed rave reviews.

But the big money wasn't big enough. The last manifestation of Other Art shot past like a comet, in a slow and increasingly brilliant flash of light.

Then it was gone.

One Saturday in mid-summer, a bailiff's Notice of Seizure appeared on the door. Vivien and I, and Bill, a poet who has been writing for thirty years though not a single poem of his has ever seen print, happened to arrive together at our customary time. We stood there, shoving at the door and reading (but not registering) the notice. Finally Vivien and I turned to go. Bill pressed his face to the glass, placed his hands on both sides of his face, and stayed absolutely still.

"I don't understand," he said. "Nothing's changed. My table's still there."

"Are you going to be alright?" Vivien asked.

"I'm almost in."

Lilla and Harvey, we quickly discovered, had already left town. Nobody knew where they were.

Four months later we received an invitation to subscribe to something called the "Imaginary Canadian Art Car Tour." Harvey and another artist were converting a '65 Pontiac Parisienne into "a visible, moving portrait of what makes Canada unique." By sending $50 to a post office box in Powell River, subscribers would get a chance to "tickle the belly of the giant." Their names would be displayed on the car and they would receive a photo of the car, a collage by Harvey, and a postcard from Houston, Texas, home of the Annual Art Car Parade.

We promptly sent our cheque.

Barry, facing a large Visa bill, sent $25. "Hold the name on the car," he wrote. "Hold the photo and the postcard."

Four months later we got our photo and collage. Folded into the package was a photocopy of page 222 of *Central America by Chickenbus*. Circled on that page was Vivien's description of the Mask Maker of Chichicastenango:

> The Mask Maker is on the same hill as the Pascual Idol. You may stop and see some of his works of art. He makes the masks for the Indian dancers to rent on special fiesta days. However, if you are looking to purchase, there is a large selection in the market. Often, no one is around the Mask Maker's house.

The Art Car, it seemed, was returning to Canada without Harvey and Lilla.

I'm convinced that they will return. But in what form?

Look in your town for a small storefront, probably in the downtown core. It will have a striking logo, prominently displayed. It will have an unusual name.

El Arte Otro, perhaps.
Maybe there will be a decorated car parked in front.
Go on in.
Buy a T-shirt, a tie, or a mask. Try the eggs-istential.
There's a chance that your life will change for good.

For a free catalogue of all New Star titles, write to:

NEW STAR BOOKS
2504 York Avenue
Vancouver, BC   V6K 1E3
CANADA

Or e-mail your request to NEWSTAR@PINC.COM